# AFTER THAT, THE DARK

# AFTER THAT, THE DARK

ANDREW KLAVAN

THE MYSTERIOUS PRESS
NEW YORK

AFTER THAT, THE DARK

Mysterious Press
An Imprint of Penzler Publishers
58 Warren Street
New York, N.Y. 10007



First edition

Interior design by Lia Kantrowitz



Library of Congress Control Number: 2025935476

ISBN: 978-1-61316-686-4
eBook ISBN: 978-1-61316-687-1

10 9 8 7 6 5 4 3 2 1

Printed in the United States of America

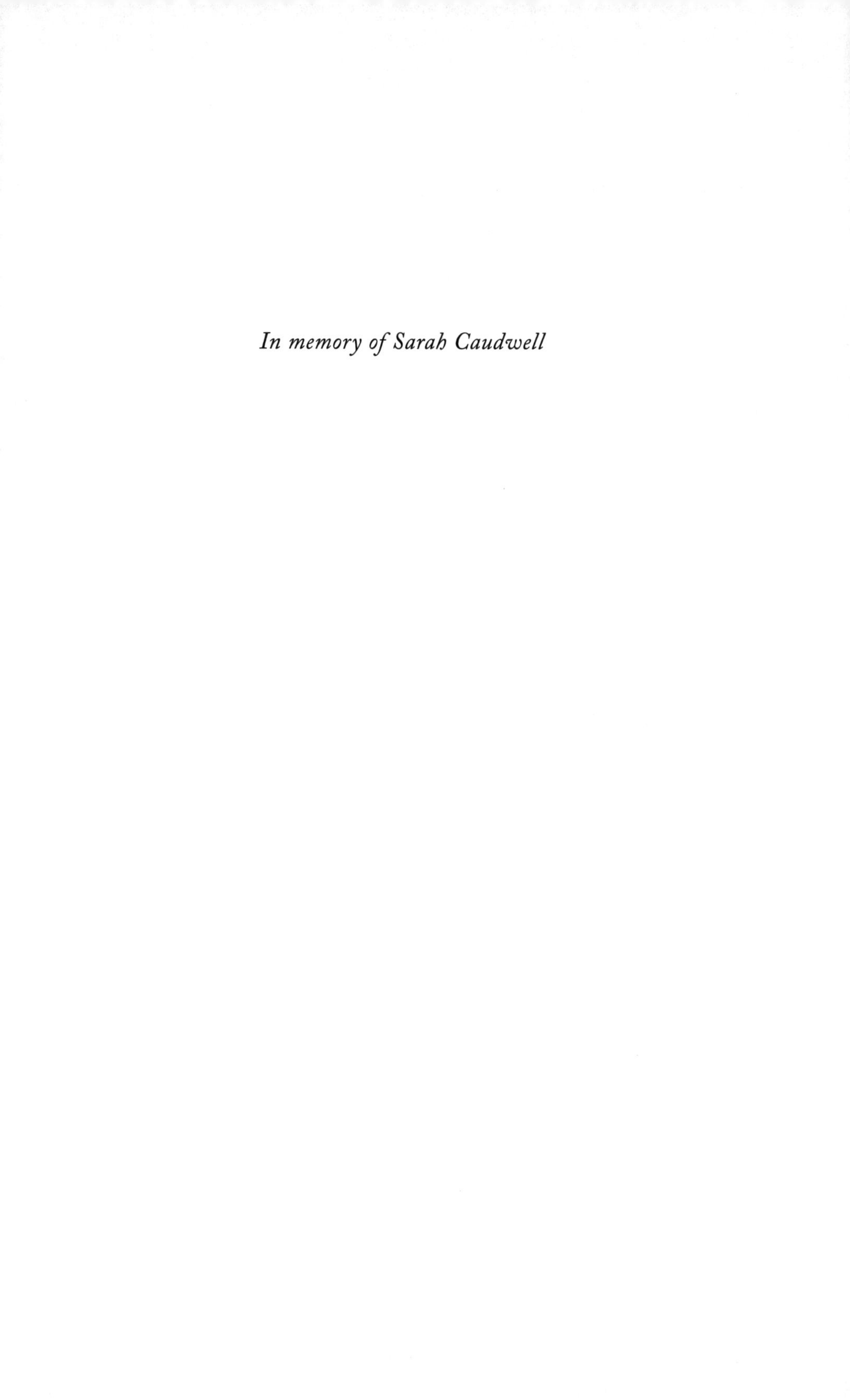

*In memory of Sarah Caudwell*

*"When an impure spirit comes out of a person, it goes through arid places seeking rest and does not find it. Then it says, 'I will return to the house I left.' When it arrives, it finds the house unoccupied, swept clean and put in order. Then it goes and takes with it seven other spirits more wicked than itself, and they go in and live there. And the final condition of that person is worse than the first."*

—Matthew 12:43–45 NIV

# PROLOGUE

Tilda Bach folded the laundry and thought about the devil. The sunlight at the basement window was just beginning to lose its edge of midday brilliance. The sun, unseen beyond the left-hand border of the long, narrow pane, had dropped behind the screen of the summer leaves. The sparse grass of the small backyard was darkening.

Tilda gazed out through the dusty glass. Her hands, moving automatically, worked a bath towel into a tidy square. She set the square down on the pile of towels atop the dryer. She reached into the plastic basket for another. But her eyes remained on the window all the while, the long, narrow window set high on the wall in front of her, just above the level of her head.

Outside, just visible at the right edge of the glass, lay the dirt path along the border of the lawn. The path led to the doorway of her husband's storage shed.

Tilda felt sick inside at the thought of what she was about to do. But what else *could* she do? The devil was in her house. Or a demon sent by the devil. She didn't pretend to know the ins and outs of such things. She didn't even know if she really believed in such things. But she did know this. Something had gotten inside her husband. Something evil. Something alive. It was taking him over. It was eating his soul away. It was turning him into itself.

At night, in bed, asleep, in dreams, he said things, horrible things, murmured obscenities full of violence. She woke sometimes to find him sitting in her armchair, his laptop on his thighs, the white light from the monitor shining on his face, his face demonic, twisted into a grin. Sometimes he went out at night. For a drive, he said. Sometimes he went into the shed and locked the door and did not come out for hours. It was not like him. It was not him at all. It was something else.

Whatever it was, she had to stop it. For his sake. For her sake. For the sake of the baby growing inside her.

She lay another freshly folded towel on the pile atop the dryer. Then she stopped moving altogether. She stood there, still, gazing out the basement window. Gazing at the shed.

She knew she needed help. She had to tell someone. Someone at the church, someone who might understand. But no one would believe her unless she brought them proof. Everyone at church knew Martin. Everyone loved Martin. If she went to Pastor Mike or her friend Gretchen, the junior warden on the vestry—if she went to them and started babbling about devils and demons and evil, they would think she had gone crazy. She herself was half afraid she had gone crazy, thinking about these things. Sometimes she was sure she had. She needed proof, proof to show the pastor, proof to show herself.

She believed the proof was hidden in that shed.

For long moments end to end, she stood motionless in front of the dryer, her arms at her sides. She went on gazing out the basement window. Finally, she drew a long, deep breath. When she let it out, it trembled. The fear in her chest was a cold fire, an icy flame that made her body feel hollow and weak. She feared that it would stop her heart. She feared that it would hurt her baby.

But she could not talk herself out of her suspicions anymore.

It was getting late. She wasn't wearing her watch, but she knew it had to be four o'clock at least. Martin had left for work early this morning, before eight. He probably wouldn't be home for another hour or so, but she couldn't be sure.

She had to go out there. She had to go out there now.

Tilda was a small woman, twenty-eight, thin except for the baby bump beginning to show at her center. Her lank yellow hair framed a sharp face with sharp features. As she drifted across the basement floor toward the stairs, she felt her own frailty. She felt insubstantial, like a ghost, like a piece of paper blowing on a breeze, in her flowery blouse and her sandals and her pale-blue shorts with the stretchy waist to fit her growing belly. She felt as if there were nothing to her except that icy fear.

She rose up the stairs as if she were floating, as if she could not stop herself even if she wanted to. Her mouth was open. Her throat was dry. The only sound she heard was her sneakers on the steps. She felt as if she must be whimpering, but she was only whimpering inside, silently.

She came into the kitchen. She moved a stride across the withering linoleum to the backyard door. She pushed out through the screen into the heat of the day.

It was odd. The houses on Linden Street were close together. She could see the Mullers' house through the leaves of the walnut tree, not far at all, a few yards away. If she turned her head to the left, she would see Bill and Mary Weber's place across the street, and if she looked over her right shoulder, there would be the side of Jeff and Abbey's house with nothing but a narrow slate pathway between the wall of her own house, hers and Martin's. Why did she feel so isolated? The late afternoon was coming on, but it was still bright daylight. Why did she feel like she was swimming in shadows? Why did she feel so utterly alone in a darkness like the dead of night?

She reached the shed. It was a worn resin box only a couple of feet taller than herself, walls of mock clapboard, dull gray. Her hand went out to it, drifting away from her as if on its own. She wanted to stop herself, but she couldn't. She gripped the handle, pressed the latch. She drew the door open.

There was the darkness, the darkness she had felt all around her. It was waiting for her inside the shed.

She stepped into it, drawing the door shut behind her.

The shed had no windows but there were vents beneath the eaves. Some light trailed in through these, enough to see by. She found the switch on the wall and flipped it. A bare bulb glared angrily down from the low ceiling.

She swallowed hard. How could she be so close to home and so afraid? Afraid of her own husband, her own Martin. She could still remember—she would never forget—the sweetness of his smile the first time she had seen him. She was serving drinks in the Bar and Grill, a place so low it had no other name, just Bar and Grill, that's all. The music there was so loud it had no tune but noise. The walls shook with it. She was moving down the line of customers, looking for empties she could refill. She came upon his smile among the cunning faces and the angry faces and the faces, as she now understood, of men who did not even know they had despaired. There was Martin, his sweet smile, like sudden water mellow in the midst of baking sand.

"How about you and me go somewhere quiet, darling, and talk about Jesus Christ," he said.

He had really said that. It had made her laugh out loud. It had got her talking with him, flirting back and forth, trading lines until she'd made a date with him for after work, good-looking boy that he was, big strong man that he was, muscles outlined in the fabric of his tee, a workingman's hands, rough and sure. She knew how it would be, but that didn't matter. It would be the same as it always was in the end, but if it was good for even an hour, that was something, wasn't it? A little dream of something, floating like a bubble, pink and pretty, in the air. A feeling like someone cared for her or at least thought she was pretty enough to be worth having. So she went with him, same as she always went with all of them.

Martin drove her in his pickup to the overlook by the lake, the usual lovers' lane. And there, in a surprise as shocking as a scene in a movie, as a ghost-monster jumping out through the glass of a mirror or the killer lurking in the house after the heroine rushes inside and locks the door, he had sat with her in that place of forlorn surrender and talked with her till dawn about Jesus Christ. He really had. Talked and talked about religion and the sadness of worldly things until she heard herself talking back to him, not just the usual jaded clichés, but real talk, just as the stars were fading, about the misery she pretended was "doing okay," and the pain she had figured was just the way things were. It all came pouring out of her into his gentle eyes and she knew with a kind of childlike wonder: she had found love.

She stood where she was in the shed. She breathed unsteadily, cold with fear. Her eyes traveled over the space beneath the glaring light from the naked bulb. The red tool chest she had bought him for his birthday. The power tools hanging on the wall. The shelves of paint cans and buckets and weed killer. The workbench with its segmented trays of electronic bits and pieces: black boxes and wires and glassy elements. They looked to Tilda like the bodies of some alien robots gathered up for burial after their starship crashed to Earth. Martin had a genius for electronics. He could fix things, make things. Toys for poor kids at church who didn't have any toys. Computer add-ons that could pick up the videos from nearby drones or trace what a neighbor's computer was doing on wireless. Some of these things—Tilda wasn't even sure they'd been invented yet. She was always telling Martin he ought to turn this skill into a business somehow. He could make real money at it. But he'd just laugh and say it was only a hobby, nothing special. Then he'd go back to rooting through the pieces splayed out over the workbench, putting them together—at random, it seemed to her—like he was a sorcerer magically transforming junk into technology.

But all those doodads were stowed away now, each in its compartment, like mashed potatoes and peas in a frozen-dinner tray. Fearful as she was, Tilda almost smiled at that. For a big, shambling, sloppy boy, Martin was neat as a prissy old maid. She had always found that kind of adorable. He liked things in their proper places, all just so.

That's why she spotted the hiding place right away.

A cardboard box stuffed with wires, shoved under the workbench where it shouldn't have been. That was the telltale sign.

She moved to it slowly. She wasn't sure she was breathing at all anymore. The fear had gutted her. She felt dead and empty. She knelt down. She wrestled the box to one side. She saw the rectangular gray metal chest hidden behind it. She drew it toward her. It scraped against the floor.

The chest was locked, but she knew where the key would be. She reached up and pulled open the workbench drawer, right at her eye level. There it was in the front compartment, right in its proper place. She picked the key out and, kneeling there, unlocked the chest.

Everything came on her all at once: all the horror and all the fear together.

Tilda lifted the lid of the chest and in the harsh, pitiless glare from the bare bulb she caught a single glimpse of an image—a printed picture—of pornographic brutality. Martin's nighttime murmurings come to life. The girl's body. The girl's face. Her wide-eyed terror. Her mouth strapped shut. There was also a stained T-shirt, bunched in a corner of the chest. *Blood*—the thought was like a siren going off inside her. *That's blood!*

At the same time, at the very same second, there came the sound of tires on the driveway outside. Martin's pickup. A sound she knew well: her husband had come home.

A noise escaped her. A single, strangled cry. She shut the chest with a clanking bang. Too loud! He'd hear her. She shoved it back in place. Was it back in place? The right place? Would he notice it had been moved? She put the cardboard box in front of it again and was already rising from her knees as she dropped the key back in the workbench drawer and shut the drawer as quietly as she could. She could hear the door of Martin's pickup opening.

The driveway was on the near side of the house. She had seconds—three or four or five, no more than that—to get out of the shed before he stepped from the pickup's cab and saw the light shining through the vents. He might have already spotted it as he was driving up. She had no way of knowing.

Another whimpering cry came out of her as she raced to the door and hit the switch. The shed went dark. The darkness seemed to tilt and spin around her. She opened the door the slightest crack. She slipped through the gap like liquid smoke. She shut the door and started walking quickly through the afternoon sunlight. She looked up toward the driveway. An instant—half an instant—later,

Martin shut the truck door and turned to see her moving toward him across the lawn.

How much had he seen? The light in the shed? The door closing? Or maybe just this, just Tilda walking toward him. Maybe she could tell him she'd heard his truck in the drive and had come out the kitchen door to greet him. Maybe. She didn't know what he knew.

Her mind was a panicked stampede of images. That girl in the printed picture. That T-shirt stained with blood. And had she put the chest away in the right place? And was her fear visible in her eyes? And was her horror visible on her red cheeks? No way of knowing.

Tilda smiled brightly, sick at heart. She waved as she walked toward her husband. He towered over her, broad shouldered and muscular in his workingman's tee, the underarms dark with sweat. He had his toolbox in his right hand. He was smiling over her. His sweet smile. But was he masking something? Suspicion? She couldn't tell.

"Hey," he said. And with his big bear-paw of a hand behind her head, he drew her up on tiptoe into a kiss. Tilda felt as if a whole world inside her were collapsing into dust.

Martin set her down and grinned and touched her belly.

"Hey there, baby," he said to the bump there. "Daddy's home."

# PART ONE

# A PERFECTLY PLEASANT ASSASSIN

*A man was murdered yesterday. No, wait. It was the day before. His name was Warren Gentry. He was an independent journalist, one of the new breed online. Started small, with a sort of blog, but landed enough scoops to begin building a real news site.*

*He was shot outside his home in Chevy Chase, in Maryland, near Washington, DC. A mugging gone wrong—that's what the police are saying. Not the usual neighborhood for muggings, but I guess these things can happen anywhere from time to time. Three bullets in the chest, according to the news sites: .38 caliber. He was fifty-seven.*

*Yes, I know, Margaret. I know what you're going to say. I know you so well at this point, I could play both our parts, therapist and patient both, talking to myself, jumping from chair to chair. Why am I telling you this, you're going to ask me. What's this got to do with anything?*

*Hear me out, though.*

*When I got back from Istanbul, I knew my situation was dangerous, maybe deadly. I'd been with the Division for several years by then. Arranging the deaths of bad men around the globe. Turning bad men against each other so they'd do the killing for me but also killing them myself from time to time when the need arose. Whatever the Recruiter sent me to do, that's what I did. He was my chief, my mentor. I believed in him. And he . . . he believed in the US of A. The sacred song of liberty. Our kick-ass Lord and Savior Jesus Christ. But what I believed in was him.*

*Then came Istanbul. I saw those pictures on the wall. The trophy room in the mansion of the human trafficker Kemal Balkin. Photographs of some of the most important men in American government—some women too—exercising, let's say, the privilege of their desires. In unforgivable ways, often with children. Even in our weary age, the stuff they were doing would get them tossed behind bars for life if they were lucky enough to escape a lynching.*

*That meant someone, somewhere had some of the key figures in the American elite on a string, marionettes dancing to his tune. It wasn't Kemal either. That fat son-of-a-Turk was a body seller, not a big-time power player. Someone was running him. Chinese, Iranian, Russian maybe. But given the way events had unspooled, it was just as likely it was someone on the inside, an American. Someone who felt threatened because the Recruiter was onto him.*

*That is, if it wasn't the Recruiter himself.*

*So now, I was like the guy in the cartoon with a thundercloud over his head, pouring down rain and lightning. Who was I going to trust? If I was going to kill, who was I killing for? And what would I do if the Recruiter assigned me an American target? I tried not to think about it, but I couldn't think about anything else.*

*And yes, I'm getting to Warren Gentry. The murder in Chevy Chase. I'm getting to it. Hold on.*

*One day, sure enough, I get the call. Come into the Division. I was across the river, in Alexandria. I was driving a cool little yellow Mustang then, black stripes on the hood. A flashy indulgence, not to mention a really easy car to follow if anyone had a mind to follow me. But why would they? The Division was so secret even I wasn't sure it existed. So I tootled into DC without checking the rearview.*

*The Division—I've told you—was a three-story brick brownstone on a corner near Capitol Hill. A nondescript sort of place in the midst of all the white-columned government temples everywhere around it. There was an underground garage across the street. I parked the Mustang in there, next to a sleek Mercedes. Only as I got out of the car did I realize two evildoers had come in right behind me.*

*They made a big show of cornering me. As I was stepping out of the 'Stang, I heard their tires screech on the concrete floor and looked up to see a black Cadillac Escalade roughly the size of a T. Rex pull up behind my rear fender, blocking my way.*

*Evildoer Number One jumped out from behind the wheel. He was a rangy Mexican punk and I knew at first sight I could kill him without getting out of breath. Evildoer Two, though, looked like more of a problem. He was young also, about my age by the look of him. Also Mexican, or something that looked Mexican. But he was smooth, relaxed, built for speed with lean muscles made to move fast. He had a round, light-brown, blunt face under a patina of black hair. Steady eyes, unnerving eyes, calm, professional, unfeeling. He had a tattoo on the back of his hand, a pentagram in a circle. I remember thinking it must've hurt to get a tat in that spot, so near the bone. Maybe that was the point of it, to show how tough he was.*

*Both men were wearing black, black jeans and T-shirts. It was summer—summer in DC—hot and thick and swampy.*

*There was a lot of stuff going through my head as they approached me. They must have known where I lived. They must have followed me from my house. Or maybe they'd been watching the Division building and just picked me up as I was parking. But mostly I was thinking about the fact that they'd made a mistake—a rookie error. I was parked next to the Mercedes, like I said, and there wasn't much space between one car and another. So I was standing in a narrow alley. Which meant these clowns couldn't come at me together. It would have to be one at a time.*

*Sure enough, the first guy, Evildoer One, goes right to it like the dope he was. Pulls a KA-BAR, a knife, snicker-snacks it open. Strides down that little alley right for me, with a big stupid grin on his face, his gold tooth showing.*

*The next thing we know Evildoer One has got a broken wrist and a broken nose and he's lying curled up on the parking lot floor clutching the place where his testicles used to be. And Evildoer Two—Pentagram Guy—tough as he is, has got no way to reach me without stepping over the body, by which time he'd be dead.*

*Just out of politeness, I asked him: "Is there something you'd like to discuss with me before I kill you?"*

*Pentagram Guy laughed. No gold teeth on him. All white and shiny. He put his hands up to show he meant no harm. Or at least he meant no harm anymore.*

*"No need for violence, my friend," he said. "My partner just got a little carried away, that's all."*

*"Your partner's an idiot," I told him. "But you seem like a perfectly pleasant assassin, so why don't you just tell me what this is all about."*

*"Isabella," he said.*

*"Don't know her."*

*"We just want to find her."*

*"Still don't know her."*

*"Your boss does. Your boss knows where she is."*

*"Well, you could ask him, I guess, but I don't recommend it. I'll just kill you in self-defense. He'll torture you for fun, then kill you. He's a religious man. He's got no pity."*

*Pentagram Guy stopped smiling. His round face went very quiet and I could feel his calm eyes assessing me. "You really don't know Isabella?"*

*"Scout's honor. Never heard of her."*

*He studied me for another second or two. "I believe you."*

*"I'm so relieved."*

*He gestured his tattooed hand toward the idiot writhing on the ground between us.*

*"In that case, if you don't mind, I'll take my stupid friend and leave."*

*"Go ahead. But if you make a move on me, the cops are going to find your head in the glove compartment."*

*He made another shrugging gesture by way of reassuring me he would not make a move. He bent down and grabbed Evildoer the Stupid by the heels and dragged him out from between the cars. Then he hoisted him onto his shoulder, easy as a sack of straw. Popped the Escalade's liftgate and plunked him inside.*

*"Sorry to trouble you, my friend," he said. "You seem like an interesting person. One day I hope to have a reason to speak with you again."*

*He smiled like a shark smiles at his dinner. Climbed behind the wheel of the Escalade and drove away.*

*I found the Recruiter where I usually found him, in his upstairs office. Very modest little place—I guess I've told you about that too. Wooden desk. Two chairs and a sofa. A flag. And pictures on the wall of George Washington and Jesus, or maybe Jesus and George Washington; I'm not sure the Recruiter recognized any difference between them. Same guy in different outfits as far as he was concerned.*

*And, of course, there was the Recruiter himself, sitting as he always sat, leaning forward in his chair, hands clasped on the desktop. Dressed in a khaki suit as if he was in uniform. The face on his shaved, blocky, dark-black head expressionless. Maybe even serious. I was never sure whether the man had no sense of humor or had nothing but. It was always possible he was one long running gag.*

*I sat in the chair across from him. "Some evil Mexican just tried to cut my throat, then question me about the whereabouts of a woman named Isabella."*

*"He wanted to cut your throat, then question you?"*

*"Clearly, the cartels aren't sending their best. There was another guy with him. More of a professional. Pentagram tattoo on the back of his right hand. He said you'd know all about this Isabella girl."*

*There was no change of expression on the Recruiter's face. There never was. And you'd be crazy to think you could read him or guess what he was thinking. But he'd been running my life for a while at this point, and I'd studied his reactions the way a dog studies his master. I would have sworn there was a half-second's hesitation before he answered me. I thought it had something to do with the pentagram tattoo. I thought he knew who Pentagram Guy was and I thought he was not happy about it.*

*"Well, Poetry Boy, as you know, I consider you to possess the sort of childlike proto-intellect that swaddles itself in fashionable but inchoate nihilism to avoid contemplating the reality of the eternal damnation certain to swallow you in the demisecond after you shuffle off this mortal coil, so I'd be happy to lie to you and tell you I have no idea what any of this is about if it will help you sleep at night like the emotional infant you are."*

*"I appreciate your confidence in me, chief. Go right ahead and lie like a bastard."*

*"I have no idea what this is about. And there is no hell, so you're fine. But this isn't why I invited you in."*

*I lifted my hand to indicate he should get down to business.*

*"Have you ever heard of a man named Thaddeus Blatt?" he said.*

*"Yeah. Yeah. I've seen his picture in the news a couple of times. Rich businessman or some such, right?"*

*"Very rich and full of business, though, in fact, he isn't mentioned in the news very much at all. He likes to keep a low profile. He organizes summits with thought leaders on private islands but doesn't attend until the final day. He sends senators and Supreme Court justices on Caribbean cruises but only joins them by chopper in the middle of the*

*night when no one's around to see. He's the sort of man who has lots and lots of big ideas about what the future ought to look like. You probably know the type. Somehow he manages to whisper his ideas in the ears of important people and somehow the ideas then show up in various papers and speeches that somehow inform government policy so that every day in every way the world looks a little more like the mind of Thaddeus Blatt, not to say a little more pre-apocalyptic than it was the day before."*

*"So you're saying he's the Antichrist."*

*I think the Recruiter snorted at that, but I'm not sure. "Just another idiot billionaire. The gap between how smart these people think they are and how smart they are in fact is almost infinite."*

*"Okay. What about him?" I asked. "Blatt. What about him?"*

*Like the raven never flitting on the bust of Pallas above the chamber door, the Recruiter did not move a muscle, just sat there, gazing at me steadfast and unreadable. That was a habit he had. Staring at me like that. It got under my skin.*

*"About three weeks ago," he said, "a story began circulating among the people who circulate stories in this town. Apparently, an idea had escaped like a noxious gas from the cesspits of academe and was being passed like a poisoned kiss mouth-to-mouth by the nation's elected representatives and other toxic ne'er-do-wells who have the ability to turn unimaginable flights of idiocy into government policy. In this particular case, the idea had to do with sharing highly classified technical information about next-generation weapons systems with our enemies. Because wouldn't the world be a fairer and more peaceable place if the Christly guardians of Jeffersonian democracy created a parity of power between themselves and the slavering psychotic priest class of a satanic imitation of true religion bent on destroying the known universe to bring their nightmare ideology to its natural fruition?"*

*He paused for such a long moment after that, I said, "Do you want an answer to that question?"*

*"From a man as godless as a turnip? What possible good could that do me?"*

*"No clue."*

*"The point is this," the Recruiter said. "The story found its way into the hands of Warren Gentry, one of these new independent online reporters who has developed a revolutionary innovation in American journalism, namely telling the truth. I believe you may have heard of him."*

*"I have," I said, though I had no idea how he could have known that. "I read his stuff. So all right. Thaddeus Blatt was floating some harebrained scheme to share weapons secrets with our enemies in the name of global peace, and Gentry got hold of it and—what? Ran the story?"*

*"Was about to run it. Then didn't."*

*"Because Thaddeus Blatt . . . paid him off, I'm guessing."*

*The office light gleamed on the Recruiter's bald pate as, slowly, he shook his head side to side. "No. Blatt contacted him, but no money changed hands."*

*"How can you know that?"*

*"I can't. I would have had to violate every law protecting our citizens from the intrusive and illegal gathering of their private information by an intelligence agency that doesn't even exist in the first place."*

*"So it's just a wild guess then."*

*"Exactly. And with the possible exception of your colleague Jerry Collins—who has vanished into the vast expanses of savage nothingness that border the Bosporus—I am talking to the one person in this country who might understand its ramifications."*

*It took me a second before I did understand, but only a second. When the understanding came to me, my stomach started to turn sour.*

*If Warren Gentry was one of the men in the pictures in Kemal Balkin's trophy room, I hadn't seen him there. But Gentry was famously gay and there were rumors he indulged in some pretty outlandish behavior, so possibly the sort of illegal stuff that Balkin would have serviced and then secretly filmed.*

*"You're saying Thaddeus Blatt might have had access to Balkin's intel and blackmailed Gentry into killing a story that would have embarrassed him and thwarted his plans."*

*"If I were saying that, I would have said it, Poetry Boy."*

*"Right."*

*But there it was all the same. The idea sat between us now, almost like a solid object on the Recruiter's desk, something viscous and fetid, sending up fumes. What the Recruiter was telling me was that Thaddeus Blatt might have made himself a candidate for the man most likely to be behind Kemal Balkin's blackmail operation. An American billionaire holding the strings that made official Washington dance.*

*In other words, as quick as that, my crisis had come. I was afraid the next words out of the Recruiter's mouth would be instructions on how to arrange for Thaddeus Blatt to fall afoul of terrorists or get hit by a train or stumble off a rooftop or, worst of all, get cut in half by a bullet from my own gun, his pieces sunk in the Dyke Marsh in the dead of night—which would be sweaty work this time of year, not to mention murder.*

*And look, just being honest here, I would have ridden, do or die, into the valley of death for the Recruiter. But kill an American citizen? The idea made me feel nauseous.*

*"It's a very big guess on very flimsy evidence, isn't it?" I said.*

*"I pity you, Poetry Boy," the Recruiter answered. As I'm pretty sure I've mentioned, he could read my thoughts as if they were running across my forehead like the news on one of those electronic tickers. "By sinking into the chic but ill-considered atheistic fog of postmodernity, you've condemned yourself to drown in a sea of nothingness with no possible basis for determining which way leads upward to the open air of righteous action and which leads downward into an inferno which you don't believe in but know in your very soul exists."*

*"Is there an assignment here?"*

*"What if there is?" said the Recruiter, his expression never changing. "What will you do then? You believe in me, I know, but that's only because you can see me. You're like a duckling imprinted on his mother. But you don't believe in the unseen Bread of Life that feeds my moral core. So how can you know whether you should trust what you can't help but follow?"*

*I laughed. Or I pretended to laugh as I was pretending not to be sick to my stomach. "Just give it to me, chief. Thaddeus Blatt. What do you want me to do with him?"*

*The pause that followed was long enough for my mouth to go dry as a stale crust of bread, even if it was the Bread of Life, which it wasn't.*

*"Find out if Blatt blackmailed Warren Gentry with information he secured from Kemal Balkin, because that might mean he's the secret puppeteer behind Balkin's trophy room and wielding vast resources of extortion over our entire corrupt power class."*

*"Then what?" I said, or tried to say. My voice was little more than a croak.*

*"Then we'll decide from there," said the Recruiter.*

*That wasn't very reassuring.*

*I can still remember the long drive home. There'd been an accident on the parkway. Traffic was bad. It made the tension grow more tense inside me. Sitting there in the Mustang, stopping and starting. Every minute felt like a rubber band being wound tighter and tighter in my gut.*

*I had wandered, lovelorn, into my life in the Division. Looking for something to do, something suitable for a man in an unmanly world. It had seemed like an accident at the time, me being there, but now it felt like fate. The fruit of my own tragic flaw.*

*Because what if the Recruiter was right? What if Thaddeus Blatt was funding Kemal Balkin's enterprise? Drawing elites into compromising situations. Filming them. Blackmailing officials to do his idiot billionaire will. What was the Recruiter going to do about it? Send us out to hunt down every crank with a crappy idea? And what would we be fighting for then? All the Recruiter's talk about Jesus Christ and George Washington or George Christ and Jesus Washington, whichever. Was that my lodestar? Would I be willing to spend my days killing in service to a theocratic madman? I mean, probably I would be, yes, but should I be?*

*I pulled into the garage below my building near the river. Rode the elevator up to my apartment. I felt sweaty, clammy. Maybe it was the heat, but I don't think so. I was so absorbed in my own anxieties, I didn't even notice the line of light beneath the apartment door. I didn't realize there was someone waiting for me in there until I pushed the door open.*

*Then I saw him. A fit, youthful middle-aged man, sitting relaxed in my easy chair by the fireplace. Drinking a glass of the fine rosé I had been saving for a summer evening just like this one. There was a man standing behind him too. A tall, thin man resting a hand on the back of the chair. They were both smiling at me. Welcoming me home to my own apartment.*

*The man in the chair was Thaddeus Blatt.*

*The man behind him was the killer with the pentagram tattoo.*

# 1

Cameron Winter paused there, probably for dramatic effect.

"So," Margaret Whitaker broke in. "Let's talk about Gwendolyn Lord?"

Winter groaned and laughed and raised his gaze heavenward. Margaret was glad to see it. They had crossed a watershed in their therapy work. Winter's crisis was past. She could tell just by looking at him. His eyes—his intelligent, watchful eyes—were bright again. The pasty pale complexion of depression was gone from his cheeks entirely. When she compared him now to the way he'd been not so very long ago, he looked to her like a patient who had recovered from a long illness—or, really, like a corpse that had come back to life.

"This is important, what I'm telling you," he said with half a smile. "No kidding. It really is. It's a big part of my story."

"So is Gwendolyn, I think. You came to me because you were living a life without love. Because your past had left you feeling unworthy of loving or being loved."

"I'm not in love with Gwendolyn, Margaret. I don't even know her."

"You have a date with her this weekend."

"Yes, yes."

"Finally."

"Yes, yes, yes."

"After waiting months before you could work up the courage to ask her. Like some thirteen-year-old boy calling a girl for the first time."

"Do boys and girls still call each other? I thought they just texted each other nude photos and went from there."

Margaret couldn't help but smile. This was the way she liked him best, confident and comical and at war with modernity. And dangerous, when you looked more closely, but only then.

Winter was not her usual sort of client. Not the usual disappointed academic or alienated student or state bureaucrat out of love with his wife. He was a former government contract killer trying to rise above a violent past that had lost its meaning for him. A sensitive thinker, not yet forty, trying to start life afresh as a professor of literature. Tweedy and startlingly handsome—with otherworldly features, she always thought, like an angel in a Renaissance painting. But also—behind the spectacles and under the longish light hair—a quick, cold, deadly man. A vital presence in a dull office decorated all in tans and browns to go with Margaret's dull, tan, brown life.

She'd had an awful crush on him ever since their first session. A transference to the nth power. It left her girly and dreamy, old as she was. She thought of herself as old, anyway. She was nearly seventy. She thought of herself as an old, nervous widow woman. She even cultivated that image of herself in her own mind, repeated it over and over. It soothed her somehow, took the pressure off her. It made her feel as if nothing much were to be expected in the life of such an ancient and fluttery biddy as herself, so she could give up on those expectations and it would be okay.

But sure, yes, she was jealous of this Gwendolyn Lord. She was Winter's first genuinely romantic interest since he and Margaret had started working together. Gwendolyn worked with children in a community center near Chicago. She was a therapist like Margaret, which made Margaret's jealousy worse, as if she were being replaced with a younger model. But jealous as Margaret was, she was also glad. Because Winter was her work, and she knew she had done her work well. He was better now than he had been since she'd known him.

"So where are you taking her on this date?" she asked.

"Just to dinner. There's a place on the lake that seems nice. No big deal. I figured we ought to keep it short and simple at first, find out if we even like each other."

"How are you feeling about it?"

"You want the truth?"

"No, lie to me. Therapists love that."

"I feel like some thirteen-year-old boy calling a girl for the first time. I'm scared out of my wits."

"Yes, I sensed that." Margaret put her hands together, steepled her fingers against her chin. She swiveled back and forth a little in her high-backed leather I-am-the-therapist chair. "What's that about, do you think?"

"Well, I know what you'd say."

"Of course you do. You could jump from your chair to my chair doing the whole therapeutic process on your own. You just told me."

One corner of his mouth turned up, a wry smile. "God, you're a pain in the ass."

She nodded her thanks.

"You do good work though," he said. "I have to admit it. I do admit it. I've been feeling . . ."

"What?" said Margaret, suppressing a smile of her own.

"Better," he said. "Much better, in fact. Really different than I felt when I started coming here. More than that. Different than I've ever felt. Maybe it's just about what happened with Charlotte. I don't know. But it's kind of remarkable. A remarkable transformation."

"And . . . ?"

He took a deep breath. Held it. Let it out in a long stream.

"And, you know, it's just dinner with a woman. I'm a big boy and all. I've gone on dates before. But there is something about Gwendolyn. I can't quite describe it but . . ." Slumped in the client's armchair, he looked up at her with that plaintive, almost childlike look of dependence that came over him sometimes. It was painfully appealing to her, that look. She really did feel a gripping pang in her heart at the thought he might fall in love with this Gwendolyn and bring his therapy to its reasonable end. She felt like a mother watching her son go off on his own, she told herself. But that was a lie, such a lie. She didn't feel motherly toward him at all.

She went on watching him, went on swiveling in her chair. Keeping silent, giving him no direction. It was time for him to learn to figure these things out for himself.

"What will I say to her, Margaret?" Winter asked. "What will I tell her about myself? Who I've been. What I've done."

Margaret lowered her steepled fingers so he could see her face clearly. "You've told me about those things," she said. "You've told me the worst of them anyway. And I'm still here, aren't I?"

He averted his eyes. He gazed off into space. He nodded to himself—sadly, she thought. "That's what I keep telling myself," he said. "You're still here."

Margaret started to speak but hesitated. Her throat thickened and she was uncertain of her voice. It was only for a moment. She swallowed hard. The moment passed.

"Our time is up for today, Cam," she said then. "Off you go."

# 2

Winter had liked Gwendolyn Lord from the first moment he saw her. More than that. He liked her in a way he found odd and disturbing. There was, as he'd told Margaret, something about her, something that touched him to his core.

She was a small woman with a slim, graceful figure, but she carried herself very straight so that she seemed taller than she was, straight and somehow serene, too, with a gleam of humor in her green eyes. Ladylike and girly at once, was how he described her to himself. She had elfin features framed with wavy brown hair down to her shoulders. Cute enough, in his judgment, but not gorgeous. There was nothing spectacular in the sight of her, nothing dazzling. It was just her way, her presence that had such a powerful effect on him.

What was odd, though, what was disturbing, what unnerved him and put that thirteen-year-old's fear into him—a fear that grew worse as he drove the two-plus hours to see her that Saturday afternoon—was the quiet, almost unnoticeable, natural flow of his attraction to her. It wasn't love at first sight or flaming passion or anything dramatic like that. It was more as if he'd known her even before he saw her, as if he recognized her though they had never met.

It was early evening by the time he pulled his Jeep SUV up in front of her apartment building, a fine summer evening, mild and warm and breezy. He was wearing a tan seersucker suit and a white shirt open at the throat. As he walked up the path toward the faceless block of the structure, he upbraided himself for wearing such an outfit. Could he have dressed any whiter? he asked himself. Could he have made himself appear any more WASPy and nerdy and professor-ish if he'd tried? Was he *trying* to put her off? Was he engaged in some sort of unconscious self-sabotage?

He came into the glass foyer. Pressed the buzzer under her name. Her voice sang out over the intercom. "I'll be right down."

His heart—so he described it bitterly to himself—was going pitter-pat. As he waited for her to appear, he spent the time reviewing every single one of his doubts and fears. He was just remembering a particularly ugly job during which he'd broken a man's neck with his bare hands when he saw her through the glass doors. She emerged from the elevator and walked toward him smiling.

He stood with his hands safely in his pockets and watched her approach. There was a novel he'd read long ago—or no, a short story. Literary man though he was, he couldn't remember the name of the author just at the moment. But the title of the story had always struck him as particularly wonderful: "The Girls in Their Summer Dresses." What man who heard those words would not understand the sweet sadness of longing in them?

Gwendolyn Lord was wearing a summer dress. It was royal blue with an irregular white floral print—a ditzy print, he had once heard it called. There was a deep V at the neck that showed off the elegance of her figure. The skirt ended at her knees and he could see her legs were very graceful and fine.

He was struck again at the mysterious quiet of her appeal to him. Like suddenly noticing the beauty of a girl you grew up with. Like a change in feeling for an old friend.

When he opened the door of the Jeep for her and she lowered herself into it past his eye level, she smiled at him again. He had the uncanny sense that everything that was going to happen between them had already happened. He was just catching up with reality.

So it seemed to him all evening long.

"I'm sorry it took me so long to call," he said, as he drove along the suburban lanes toward the lake.

"No, I'm happy you called at all. I wasn't expecting it. I thought I'd made a total fool of myself, running out and accosting you like that just as everything was going to pieces."

He was off the hook for his delay. There was no need to continue. But he'd rehearsed these lines and he couldn't help saying them. "I just had some old business to attend to."

"I completely understand. Of course you did."

These words had not sounded the same to him out loud as when he'd practiced them in his mind. They sounded like there'd been some other relationship he'd had to weasel out of. And now he felt he had to correct that impression, because while it was sort of true, it wasn't really true, and he knew if he let himself start lying to her, he would go on and on lying to her because he couldn't bear the idea of telling her the truth about his life and more than anything he just wished he had shot himself before he'd called and asked her out.

What it was about this woman that reduced him to preadolescent insecurity like this, he really didn't know. And yet even this—this moment of tweener lunacy—seemed weirdly comfortable to him, as if it had happened before, as if it were all more like a memory than a present event.

What was wrong with him? It was more than he could unravel.

The restaurant was good enough, a typical suburban steak house, all white tablecloths and oversized windows. But the views were excellent. They were seated above the lakefront. The late sun lay in a sparkling line across the riffling surface of the water. The pretty weekend sloops sailed by on the first breath of dusk.

He ordered a bottle of that rosé he liked to drink in summer-time. And as the waitress walked away from them, he stole a glance at Gwendolyn's left hand.

"Yes," she said. "I took it off. See? You had a good effect on me."

He smiled, embarrassed. She'd been wearing a wedding band when he'd met her first. Still mourning her husband, a marine who was killed in the wars. Now the ring was gone.

"I'm not sure how I feel about your reading my mind like that," he said.

"Sorry. My therapist training. Watching eyes. Expressions. I can't stop myself off-hours."

"Well, I'm glad if I was helpful."

"It had to happen sooner or later. It was just the suddenness of it, you know. Brett dying the way he did. It was like a story that didn't have a chance to end, or even to get started really. We barely knew each other when we got married. He was a very hard man not to fall in love with. Like a hero out of books. We'd only been married two months when he was called up, and I never saw him face-to-face again."

"I'm sorry."

"I never really got to be his wife, so it was hard to figure out how to be his widow. Or how to stop being his widow."

What could he say to all that? He only nodded, jealous of the dead man, sorry for her.

A fussy, mustachioed cartoon of a sommelier came with the wine and rescued them from the awkward moment. Uncorking. Tasting. Pouring. Hanging about. As soon as he left, the waitress descended on them, but Winter shooed her away so they could drink and talk awhile in peace.

"I'm not very good at this, am I?" she said.

"At what?"

"You know: being on a date, making conversation. I haven't been on a date since Brett. It's been literally three years."

"Well, the ring . . . It was discouraging."

"Well, that was the whole point of it, wasn't it?" She made her hand into a pistol and put it to her head. "And now, I've dumped all this on you before we've even gotten to know each other. I'm sure I've made you completely uncomfortable."

"No, no."

"Tell me what you're thinking. I'm feeling really insecure." Winter gestured helplessly. "No. Go ahead," she said. "Give it to me straight, professor. I can take it."

"I was thinking . . . some lines of poetry, to tell the truth. Poetry has a way of cluttering up my mind. I was thinking, 'They shall grow not old, as we that are left grow old: / Age shall not weary them, nor the years condemn. / At the going down of the sun and in the morning / We will remember them.' It's about soldiers who've died in a war."

"Oh, it's beautiful."

"'For the Fallen,' it's called. Laurence Binyon."

"And you just have that in your head like that?"

"For lack of anything useful, yes."

"No, I love that, it's wonderful. I think it's wonderful to be able to do that. I haven't read much poetry at all. Is that really what you were thinking?"

He sipped his wine and sighed. "Well . . . I think it was my way of saying to myself that it will be hard to compete with a fallen hero out of books."

She went quiet and lifted her chin as she understood him. "Oh!" she said. Then she studied him, her green eyes soft and bright. A corner of her mouth turned up. "I don't believe you," she said finally.

"No, it's true. That's what I was thinking."

"Yes, it's true that you were thinking that. But I don't believe that it will be hard for you to compete." She sat back in her chair, considering him, glass in hand. Swirled her wine, the lake glistening out beyond her. He watched the intelligence working beneath her features. "You came into this town out of nowhere," she said. "And when you left, the corruption was gone, and the gangsters were gone, and a murder was solved, and all as if by magic with you doing nothing to make it happen. Like dominoes falling, but all by themselves. And then there was the story I heard on the news about the girl at your university. The one you rescued."

"The news reports made it sound more exciting than it was."

"Mm . . ." she said. She considered him. "I've thought about all that a lot since then. During all that long, long time you didn't call me," she added teasingly.

He laughed. "I really am sorry."

"Who are you, Cameron? Will you tell me?"

"I'm an English professor," he said automatically, but then he immediately waved the words away. "But before that, I suppose I was a kind of warrior too. The secret variety. It was violent sometimes. Oftentimes. That was the old business I was referring to before. The old business I had to take care of. It had an effect on me, on my mind."

"Of course it did. Of course," said Gwendolyn.

"It made an evening like this one fraught. Difficult."

"That's all right. It's difficult for me too. I guess we were both wounded in the wars, weren't we?"

He found himself going on before he had decided to go on, before he had decided what he was going to say.

He said: "Someone once told me that a soldier can never come back to the country he fought for."

"Yes. Yes. I worked with soldiers for a while. As a kind of therapy. Or penance maybe. After Brett died. To do what a soldier has to do, it's not enough to believe the enemy is bad. You have to believe your own country is good. And then you come home and . . . Well, no country can really be good, can it? They've all got people in them, and you know what they're like. And no one understands what you did or is grateful for it, except in that offhand *thank you for your service* sort of way. So what was it all for?"

Winter found himself gazing at her in a daze. He was startled to find he had spoken so plainly to her so quickly. The very thing he'd been afraid of telling her he'd told her almost without a thought. Again, as if all the preliminaries, the chitchat, and the getting-to-know-you and so on had already been taken care of in some weird way.

"So now," said Gwendolyn, off a swallow of wine. "Now you use your—what did you call it?—your strange habit of mind—you use your strange habit of mind to make things right where you can. To do good where you can and . . ." She spoke with mock drama. ". . . solve impossible murders. Do I have that right?"

He opened his mouth to speak, but he didn't speak. He didn't know what would come out of him. He didn't trust himself.

Gwendolyn suddenly transformed her tone. She must have sensed his distress—sensed it and, on a kindly impulse, changed the mood. She became playful and girlish, leaning toward him across the table.

"Ooh, I know a good one."

"A good . . . ?"

"An impossible murder. I know *about* one, anyway. I just heard about it recently. It's a really creepy story too. Can I tell you? Or would that be like telling an artist what picture to paint? I don't want to be *that* girl."

Winter smiled, glad to go along with her. This feeling he had, this feeling that he had walked into the middle of something that was happening before he arrived, so deep in the middle he worried he wouldn't be able to get out—it was too much for him to think about just then.

Out of the corner of his eye, he caught the waitress circling. He waved her off again.

"Let's hear it," he said.

"Oh, good!"

She launched into her tale with wide-eyed relish, like a counselor at a summer campfire telling the story of the ghost who haunted the surrounding woods. Winter took the opportunity to study her small features—those features he had decided were cute—and the sound of her voice, which he found intelligent, pretty, and soothing.

"Okay," she said. "So I had this friend in grad school. Livy Swain, her name was. Kind of a—I don't know what you'd call it these days—we used to call it a tomboy type, something like that. Very gung ho, athletic, roll-up-your-sleeves-and-get-her-done sort of girl. I think that's why we got along so well, because we were polar opposites. I can sit in a window seat and daydream for days on end. Not Livy. She was interested in forensic psychology, dealing with criminals. And after we graduated, she got a job down in

Tulsa, Oklahoma, at a jail there. Doing assessments and sometimes giving testimony in trials and stuff like that. Very exciting. Perfect work for Livy too. I can just picture her doing that sort of thing."

Winter's mind had drifted. He was thinking about kissing her cheek very softly, or very softly at first until she turned to face him.

"Are you with me? Is this boring?" she asked.

"No, I'm listening," he said and forced himself to listen. "Go ahead."

"All right. So she visited the other day. Livy. She told me this story. This is something that happened about four, five months ago, she said. One day, there's this terrible murder. This is not the impossible murder. This is a different murder, before that. But it was very shocking. This man whose name I can't remember. Owen. Owen Something. He suddenly murders his wife and son, stabs them to death. And what's so shocking about it is that he's been living in Tulsa for several years and he's more or less been a pillar of the community. He has an independent IT shop, doing computer upkeep for several businesses in town. He's an honest guy, well trusted. Goes to church. Umpires Little League games at the Y. Everyone likes him. The last man you'd expect, right? But suddenly, for no reason, he goes crazy. Stabs his wife and his year-old son to death. Neighbors hear the screams. Call the police. The police come and they bring him to the jail. And he is absolutely raving. Screaming, fighting with the officers and so on. They have to put him in restraints and shove him in what they call a safety cell. A padded cell. Now, this cell is just a small room with absolutely nothing in it but a drain the prisoner can use for a toilet. No furniture. Because they don't want him to be able to stand on anything and reach the lights and hurt himself. So it's just a tiny rectangle of a room. There's no camera in it, but there is a small square of a window in the door so they can look in and check on him and there's a camera outside so they can see if anyone goes in or out.

"They bring him in and they have to take his clothes off to make sure he can't hurt himself. So now he's just wearing his boxer shorts. And he's in shackles, hands and feet. And they throw him in the padded cell. Okay?"

Winter was focused on what she was saying now, and only lost a sentence or two occasionally when his eyes traced the elegant length of her throat to the gold cross she wore above the V-neck of her summer dress and then flitted down into the V-neck imagining the places where he would one day kiss her.

"I'm listening," he said again, and tried harder to listen.

"Well, they can't keep him in the safety cell for very long without getting an assessment from Psych Services. That's Livy, that's my friend. Also, if they need to sedate him they have to get her approval for that too. Her office is upstairs from the cells. So one of the guards goes to fetch her. And this man, this murderer, Owen Something. Owen McKay, that's his name. Owen McKay has gone quiet now in the safety cell. One of the guards looks in on him through the square window. And he's pacing around in his shackles, but he seems to be calming down. So the guard goes back to his station, where he can monitor the—what do you call it?—footage, the video from the security cams. He can see that no one goes in or out of the cell. It's down this little corridor off by itself. No one even goes near it.

"Now, Livy comes down in the elevator to do an assessment. She goes to the safety cell and looks in. She can see Owen McKay is now lying face down on top of the drain. So Livy calls the guard. The guard opens the cell and they go in. They call Owen's name. He's nonresponsive. The guard turns him over. He's dead! All right? He's been shot in the heart. He's been murdered! Right there in the cell."

Gwendolyn sat back in her chair with an air of satisfaction. "That's good, right? It's like one of those—what do you call 'em? That they have in books and television shows."

"A locked room mystery," said Winter, amused.

"Exactly. Like in a novel, right? A locked room mystery. So? What do you think? Should I book you a flight to Tulsa so you can go and solve it?"

"Can I finish my wine first?"

Just then, the waitress returned and this time there seemed to be no getting rid of her. They ordered dinner.

Winter admired the way Gwendolyn had handled their awkwardness. He could see it had been well done. He imagined she had prepared that murder story beforehand, in case the conversation lagged. But she had used it instead to dispel the heavy mood that had descended on them after they had exchanged intimacies too quickly, too soon.

Now, when they returned to chatting, everything was easier between them. They got down to the usual sort of subjects. Her work with children at the community center. His study of the British Romantic poets. The ordinary first date back-and-forth. But even this, maybe especially this—this ordinary atmosphere between them—seemed remarkable to Winter. Because so easily, so smoothly, so oddly well, they had moved beyond the truth he had feared to tell her. And now it was done, he had told her, and it was all right. Like Margaret Whitaker, Gwendolyn was still here.

When they finished dinner, they walked down to the lake and strolled the asphalt path along the shore. It was night now, a bright gibbous moon risen above the distant screen of trees. The sloops had all sailed for home. The empty water lapped and rippled. The silver moonlight shimmered on the little waves. Crickets twittered.

Frogs croaked. The noise of traffic seemed far away. Somehow a sense of closeness had sprung up between them. Winter was surprised to find he had taken her hand. It was like everything else about being with her, done before he'd done it, suddenly there.

"Are you religious at all?" she asked him.

With the water and the night and the big bright moon, it seemed natural to move on to more personal subjects.

"Not really, no," he said. "I mean, I can see there's some sort of mystery to it all. It's just with religion, I can never get past all the priestcraft and hocus-pocus. The fussiness about other people's personal lives and peccadilloes . . ." He added quickly: "I don't mean to be . . ."

"No, it's all right."

"I noticed your cross. I remember you mentioned you had a church last time I saw you. You are religious, I take it."

"I am," she said. "Very. Total Jesus girl. Since I was little. I don't know what I would have done without him and without the church these last few years."

"Oh, yes, sure. Does it bother you that I'm not?" he asked her. What he really wanted to ask, of course, was whether there would be some sort of religious prissiness when it came time for them to sleep together, but there was no good way to ask her that.

She considered her answer for a moment. "No," she said slowly. "It doesn't bother me. I'm not sure why but . . . I don't think it does anyway. No. No, it doesn't."

They were quiet for a few seconds after that. Then, impulsively, he asked: "What do you want, Gwendolyn?"

He wasn't certain in the dark, but he thought her answer sounded hesitant. Wary. "What do you mean?"

"In life. You know. What do you want your life to be?"

She did not answer for a long time—so long he was about to ask again. But then she said: "My mother specifically told me not to talk about that."

"Your mother?"

"She says it scares men away. Ever since you called me, she's been phoning me with advice. She's got a lot riding on this date. My brother's a bit of a wild child, and Mother's desperate for grandchildren."

Winter laughed. "Tell her I don't usually impregnate women on the first date, but for her sake, I might make an exception."

She laughed too and slapped his shoulder with her free hand. He began to wonder what Total Jesus Girl might make of it if he really did kiss her.

"Anyway, if a man is going to be scared of your dreams, shouldn't you find out sooner rather than later?" he said.

"Oh, I don't know."

"Well. I wouldn't want to contradict your mother. I withdraw the question."

They walked in silence, hand in hand. The woods across the water drew into silhouette as the night deepened.

All at once, Gwendolyn said: "Children. Lots of children. And a big rambling house to put them in. And I want to homeschool them with the other homeschooling mothers in my church. When I hear them talking at coffee hour, I'm so jealous sometimes it's like I'm being boiled in oil. And I want a husband who comes home at night and all the children shout out loud and run to greet him. And he's happy, you know, because he's living in Proverbs 31 and Ephesians 5 and he thinks it's the greatest thing ever. That's what I want."

When he glanced at her, he saw the moonlight swimming in her eyes, and he realized the effort of telling him this had made the tears rise in them. Her voice was unsteady when she said to him: "So was my mother right? Do you think I'm terrifying now?"

*I think you're magic*, he wanted to say to her, but he couldn't get the words out. The best he could do was to lean over and kiss her once, very quickly, very gently, a kiss which she quickly and gently returned.

Then they walked on in silence again, hand in hand.

# 3

Winter did not think again about the murder of Owen McKay until suddenly he did. It was the Monday after his date with Gwendolyn. He was home again, just off campus, sitting in the Independent coffee shop not writing his book.

He always liked the Independent and he liked it especially now, in July. With school out, it was often nearly empty. In the later afternoon, after the government workers trudged back to their offices to do whatever it was government workers did, he had his choice of tables. He could grab a coffee and croissant and nab one of the seats right by the big window. And he could sit as long as he wanted, watching the sparrows in the trees and the bright goldfinches and occasional cardinals, not to mention the girls in their summer dresses walking by beneath the branches. It made not writing his book a very pleasant occupation.

The book was supposed to be about the cultural forces that had shaped the transition from the first generation of Romantic poets to the second. He had been not working on it for months now, and the number of pages he hadn't written had grown and grown. He was beginning to suspect that he was not very interested in the cultural forces that had shaped the transition from the first generation of

Romantic poets to the second. In fact, he was becoming pretty well certain he didn't give a damn about them.

His procrastination had begun long before he'd gone out with Gwendolyn. But now he had gone out with her so he could not only avoid writing but avoid writing while thinking about her, which seemed at least to give him some kind of excuse.

Their date had been an event for him and he knew it. He had sent her flowers afterward. He had called her. He had asked her out again. And she had said yes without hesitation, which had made him immoderately glad. But there were questions nagging at him. For instance, this business of her religion. If she was so totally Jesus-y, why didn't his agnosticism bother her? Why was there no man at her church eager to live out the Bible verses she'd mentioned? And what were those verses? Winter didn't know them and had forgotten their names and numbers so he couldn't look them up. And why, after three years a widow, wearing her husband's ring—why had she chased after him to tell him she was single? Why had she taken the ring off for him? Why him specifically? As if she felt as he did, that they had somehow stepped into their relationship in medias res.

It was because he could solve none of these puzzles that he returned to the puzzling murder of Owen McKay. It was a way of thinking about Gwendolyn Lord without constantly thinking about Gwendolyn Lord.

He did not find the murder itself particularly interesting. He never really understood why the murders that drew him drew him. But it wasn't for the pure puzzle of them, he knew that. He did not read mystery novels very often, and when he did, it was never one of those conundrum stories about impossible circumstances and locked rooms and the like. He always found the solutions to such books too ridiculous. *The murderer used a mirror to make it seem as if he had disappeared, then used a blowgun to inject an untraceable poison before lowering the body through a trapdoor into a ventilator shaft and . . .* Why not just shoot the bastard and dump the body in the ocean? That's what guns and sharks were for.

Still, reading about Owen McKay was better than worrying over questions he couldn't answer—and better than just sitting there stuffing a croissant in his face while not writing his book. So he pushed the plate with its half-eaten croissant to one side and opened his laptop on the table.

McKay's death had occurred six months ago, as it turned out. Much of the rest of the story was as Gwendolyn had told it. McKay's murderous rampage had been completely unexpected. Before that, he was a well-liked, even-tempered man of thirty-seven. He was widely considered decent and reliable as both a friend and a businessman. No one close to him had noticed any change in him that forewarned he would go mad. He had recently complained about having the flu, one neighbor told a local news site. But it was February then. Everyone was suffering with some sort of ailment or other. McKay had missed three days of work, that was all. Then, suddenly, late one night, there came the screams from the bedroom of his modest brick-faced house in the Brookside district.

A local television station had broadcast cell phone video of McKay's arrest. As fretful neighbors gathered to watch, an armored city police officer marched out the front door in the lead. Then two officers followed with the handcuffed McKay between them. A fifth officer trailed huskily behind them.

McKay was a midsize white man, well made, broad shouldered. He had thinning red hair, now standing on end, and a goatee. Though the weather was chill and gray, he wore nothing but jeans and a white T-shirt. There were tattoos on both his muscular arms. His T-shirt was stained with blood.

As the officers hauled him to the patrol car at the curb, he struggled in their grip, but only intermittently, like a landed fish. The rest of the time, he simply flung back his head and howled wildly into the bleak darkness of the winter sky.

It was an animal cry. A wolf's howl. At first, Winter could not make out the words he was saying. He had to rewind the vid and lower the volume. Finally, it became clear.

"It's still there! Still there!" cried Owen McKay. "Still there!"

As the officers lowered him into the patrol car's rear seat, his body went slack. He hung his head and began to weep silently.

Winter watched the video three times over. He had to admit there was something disturbing about it. McKay's son had been only eighteen months old.

"They were a nice family," one neighbor, a woman in her fifties, told the local TV reporter. "You'd see them walking together, very nice, very loving. They were always nice. This is such a shock."

Winter moved on to the story of McKay's death. He saw the headline: ACCUSED KILLER COMMITS SUICIDE IN COUNTY JAIL.

He thought: *Suicide.* Gwendolyn had said it was murder.

But before he could go on reading, he sensed a presence looming over him. He glanced up. His stomach dropped like a man on the gallows. There was Lori Lesser standing before his table, smiling down at him with what he took to be a predatory smile.

The dean of student relations—or as he sometimes thought of her, La Belle Dame sans Merci—was, to him, a strangely cuddly monster. She was a pile of mismatched secondhand clothing with a shock of frizzy hair on top. Her pert features seemed spotlit by eyes bright with fanaticism. She was, Winter thought, a dangerous character in her own loopy way. And yet, he could not help it: He found her strangely attractive. She had a nice, full figure, so that was one thing. But also, he was never sure whether she was going to try to destroy him or seduce him. Which he just found kind of sexually interesting.

Lori's job, when she was not torturing the faculty, was tormenting the students. She patrolled their attitudes, ideas, social media posts, and sex lives. Whenever one of them violated the university code of conduct, she would launch one of her dreaded inquiries. The inquiry always began with Lori smiling and "just trying to understand what happened." It usually ended with someone's career or reputation in tatters. Given that the code of conduct had a lengthy section covering sexual relations, and given that the students were in their teens and early twenties, one of these inquiries was almost always in progress.

Except for recently. Recently, Lori had been on a six-month sabbatical. According to some campus rumors, Winter's retrograde attitudes toward gender, race, and the teaching of poetry had so exhausted her, she needed to undergo some sort of treatment to restore her psyche. Apparently, Winter was a painful enigma to her. He had no tenure. He taught the poetry of dead white men from their own points of view. He was blithely untroubled in his heterosexuality. He had even had an affair with a student once, though that was before such relationships were explicitly forbidden by the code. Yet for all that, Lori could neither get him fired nor convince him to sleep with her. According to the rumors, this state of affairs had played havoc with her peace of mind.

Possibly these rumors were strictly satirical. Winter wasn't sure. But in any case, he had not realized how much he had enjoyed Lori's absence until the moment—this very moment—when it abruptly came to an end.

"Lori," he said in a pathetic imitation of enthusiasm. "You're back."

"How are you, Cam? Do you mind if I sit for a minute?"

He had even managed to forget the irritating buzzy sound of her voice. Like a nest of adenoidal wasps. "Of course," he said. "Please."

She was dressed in something flowery and fluttery with a flowery, fluttery shawl wrapped around it. The whole shambolic package wafted down into the seat across from him.

"I hear you got yourself into quite a situation while I was gone," she said.

"Did I?" said Winter. "Oh, you mean the girl and the gun and all that."

"Everyone's talking about it. They think you're a hero."

Her voice took on an ironic, insinuating tone when she said that. That's what Winter heard anyway. *They think you're a hero but you and I know better, don't we?* That's what he thought she was trying to tell him.

"How was your sabbatical?" he asked her.

Her answer went on a long time. It seemed there had been a conference of some sort in a watering hole in Sedona, Arizona. Something about decolonizing the student mindset. Lori was very animated in her descriptions of the event. But Winter's eyes kept drifting back to his laptop screen.

> *Owen McKay, a 37-year-old computer repairman charged with brutally stabbing his wife and baby son to death, shot himself in county jail yesterday afternoon after somehow managing to smuggle a manual nail gun into a padded safety cell,* the story began.

*A nail gun?* Winter thought. He lifted his eyes to Lori and smiled as if he was listening to her. Instead, he was trying to imagine what part of McKay's work in information technology would require a nail gun.

". . . widespread reimagining of the liberal arts curriculum—something I'm very much hoping you and I will be able to collaborate on," Lori was saying.

"What do you mean?" Winter replied vaguely. He was not exactly sure what she had said, but it had set off an alarm in the part of his mind that was keeping track of her.

"Well, I know we're all reluctant to experience change," Lori went on in a tone of mock self-mockery. "But seeing as the attitudes that come across in our teaching even unintentionally are complicit in the formation of young minds . . ."

*Leann Snopes, a spokesperson for the Tulsa County Sheriff's office, says an investigation is underway into how the inmate managed to hide the nail gun in his jeans despite the jail's usual intake searches,* Winter read, discreetly glancing at his screen.

*In his jeans?* he thought. Gwendolyn had said McKay was stripped down to his boxer shorts.

*"Mr. McKay was brought into the safety cell because of his state of violent agitation," Ms. Snopes told reporters. "That may have created a necessity to hurry during the intake process so that the weapon was overlooked. Our investigation is ongoing."*

"Just for an example," Lori went on. "Obviously, you'll want to come up with your own ideas, but next year, you're scheduled to teach a one-oh course in English Romantic poetry to fulfill the breadth requirement. And I was thinking, 'Wouldn't it be fun if, instead of the usual boring suspects everybody knows already, we could incorporate the voices of Indigenous people of color in that curriculum?' "

Without thinking, Winter laughed out loud.

When he thought about this moment later, he recalled an obscure sonnet by John Keats:

Why did I laugh to-night? No voice will tell
No God, no Demon of severe response,
Deigns to reply from Heaven or from Hell . . .

*Likewise,* Winter thought. He wasn't sure what had brought the laughter out of him. It may have just been Lori's idiot notion that he would ever agree to teach English Romantic poetry through the works of Indigenous people of color who—outside of Wordsworth's sonnet on the Haitian slave rebellion—had had no meaningful part in it. What color would the Indigenous people of eighteenth-century England be? Blue? But he might also have been reacting to the idea that a man could hide a yard-long nail gun from even the most rudimentary intake search, especially if he was only wearing boxer shorts, but even in his jeans.

In the end, he knew, it didn't really matter why he laughed. "O mortal pain! / O Darkness! Darkness! ever must I moan, / To question Heaven and Hell and Heart in vain." The simple fact was, he had laughed—and Lori could not have looked more shocked and offended if he had leaned across the table and slapped her in the face.

"I'm sorry, did I say something funny?" she asked him. And there was that just-asking-questions smile that usually began one of her inquiries.

It was in that moment that Winter decided to investigate the death of Owen McKay. For once, he understood his own motives. He wanted to solve the impossible murder in the hope of impressing Gwendolyn Lord.

It was Lori's blather that brought this on. Normally, his feelings toward Lori ran the gamut from irritation to a lot of irritation. Today, though, he just found her depressing. Why was she talking to him about poetry? If she knew the first thing about poetry, he thought, she would not behave as she did.

Winter's love of Romantic poetry was a blessedly simple thing. He loved it because he found it beautiful. The beauty connected him to something—a mysterious truth outside himself—a truth that could be described in no other way but through the poem. For all his questions about his evening with Gwendolyn Lord, he realized in this moment that he felt the same way about her. At first sight, something about her resonated with him, connected him to something beyond them both. He couldn't quite say what that something was. But the same was true of poetry. There was something in its beauty that was truth itself, and so it was with Gwendolyn.

What Lori was talking about was not that. It was the opposite of that. It was the nonsense of the moment, a fad of the age. He wanted to get away from her as quickly as possible and get back to the things that mattered to him. She was making him feel sad.

He smiled at her. He knew it was an acid smile, but it was the best he could do. "I have to go, Lori," he said. "Welcome back."

Her face turned a dark and stormy red. Her eyes grew so bright, he seriously wondered if she was clinically insane. "No, no, wait a minute," she said. "Why did you laugh? It's important. I think we should discuss this."

"I know you do," Winter said. He shut his laptop and slipped it into its bag. "But I really do have to go."

He could feel those bright eyes on him as he walked out of the coffee shop. A stare like a bullet, right between his shoulder blades. He stepped out of the air-conditioning and into the blue warmth of the day. A white sun glared through the sidewalk canopy of green leaves. As he walked away, his hand went into his pocket for his phone. When he reached the corner, away from the coffee shop windows, he paused beneath the branches of a small hickory tree. He called up an airline site and booked a trip to Oklahoma.

# 4

He began his inquiries with Livy Swain, Gwendolyn's friend from grad school.

He met her in a Tulsa tavern the next day. It was early evening, still light. The air was heavy outside, ninety degrees under a gray sky. The tavern was in a line of low Western-style red-brick buildings in a stretch of concrete under a big sky.

He had rented a sleek Audi A5, snazzy blue. He parked it in one of the slanted spaces at the curb. It looked out of place in a row of compacts and pickups, all American made. As he stepped out, the heat hit him hard. He looked up and down the wide street. It was almost empty. A car or two passing. No pedestrians. The air hung like lead. To Winter, the place looked like the middle of nowhere.

Walking through the tavern door was like passing from a foggy atmosphere into an even foggier atmosphere. Apparently, people still smoked cigarettes indoors in Oklahoma. The little room was blurry beneath a gray fug. The tavern was about half full, at both the bar and the tables. The faces around him looked pale and far away under the hanging white cloud. There was music playing, but it was not too loud. That was a relief, at least. Winter hated modern music. He was not all that fond of modernity in general. The eighteenth century was his Happy Place.

Livy Swain was sitting at a small round table in a corner way in back, right next to the men's room door. He had asked Gwendolyn to call her to help set up the meeting. Livy had agreed to meet but she'd told Winter on the phone she didn't want to be seen with him at her place of work. Winter took that as a sign of secrecy and trouble.

There was a box of filtered Luckies on her table, a yellow plastic lighter, a black plastic ashtray, and a long glass of beer. She had one cigarette in her hand already, nearly burned out. When she saw Winter, she laughed and shook her head.

"What's so funny?" said Winter, smiling. He slipped into the chair across from her.

"You," Livy said. "You and Gwendolyn. Gwendolyn and her handsome heroes."

The waitress hurried over to them. Winter spoke to her over his shoulder. "I'll have what she's having." He turned back to Livy. "I'm her type, you mean."

"You should have seen Brett, her husband. He must have bought his jawline at a comic book store. What are you, like a Navy SEAL or something?"

"I'm an English professor."

Livy laughed and shook her head again. "I'll bet."

Winter liked her. He could see right away she was smart and humorous—and just bitter enough to be amusing. She was short and curvy, big breasts, big hips, but fit and narrow at the waist. She had an angular face, permanently *stuck on cynical.* Her eyes were lively and hard behind her small, round glasses. Her dark, lank hair ending jaggedly at her earlobes. It looked like she had cut it with a dagger as an act of revenge.

"And you want to know about Owen McKay," she said.

"I study odd crimes sometimes," Winter said.

"And rescue kidnapped girls and arrange for gangsters to get killed. As English professors do."

"It's a comprehensive curriculum."

Livy took a last draw on her cigarette then jabbed it out in the ashtray. "Gwendolyn. She is such a character. Such a girly girl. Don't get me wrong. I love her to death. Has she told you about Jesus yet?"

"A bit. Jewish man. White robe."

"That's the one. I guess you guys are on your way. So what can I do for you, English Professor?"

Winter was sorry to change the subject. He wanted to hear more about Gwendolyn and what she thought of him. But he knew enough about women to know that anything he said to Livy would be repeated to her friend. He figured it would be wiser to get down to business.

"The way I understand it," he said, "the sheriff's department believes Owen McKay smuggled a nail gun into a county jail in his boxer shorts, then shot himself in the heart with it while he was manacled inside a locked padded cell."

"If you can't trust the government, who can you trust?" Livy said dryly.

"You seem dubious."

Livy lifted the cigarette pack off the table and shook out a filter. She offered it to Winter. He waved it off. The air in the room being thick as it was, he felt he had smoked half a pack already.

Livy shot the cigarette between her teeth. Winter swept the plastic lighter off the table and held the flame for her.

"Thank you," she said. "A hero and a gentleman."

"And an English professor," said Winter.

"Right." Livy took a drag. The smoke poured out of her as she spoke again. "The whole thing is bug-eyed crazy. There were no drugs in McKay's system. No history of violence. He was a pillar of the community. Suddenly, he knifes his wife and baby to death. He comes into jail the next day raving and struggling. They put a spit mask on him. They strip him and put him in chains. They toss him in the safety cell practically naked and they call me for an assessment so they can dose him. No one goes in or out of the cell. I come down fifteen minutes later—and he's dead. A nail in his heart. And he's lying face down over the piss hole so the blood goes straight down, no stain on the floor."

"What about the nail gun?"

"I only saw it for a second. The guards rushed me out of there in a big hurry."

"And?"

Livy shrugged. "What do I know about nail guns? It was made of wood."

"Wood?"

"Don't ask me. I looked it up online. You can make a nail gun out of wood, but not like this. It was small. Like a cannister. That's all I saw."

Winter sat back in his chair. He tilted his head back, looking up through the hanging smoke at the beamed ceiling. In fact, he did know how to make a nail gun the size of a cannister out of wood. But then, he was an assassin.

He lowered his eyes to Livy. "He was murdered then."

She made a riffling noise. "Ya think?"

The waitress plunked Winter's beer down on the table beside him. Winter took a swig. He wished he could breathe the beer instead of the air in the room. The place was a box of poison. He coughed.

"You have a theory of the case?" he asked.

The sharp eyes behind the round lenses took a long appraising look at him. "My theory is: People are lying and people are scared. I know I'm scared. And nobody talks about it. Not even gossip. It's just a thing that happened that no one ever says a word about." She leaned toward him, close enough so he could smell the cigarette on her breath even in the ambient smoke. She dropped her voice so that her words were almost drowned out by the low music. "The more I think about it, I don't even know if Owen McKay did the original crime. Killed his wife, his kid. I don't even know if he did that. I don't know anything. Well, that's not totally true. I'm a forensic psychologist. I know some things. For instance. I know that that sort of break—where everything's fine, then you suddenly stab your wife and child to death: That's not a thing that actually happens. People are evil and kill people. People are mentally ill and get violent. People take drugs and go nuts. People have passions. They have affairs and kill their spouses or their spouses have affairs and they find out about it and kill them. There's gotta be something, some kind of trigger. And there was nothing like that here, or if there was, I never heard about it. What I heard was a lot of people in positions of power telling me that he smuggled in a nail gun and committed suicide. Nice people mostly. People I like and respect. But, while they're telling me this, they're looking me in the eyes in a way that says: 'Don't ask the next question, Livy. Don't ask any questions, if you know what's good for you. Just go on with your life and forget about it.' So . . ." She gestured with her cigarette. She lifted one shoulder. "That's what I did."

"Except with Gwendolyn. You told her."

Livy shrugged. "I was in town for a visit last week. Girls' night out. One umbrella drink too many. It just came out of me somehow. I had to tell someone." Holding her cigarette in one hand, she reached under her glasses to rub her eyes with the other. "Even then, I tried to make a joke of it. My very own locked room mystery and all that. You know what, though, English Professor?" she said. "It's not funny. It's ruining me. It's ruining my life. I'm going to have to quit my job. I'm gonna have to move. I mean, look, I'm not Super Fem Jesus Girl like Saint Gwendolyn, but I'm a good person. I try to be a good person. I don't know who to talk to about this and . . . and when I said I was scared? I was serious. I'm scared to talk to anyone. I'm scared to be talking to you. Something happened here. Something not good."

Winter nodded slowly. He believed her.

"So go do your English professor thing, okay?" said Livy Swain. "But do me one favor too."

"I'll keep you out of it."

"Yes, that. But that's not what I meant." She took a long draw on her Lucky. Blew the smoke out into the general fug. "Gwendolyn had her heart broken into a million pieces when Brett died," she said. "If that happens again, even Jesus won't be able to bring her back."

Winter made a little noise of surprise. "I've only been out with her once, Livy. I don't think I could possibly be that important to her."

Livy rolled her eyes. "Right. Right. But see, you only think that because you're a man and men are idiots. No offense. Stupidity just comes with the equipment." She opened her hands. She blew more smoke out of the side of her mouth. "Don't try to think about it, just do this one thing for me, okay?" she said.

"All right. What's that?" said Winter.

"Don't get yourself killed."

# 5

Winter spent the night in a hotel downtown. He had a whiskey nightcap on the balcony of the rooftop bar, eight stories up. The worst of the heat was gone and a fresh breeze was coming in off the Arkansas River. He nursed his whiskey and watched the club district down below, the landmark Blue Dome Building and a general glitter of lights all around it, washing away the stars. A silhouetted skyline rose against the blue-black dark.

He thought about his conversation with Livy. It all made sense in a strange sort of way. The solution to an impossible murder was never going to be some intricate plan involving mirrors and blowguns and ventilator shafts. It was far more likely to be simply this: Things weren't what they seemed. Someone was lying.

Someone was lying, and whoever it was, it was someone with power. Maybe several someones. Maybe a lot of power. Small people, powerless people, can't afford to get caught. They have to evade detection. They have to tell plausible lies. Otherwise they'll be exposed and punished. Only big people, powerful people, can tell big, stupid lies that no one believes. They don't care whether anyone believes them or not. Why should they? They're untouchable.

A shackled madman in his underwear killing himself with a hidden nail gun made of wood—that was a lie big and stupid enough to require several powerful people working together. A whole conspiracy's worth of them.

Winter lifted his glass to his lips. He paused with it there, drawing in the vital tang of the good scotch smell. His mind drifted. It was funny, he thought. The way Livy Swain talked about him and Gwendolyn—after they'd only had one dinner together. It was that same odd way he felt about Gwendolyn himself. As if he and she were in the middle of something instead of at the beginning.

And this was funny too. Funny odd. It made him feel good when Livy talked like that. He tried to remember the last time he felt good like this, good in quite this way. Then he did remember. Never. He had never felt good like this before.

He knocked back the last of his whiskey and set the glass down on the table, *plunk*.

"Don't get yourself killed," he said aloud.

---

He had managed to gather three other names. Three people who had agreed to talk with him. He went to them the next day, one by one.

The first was a Catholic priest. Owen McKay's priest. Father Lowe. He was a man of around sixty. Large slumped shoulders, heavy arms, a soft middle. He had a jovial, flabby, rectangular face under short silver hair. Wireless glasses perched on his nose. A priest's black robes, collar and all.

Winter went to him early in the morning, 8 A.M. He entered a bold-white stone church near the lanes of small houses where the McKays had lived. The church had an almost flat facade, bold and aggressive, like the front of a fort. It had a small cluster of spires up top to give the fort a more religious look.

Winter sat with the priest in a cluttered office in a basement directly beneath the altar. There was one top light here, lots of shadows. Books spilling off the shelves. Books on all the surfaces around. It reminded Winter of his own office back on campus, only bigger, less cramped, and all the books had crosses on their covers.

"What can I tell you?" said Father Lowe, leaning back in his desk chair. He lifted his large pink hands off his middle and made a helpless gesture, like birds taking flight. "Owen was a good man. A good man, sure enough. He must have kept a lot of secrets hidden away inside him. To seem the way he seemed and to be what he was at the same time. A lot of secrets, yes." The priest had a rhythmic way of talking. As if he had an Irish brogue, Winter thought, except he didn't.

"I wouldn't think a man would keep secrets from his priest," Winter said. "That's why I came to you. All the neighbors say there was no change in the man, then suddenly there was. That makes no sense to me."

"Ah well. You see. A man doesn't talk to his priest so much as confess to God through the priest who's been commissioned to hear him. You might not know that. That's why the seal on the confessional is inviolable, even after death. Only God hears what the priest hears, only God knows what he knows."

Winter nodded. He tried to look sincere. But he was unconvinced. Behind the lenses of his wireless glasses, Father Lowe had twinkling eyes. Not merry but amused and maybe scornful too. Winter looked into those eyes and felt almost certain the priest was holding something back. He thought the priest knew Winter knew he was hiding something. He thought that was why his eyes were twinkling—because he was amused that Winter knew. He didn't care.

"So you didn't see any sign that this was coming? Outside the confessional? Anywhere? Anything?"

The priest gave a small smile. "You know, I saw an exorcism once," he said.

"Sorry, what?" said Winter.

"Sure as I'm sitting here right before you. I was traveling—in Budapest at the time. Little Hungarian lad there was. Little lad in a sad little attic flat in Józsefváros, District Eight. Ten years old he was. Twisted up like a pretzel on his little bed. Like a pair of great mighty hands had tied his body in knots. His jaw locked shut. Drool bubbling out between his teeth. Then every now and then his mouth would move like a puppet's, like one of those ventriloquist dummies, don't you know. And he would let out a stream of the most obscene thoughts you can imagine. In a voice that seemed to come from far away, like insects chittering in the cellar. Sad, sad, sad. And it was all in Latin! Swear on the Bible as I sit here before you. The little muggins was speaking perfect Latin, which, of course, he'd never learned."

The priest shook his head in sorrow and wonder. He leaned forward in his chair, his hands clasped atop a book that lay open face down on the desktop.

"Well, the local father went to work on him, me standing by as a witness. And so help me, there was a great long battle in that little room, like there were two unseen wrestlers locked in each other's arms, neither moving, just frozen together in their struggle. Then the battle broke our way and, as God is my witness, for one brief second, I saw a dark thing rise up out of that boy. Like a crawling beast of smoke, black as a mink and boiling with rage. We all heard the cry that came out of it as it plunged down through the floor and back where it came from. It was just there before us for a second, mind. Could have been the emotions of the moment, a joint hallucination maybe, I don't know. But for that one second, I was sure I was seeing it there before me, clear as I see you now. We were all sure."

He shook his head. He sighed. He sat back in his chair, his story done.

Winter gave a small laugh. He rubbed his eyes wearily. "Demonic possession. You're telling me—what now? You saw signs of this in Owen McKay?"

"Ah," said Father Lowe, only one pink hand flying off this time. "As I tell you, friend. A priest hears nothing but what he hears on behalf of God."

"Right. Unless you saw these things outside the confessional. Or saw something anyway."

"You said you were an English professor? Is that right? An English professor writing a book on impossible crimes."

Winter no longer looked sincere. He was no longer trying. "Yes," he said.

"Well, if you're an English professor, you should know," said the priest. "There are more things in heaven and earth than are dreamt of in your philosophy."

Winter's wearied gaze met the priest's.

The priest's eyes twinkled.

---

The second man, the second name on Winter's list, was Ralph Lorenzo. He was the guard—the detention officer—who led the intake team at the county jail the night the police brought in Owen McKay.

"The afternoon shift was me, Charlie Bookman, and Lew Jerome," he said. "We wrestled him to the ground. Stripped off his clothes and got him in restraints. He was totally out of control. Cursing. Foaming. Spitting. Howling. I mean just howling, like a wolf howls at the moon."

Lorenzo was a big man and thick around. The sort of man who could slam into you like a wrecking ball, Winter thought. He could see the power in him, even as Lorenzo lazed in his folding chair on the scraggly patch of grass outside his trailer home. He wore blue tracksuit pants and a Thunder sweatshirt, but the baggy getup didn't hide the shape of him, the heavy, muscular arms, the big gut, also muscled. He sat back, beer can in hand, legs stretched out. Had to be six feet four or five at least. The trailer with its yellowed vinyl siding sat shabby and sad behind him. Winter could see the pale line on his finger where the wedding band used to be.

Lorenzo had set out another chair for Winter. He pointed an open hand at the plastic cooler sitting blue on a brown patch of grass. Winter took the chair but declined the beer. It was only eleven in the morning.

Winter made himself look relaxed, but he was watching Lorenzo closely. He was surprised by his open welcome. The man's easy manner somehow put him on his guard. Livy had told him everyone was scared, no one was talking. Lorenzo must not have gotten the memo. He was talking just fine.

"I'd like to ask you about the death of Owen McKay," Winter had said to him on the phone.

"Sure," Lorenzo said. "I've got a day off. Come on over. Ask away."

They sat side by side in the dappled shade of a spindly oak. The sky beyond the leaves was pale blue. The heat was bearable but rising.

"I guess the big question is, how did he get the nail gun in there?" Winter said.

"I'll say. And it beats the hell out of me, let me tell you." Lorenzo had a bland face, big and flat and so fleshy it was almost featureless. He had a big laugh that made his big belly quiver. Winter could picture him in his DO uniform, an intimidating presence. "I was the last man with him in that safety cell," he said. "The guy was wearing baggy boxers and chains, that was all. He was fighting so hard, we couldn't even get the county greens on him. I've seen guys go nuts before. In the jail, but also overseas. In the wars, I saw a couple guys flip out. But McKay, he was next level. Nothing left of him but crazy. So we muscled him into the cell, the three of us, me and Lew and Charlie. He was still agitated but settling down in the restraints. He knew the fight was over. Lew and Charlie backed out of there while I held him down and then I stayed behind for a few seconds to give him the talk, you know. 'You treat us with respect, we treat you with respect. You calm down and act like a man, we'll let you sit out in the chairs where the TV is. You work with us, we work with you. Mutual respect,' and so on. That's the drill. And it was working. Usually does. You talk to a man like he's a man, he'll act like a man. Makes sense, right? McKay was nodding. Calming down. I promised I'd check on him every fifteen minutes and let him out if he gave a good showing of himself. When I left the room, he was sitting against the wall. Muttering to himself a little, but peaceable enough.

"I sent Charlie upstairs to fetch the shrink. I stayed behind the desk and kept an eye on the security monitors. The safety cell is in this little nook of its own off the corridor. No one went in there. Not a single person. I was watching the monitor the whole time. Fifteen minutes later, I checked on McKay myself through the safety cell window, just like I promised I would. He was right where I left him, sitting on the floor, back against the wall. Eyes open, muttering to himself. Shaking his head about something. I went back to my station. Maybe five, ten minutes after that, the shrink comes down. I take her to the cell. We open the door. Well, you know what we saw. He was lying there face down, dead as a politician's soul."

He drank his beer, gazing off across the pebbled walk at the trailers on the other side. Gazing off as if into that moment when they'd found the body.

He screwed up his big face. "I tell you. I never saw a device like that gun before. Made all out of wood like that. And small. A normal nail gun—a manual—is about yea long." He drew his huge hands a yard apart. "This one?" He narrowed the distance to about a foot, a little less. "You wouldn't think you could get the kinetics to drive the nail with a gun that size."

"Had you searched him?" Winter asked. "Before you put him in the cell."

Lorenzo wagged his head. "We did our best. Wrestled him through the metal detector anyway. Patted him down. But the situation was what it was. We had to get him out of harm's way."

"Could he have secured the gun on his person?"

"Shoved it up his ass, you mean? Brother, you can't imagine the things I've seen come out of a cellbird's hole. Some of these guys, it wouldn't surprise me if they farted out a truck and just drove the hell away. We didn't spread him if that's what you're asking. We figured we'd do all that when we got him under control."

He gave another big laugh.

"How did it get there?" he said, shaking his head. "I mean, really, professor. On this one? Your guess is as good as mine."

---

The third man, the last man who'd agreed to speak with him, was Billy Whitefield, a pathologist from the medical examiner's office. The minute Winter saw him, he knew he had something important to say.

The priest, Winter thought, was hiding something, but who knew what? Maybe it really was just an untellable confession. Maybe it was just his own superstitions. Demon possession. Some other kind of craziness. Who could say? As for the guard, Lorenzo, he seemed to only know what he knew, what he'd seen with his own eyes. He was right about one thing though: Building a nail gun small enough to hide yet capable of creating enough force to drive a projectile into the heart was not an easy project. It could be done, but it took some training, some skill.

As for this guy, though, the pathologist, Whitefield—he knew something and he wanted to tell it. He was electric with emotion. Eyes buggy. Scared looking. Guilty looking. Desperate to get something off his chest.

It was noon now. Lunchtime. He met Whitefield in a park by the river. He was standing on a path that ran along the water. Bikes were whizzing past him. Mothers were chasing their toddlers around an adjacent patch of lawn.

Whitefield was small, thin, jumpy. He was bouncing on his toes, clapping the heels of his hands together soundlessly. Like a bird caught in a cage, Winter thought, beating against the bars, trying to escape. Only his face was slack, blank, abandoned by a mind lost in some inner haze–land of anxiety. He stared as if unseeing at the snaking, sluggish green water that swallowed the light of day.

"Dr. Whitefield," Winter said. He thought the man would blast off like a rocket at the sound of his voice. Shoot up through the overhanging maples and away into the light-blue sky.

The bone-man looked about fifty. He had black hair flecked with gray. His face was thin, his eyes big, his nose pointed, his lips very thin. He looked like he needed something to eat.

"Thank you for meeting with me," Winter said. Whitefield didn't answer. He looked around as if surprised to find himself where he was. "I understand you did the postmortem on Owen McKay."

Whitefield nodded with his whole body, bouncing on his toes. He went on nodding for so long Winter began to wonder if he was having some sort of seizure. But he finally said: "Did you read it? The autopsy report?"

Winter shook his head. "I haven't been able to get a copy. I will though."

"Don't bother. It's bull hockey. Not worth your trouble." He waved his hands around his face as if chasing off flies.

"Which part? The nail?"

"The nail was wood. Resined beech. Hard as metal, but you can get it through a detector. That's not in the report. And the gun disappeared, did they tell you that?"

"No."

"Never made it to the evidence lockers. That's not in the report either. My guess is the nail was fired by compressed gas in a plastic cannister with some kind of wooden trigger. The whole thing just as lethal as a gun but undetectable by a metal detector."

Winter nodded. He knew all about it. "You'd need a pretty long wooden barrel though. For the torque, right?"

Whitefield gave him a startled look. "You do your research. That's an assassin's weapon. You can bring it on a plane. Into a prison. Anywhere. You're an English professor, you said?"

"Could he have hidden a weapon like that on his person? Inside him?"

Whitefield gave a quick little shrug. “Maybe he could’ve. But he didn’t. It would have left traces. I’d have known. That’s not in the report either.”

“Why not?”

Whitefield sighed and ran his hand up over his hair. Winter could see the sweat on his brow. He was wearing a polo shirt and there was sweat under his arms too. He shook his head back and forth so fast, his lips fluttered. The man was a nervous wreck. It was contagious. He was making Winter nervous as well.

After a long moment of fretting and shaking and moving his hands, the little man finally looked at Winter straight on. “Also? There was a thing in his head.”

“A thing?” said Winter.

“In his brain. Like a spider.”

“A living thing?”

“No, no, no, no. Just listen.”

Winter listened. Maybe he really was catching Whitefield’s agitation. As the story got stranger and stranger, he was beginning to feel his blood rise in a low boil. He suspected that what he heard next was going to change everything. He suspected that after this, there would be no turning back for him. He would have to see this through.

“There was a thing, a metal gizmo of some kind, with wires attached to it so it looked like a spider. It was implanted in the back of McKay’s skull with the wires linked into the areas around the amygdala and hypothalamus.”

“So it was like—like what? You mean like a transmitter?”

“I don’t know. Maybe part of a DBS device? But not like one I’ve ever seen before.”

“I don’t know what DBS is.”

"Deep brain stimulation. They use it for epilepsy and like that. Seizures. Sometimes schizophrenia. Addictions. Like an electric brain massage. This could have been something like that, I guess. Like I said, I never saw anything like it before, so I'm not exactly sure what it was."

Winter cursed softly. He thought of Father Lowe and the boy in Budapest. His lips had gone dry. He touched his tongue to them. "I take it this isn't in the autopsy report either."

Whitefield went through a series of jerky movements meant to signify that no, it wasn't. "Don't get me wrong. I put it in there. Like the nail and the gun. I put everything in the report. I told the lead detective about it too. Langley. Jay Langley. I told him everything I'd found. I was planning on doing some research in the morning, see if I could find out where that spidery gizmo was made, what it was supposed to do."

Winter had already called Detective Langley. Langley had laughed and hung up on him. Why would a lawman talk to an English professor?

"So why wasn't any of this in the report?" he asked the pathologist.

"Listen," said Whitefield.

Winter listened.

Whitefield swallowed. He licked his lips. He swallowed again.

"I got four kids, okay?" he said. "Little kids. Just little. Three, four, five, and six years old. And my wife. She's just a little thing herself, my wife. Five foot nothing, if that. No hips at all to speak of. Still. Turns out one baby after another. Like a factory. She's pregnant now again, it looks like. The doctor said to her, 'Let me tie you up.' Her tubes, you know. Tie up her tubes. She won't do it. She's a good Bible-believing Christian. I look at her across a crowded room, she has another baby." He laughed fondly, thinking of his wife. Then, abruptly, he stopped laughing.

"Why are you telling me this?" Winter asked him. "About your children. Your wife. What have they got to do with anything?"

"I'm a good Christian too," Whitefield went on. "Did my premed at Oral Roberts University. I believe in heaven and hell and all that."

A cluster of bicyclers went spinning swiftly by on either side of them, bright-purple, skintight polyester suits clinging to their stringy man-shapes as they curled by the river on the walk. Whitefield fell silent as they passed, his hands on his hips, his head down, eyes on the ground. A baby started crying on the nearby lawn. Winter glanced at the baby as her mother lifted her from her blanket. He felt the boil of excitement still rising inside him. What the hell was he listening to? What was he about to hear?

"That night. After the postmortem on McKay," Whitefield went on. "After I found the wooden nail and the spider in his brain and put them in the report and told Detective Langley. That night, I'm lying asleep. Fast asleep in my bed. Everyone's asleep. My wife. All the little ones. Then suddenly I'm awake. Just like that. I open my eyes. There's a man standing over me. A naked man."

"What?"

"Yeah. Totally naked. Really muscular. All covered in tattoos. His whole body, neck to . . . I don't know. As far down as I could see, all tattoos. He's standing right over me and his . . . his thing—this big, this enormous penis he's got—is dangling right at my eye level. That was the only part of him that wasn't covered in tattoos. That and a sort of line running from his chin to his forehead. He's standing there. He's grinning down at me with his thing in my face. And I'm staring up at him and I feel like . . . like

I'm staring at death. At my own death. Like he's hooded Death with a scythe except he's just a naked tattooed man grinning down at me, these big muscles all over. His teeth all white in the darkness. And my wife is asleep right next to me, understand. You understand what I'm saying?"

Winter cursed again. What the hell kind of a crazy story was this?

"And this naked man, grinning," Whitefield says. "This naked man, he raises his finger to his lips. Like 'Shh.' You know? Like *Be quiet.* That's all. And then, real slow—he's got all the time in the world. You understand? Real slow, he turns around. Showing his butt to me, his naked butt. And he walks out of the room. Like it's his house. Like he owns the place. Like it's his world. His universe."

Winter had the oddest feeling now, a feeling that the park around him—the trees, the path, the pale-blue sky, the dull-brown water of the big river, the mothers with their children and the bikes going by and an elderly couple walking arm in arm—that they had all receded from him into a faraway reality, leaving him here with Whitefield in Whitefield's midnight world of dreams.

"I lay there frozen, just frozen," Whitefield went on. "I never felt anything like it. That kind of fear. That kind of pure terror, like it was part of me. I lay there staring at the place where the naked man had been until, after I don't know how long, I heard the front door open and close downstairs. That did it somehow. That brought me out of it. My heart was going a million miles a second. I jumped out of bed so fast, my wife cried out in her sleep. I went running into the kids' rooms. First the one with the two little ones in it. Then my son's. Then my daughter's. To make sure they're all all right, you know. And they were. They were all lying there in their beds fast asleep. Totally fine. Everything was fine except . . ." The look Whitefield turned on Winter then was such a haunted look that Winter thought he could see the memory of this long night playing like a video inside his eyes. "Except in Jilly's room. Jilly's my six-year-old. In her room, on the dresser near her bed, one of her little dolls was sitting there? Its head was gone. Its head was off its neck. It was sitting . . . The head. It was sitting on her legs, on the doll's legs. The head was. And it . . . it wasn't like that when I put her to bed. Jilly's there sleeping peacefully, but the doll, its head is off its neck, sitting on its legs."

He frowned. Shook his head at the ground. "When I went into work the next morning? The first thing I did was I called up the autopsy report on Owen McKay. And the thing, the spider, the nail and the spider thing that was in his brain, they weren't in the report anymore. The whole report had been rewritten and all that was just gone. And I knew—I knew I had to tell somebody. I knew I had to say something to somebody. But to who? Who could I tell? Not just anybody could've gone in there and changed a report like that. You have to have clearance. The password. So who could I tell? Who could I trust? The doll's head . . . you understand what I'm saying? The doll's head was off in my little Jilly's room . . . She's only six years old." He choked up and fell silent.

Winter stood silent too. He kept expecting the surrounding park, the people—reality—to come back from its far-off places, to come back and find him in the crazy midnight dreamworld he was in. But reality did not come back. There was just him and Whitefield's frightened face and the image in his mind of a naked man covered in tattoos with his finger to his lips.

*Shh.*

"Why . . . ?" Winter started to say, then stopped, then said: "Why did you tell this to me?"

Whitefield reached into his back pocket. He came out with a piece of paper. It was folded up into a small square. He stuffed the square into the breast pocket of Winter's short-sleeve shirt.

"I was afraid to even follow up on that," Whitefield said. "Afraid someone might be tracking my computer searches. I have to protect my children, you understand that. But I . . . I couldn't just stay silent. I had to tell someone." His voice cracked. "I'm an honest man. I'm a Christian man. A Bible-believing Christian, like I said. I've been praying and praying about it. I prayed to God to send someone I could talk to. Someone I could trust. I figured you were the one he sent. Man, you better be."

Whitefield turned then—spun on his heel, almost like a soldier on parade—turned and hurried away across the grass crowded with mothers and children.

One more time, Winter cursed.

# 6

"Do you believe in demonic possession?"

"Of course," said Gwendolyn. "Of course I do. Why? Don't you?"

"No!" said Winter. "Of course not. In fact, I was calling you in the hope of talking to someone sane for a change."

She laughed. "You must have dialed the wrong number."

It was night now. He was driving his Jeep SUV from the airport toward home. The highway was glaring with white headlights and red taillights. The drab scenery, the humps and shrubbery of the surrounding flatlands, was draped in dull moonlight off and on. The moon was still big, still bright, but a thin screen of clouds kept rolling over it. He could see the moon flashing on and off in the windshield like a wonky bulb. The approaching skyline below went in and out of shadow.

He had called Gwendolyn as he drove. He was glad to hear her voice fill the car. He liked the warm sound of it and the intelligence and the humor. He could picture the spark of humor in her eyes.

"This priest I talked to hinted that Owen McKay was possessed by demons," he told her. "He hinted that that was why he killed his wife and child."

"That's terrible! And what, you don't believe him?"

"There's no such thing as demons, Gwendolyn."

"Of course there are demons. Jesus casts them out of people. It's in the Bible."

Winter laughed, but silently so she wouldn't hear him. *What a loopy dame,* he thought fondly. "Well, Jesus apparently forgot to take some sort of transmitter out of McKay's brain. The medical examiner's pathologist found it in the autopsy. His photographs have all mysteriously disappeared, so he made a drawing of it and gave it to me. I'm not sure what it was, but I'm guessing it's what drove McKay out of his mind so suddenly like that. Maybe someone used it to control him, make him kill his wife and kid."

"That's awful. Who would do that?"

"I don't know. But whoever it was, they don't seem to want anyone to find out about it."

"Well . . . Okay, maybe that's what happened," said Gwendolyn doubtfully. "But that doesn't mean there are no demons."

"Listen, Demon Girl, I'm taking you to a show on Saturday. Have a snack before I pick you up. We'll eat a late dinner afterwards."

"That sounds like fun. Are we going to a concert or something?"

"No. A play."

"Oh, all right. What kind of play?"

"A play-play. It's like a movie only with real people in it."

"I know what a play is, thank you, Professor. They used to put them on in my high school. I haven't seen one since then though."

"You haven't been to the theater since high school?"

"I've been to theaters. For concerts and things. Just not to a play."

"Really? Not even Shakespeare?"

"I can never understand what people are saying in Shakespeare. I should probably try harder, but it's just mush to me."

"My God, girl, you're an unschooled savage," Winter said. "No wonder you believe in demons."

"Well, you don't know your Bible, that's all."

This time, Winter laughed out loud.

But after the call ended, he decided he'd better trade in his tickets for *The Cherry Orchard* at Second City and find something a little less daunting. Maybe a musical or a comedy or something. Fortunately, Chicago was a good theater town.

*Demons*, he thought, shaking his head and smiling to himself. *Loopy dame.*

He parked the Jeep in the garage beneath his apartment building. He lingered there behind the wheel a moment and tried to call up a ticket site on his phone, but there was no signal. He tried again in the elevator riding up to his apartment. He found the site just as he reached his floor and the elevator doors came open.

As he walked down the hall, he held his small overnight bag in his left hand while he worked his phone with his right. He traded his *Cherry Orchard* tickets for a revival of the musical *Phantom of the Opera*.

Still looking down at his phone, he approached his apartment door. *Chekhov!* he scolded himself. What had he been thinking? He had never seen *Phantom*, of course. For him, the art of music died with Schubert or, if he was being broad-minded, Cole Porter. But he knew of the musical and it seemed as if it would be perfect for the occasion. A love story. Big special effects. Overly lush, sentimental ditties. A girl like Gwendolyn would like that sort of thing. How could he go wrong?

He was so absorbed in the task, he didn't notice the line of light at the bottom of his door, even though his eyes were turned down, looking at the phone. He didn't see the light go off as he approached, or if he did, it didn't quite register with him, not right away.

He set down his overnight bag. Slipped the phone into his pants pocket. Unlocked the door. Picked up his bag and stepped into the dark apartment.

The tattooed man leaped at him, thrusting the point of a knife at his belly.

# 7

Winter must have seen the light. With his eyes turned down on the phone as they were, even with his mind engaged with securing those *Phantom* tickets, with congratulating himself on a choice Gwendolyn was sure to like, that giveaway line of light must have hit his brain in some way; he must have seen it even though he didn't know he'd seen it. Because just as he was stepping through the door, some old instinct flashed an alarm at him, and he knew he had made a terrible mistake.

The tattooed man's blade flashed in the light from the hall as it shot through the air quick as a cobra strike. With that alarm going off in his mind, Winter was dodging sideward before he even saw it. The dagger swept by so close, he felt the breath of the steel on the front of his shirt. But he didn't pause. He was all motion, no thought, just red nerves blasting beneath the skin. He hit the tattooed man's arm with his bag, losing his grip on the bag so that it flew from his hands and hit the open door. The killer stumbled only half a step. Then, as the door began to swing shut, he brought the point of the dagger slashing viciously back at Winter's face.

But Winter was already gone, spinning deeper into his apartment, the spaces barely visible to him in the sudden shadows.

For a single second more, the light from the hall spilled in. He saw the tatted assassin clearly. Naked except for a jockstrap. His bare flesh shadowed with illustrations except for the teeth gleaming in his grin.

Then the killer leaped at him and the door shut. Winter saw the man start to charge. Then darkness fell, and the killer was invisible.

Thinking with wild speed, Winter tried to access his mental map of the rooms. He was still turning with the movement of the block at the door. He used the motion to carry him out of the foyer into the living room.

He could see again, though only dimly. The light of the city was coming in through the glass doors to the balcony. He raced around the black edge of the silhouetted bar and grabbed a bottle of something by the neck as he went. Uncertain where the killer was, he planted himself suddenly, swung around again, sweeping the bottle through the air.

A lucky blow. The thick of the bottle hit the assassin hard in the side of the head as he moved in for the kill. It was a solid connection. The tattooed man grunted and slowed for a second. That was all. He steadied. His knife whipped out with that same cobra speed. But Winter hadn't waited for it. He was already backpedaling into the open space of the living room floor.

There, the two men squared off, just for a moment. Winter was puffing for breath, every nerve bowstring tight. By his calculations, his chances of survival here were little to none. In the brief pause, in the dark, he heard the killer give a groan of malevolent laughter.

Then the assassin attacked again. A blur of shadow. A glint of steel. Winter swept the bottle down desperately. Hit the killer's forearm. Knocked the blade aside. Struck out for the killer's face with his free hand stiff. Another lucky shot: he caught the man in the eye.

The tattooed man cried out—but struck back quickly, an awkward spin of the knife at the place where Winter's face had been half a second before. But Winter dodged back. Instinctively, he caught the assassin's hand. For an instant, the tatted hand, the gleaming blade, hovered before his eyes. Then in a spark-fast triple movement, the killer pressed his wrist into Winter's grip, yanked it free, and jabbed at his face again.

Once more, Winter leaped back into the shadows, the blade missing his nose by half a centimeter. The assassin paused. The light was dim. The shadows were deep. The apartment was Winter's. It was Winter's battleground. Where was he?

Then the tattooed man saw him. Came after him, quick and low. Winter had no time to break the bottle and get a cutting edge on it. He was trying to reach the bookshelf against the far wall. It was the only weapon he could think of. He passed his worktable. Grabbed a chair. Turned it over in the assassin's path. The killer knocked it aside and rushed at him. No time to kick the man in that jockstrap of his. No time for anything but to spin away.

Then Winter's back hit the wall. His shoulder touched the bookshelf. He saw the killer's silhouette and his white grin. He grabbed the edge of the shelf. The energy pumping through him doubled his strength. The weight of the shelf was nothing. He flung it over—practically hurled it at the oncoming man. Volumes of first- and second-generation Romantic poets and their critics—all the material Winter wasn't reading for the book he wasn't writing—and the shelves themselves and the shelf unit all came smashing down on the assassin's head.

It should have driven the man to the ground. It didn't. He roared like an animal and threw the shelf aside. It went crashing over onto the floor, books fluttering and pattering down all around it. But the assassin's knife was gone. At least Winter thought it was gone. He thought the shelf must have knocked it out of his hand, but it was hard to tell in the darkness. Winter had to decide. Stay back, keep moving, or attack and risk the blade.

He attacked. Swung at those white teeth with the bottle—swung hard. The assassin leaped back and chopped Winter's wrist with the edge of his hand. Winter grunted, dropped the bottle, staggered backward. Planted for a fight.

But the assassin was suddenly gone.

The move took Winter by surprise. It was a moment before he could locate the figure in the darkness. Then, outside, the moving clouds parted. A beam of moonlight shot through the balcony doors.

There the tatted killer was—a wild illustrated figure against the balcony doors, against the moonlit sky, against the glow of the lights around the Capitol dome. He glanced back once over his shoulders and grinned.

Before Winter could go after him, the assassin had the door open and was gone—out onto the balcony, vaulting over the rail. Vanished. A death drop to the street far below.

Winter didn't follow him out to watch him fall. He wouldn't fall. He was no reckless thug. He was a trained killer. He must have cased the place before he entered. He must have known he could drop to the balcony on the floor below. Winter knew it. So would he.

So Winter ran for the apartment door. He nearly tripped on the chair he'd tipped over. He saw it just before he hit it and hurtled it and kept stumbling toward the door and nearly tripped on his overnight bag and hurtled that too.

Another moment and he was out in the hall, racing down the length of it to the stairwell. Then he was through the door, at the top of the concrete stairs.

But he stopped there. He could hear the killer's footsteps far below. Too far—and moving too fast for Winter to catch up to him.

Winter stood on the landing, panting. It was only then that the full fire of fear caught up with him.

He knew that fear would not leave him soon. It would never leave him—not entirely—not until one of them, he or the assassin, was dead.

# 8

Winter awoke with a gun in his hand. It was morning. Where was he? he wondered.

His phone was buzzing. He looked at the screen. The number was blocked. He took the call.

"Mr. Winter." A woman's voice. Gentle, soft. Asian inflection. Chinese, he thought.

"Who is this?"

"My name is Fulu. I'll be at the Nomad Tavern at eleven. You had better come. It's urgent."

"I don't know . . ." said Winter.

"It's about the Recruiter," she said—and the line went dead.

Winter sat with the silence, holding the phone, trying to clear his mind. He remembered the night before. The tattooed killer. The fight in the dark. He was in his bedroom now. His gun in his hand. The door locked. He had thought that would give him an extra second if the assassin should return to finish him.

He got out of bed. Stepped out into the living room. He was wearing nothing but his boxer shorts and the Glock. The place was a mess. The bookshelf turned over. The books splattered everywhere. The desk chair on its side. It made his stomach sour.

Because he knew the killer would be back. When a man like that comes to kill you, he means to get it done.

He went into the bathroom, locking the door behind him. He left the gun on the tank of the toilet as he brushed his teeth and shaved. He tried to think things through, but his mind was overcrowded with images and flashbacks. He kept seeing that killer leaping at him from the shadows. Something strange about that attack. And then the moment when he caught the man's wrist and his hand hovered before him . . . But before he could work it through, he was thinking about the voice of the Asian girl on the phone. Talking to him about the Recruiter. His old boss, his old mentor. Retired now. Hounded out of service. Scolded by congressional hacks who pretended to be shocked he even existed. His agency—the Division—the smallish collection of government death merchants of which Winter had been one—was disbanded and condemned. There were closed-door hearings. A smattering of anonymously sourced news stories, all untrue. Then the Recruiter was an exile in disgrace. Abandoned. But not by everyone. To this day, flights of assassins would speed to the Recruiter's side whenever he called them. The Invisibles, as Winter had christened them. Because you would never see them coming.

Winter had a license to carry a concealed weapon, but he never did. Why would he? He was an English professor. But today he was an English professor with a Glock strapped under his arm and a windbreaker to hide it, though it was already eighty degrees at 10:50 in the morning, and likely to get hotter fast.

As he walked to the Nomad Tavern, his eyes moved over the pedestrians around him, flicking from face to face. The streets and sidewalks were summer quiet. The students gone. The state government out of session. Winter didn't think that tattooed freak would come after him here, out in the open. But this morning, he didn't feel like taking any chances. He didn't want to miss *Phantom of the Opera* on Saturday. He wanted to see Gwendolyn again. He remembered what Livy Swain had told him. He was not allowed to die.

Winter stepped out of the blazing sunlight into a room of stained wood. The Nomad Tavern had just opened for the morning, getting ready for the lunch crowds. The screens behind the bar were still dark. Only a single waitress was there. Ann or Nan or Fran—something like that. She was plucking last night's beer steins out of the dishwasher, a harvest of glass. There were no customers, not at the bar anyway. The tables were empty too. Except one of them, the one at the back, by the kitchen door. There was a woman sitting there, a diminutive Asian woman sure enough. She had a small round face, shoulder-length hair dyed pink, possibly a wig. She sat very still, holding some sort of tall drink in front of her.

Winter walked the length of the tavern, nodding good morning to Ann or Fran as he went. He sat down at the woman's table.

"Are you Fulu?" he asked.

She nodded. "Fulu Fulu," she said.

Winter didn't understand. Then he did. His lips parted in surprise. He gaped at her—at him. The Asian woman was Stan "Stan-Stan" Stankowski, undercover federal agent and borderline insane person. The last time Winter had seen him, he had been a six-foot-two, broad-shouldered, barrel-chested fisherman guide, skin white, with a large face and a big Hemingwayan beard. Now—impossibly—he was slender. He looked like he was about five feet tall. He looked like he was female. He looked like he was Chinese. Winter shouldn't have been surprised. Stan-Stan could do this sort of thing. In Stan-Stan's head, he was the star of a television show in which he played an undercover agent who treated each new assignment like an actor treats a role in a television show. As far as Winter was concerned, the man belonged in a hospital psych ward.

"You have to be kidding me," Winter said. "Fulu?"

"Fulu Fulu," said Stan-Stan again. "Fulu once, shame on me . . ."

"Yeah, I get it," said Winter.

"It's an honorable name. It means I possess the fragrant and precious beauty of a gemstone."

"Good for you."

"It's also a magic talisman."

"Swell. I thought you were hunting illegal Mexican dope farms in the forest," Winter said.

"Well, the Mexicans sell the drugs. But the Chinese, they launder the money."

"I don't want to know what you're going to do to get information out of them."

"If I may say so without immodesty, I am expert in the ancient Chinese arts of love."

Winter shook his head. He muttered under his breath.

Stan-Stan went on. "But have you not wondered why I risked exposing my carefully cultivated disguise in order to get in touch with a Kewpie-faced poetry professor who is supposed to be out of the business?"

"Not in those words, but generally speaking, yes, I have. You said it had to do with the Recruiter."

The diminutive Chinese woman nodded. She spoke with a submissive gentleness that Winter found disturbingly appealing. He did not believe the federal government should allow Stan-Stan to wander around free.

"You perhaps remember the name Warren Gentry?" she said—he said—whatever.

"I remember," said Winter. "The indie journalist. I heard he was shot dead a few days ago. The news sites said it was a mugging gone wrong."

Fulu brushed back her pink hair with a knowingly sensuous gesture. Winter wanted to punch him in the face. Fortunately, the waitress interrupted, coming up behind him with a coffeepot.

"Coffee, Professor?"

"Black please, thank you," he said. *And a baseball bat to beat my friend to death with*, he thought. He remembered he had the Glock under his arm. He found that comforting.

The waitress poured him a mug of coffee and retreated to the bar.

"There is a feeling among many members of the intelligence community that Mr. Gentry may have been murdered," Fulu went on.

Winter nodded. He thought Gentry was murdered too. "What's that got to do with the Recruiter?" he asked.

"Do you not know that Gentry played a role in his downfall?"

"I didn't know but I guessed," said Winter. "So what? They're going to try to pin Gentry's killing on the Recruiter? That's ridiculous."

"The dragon of power breathes the scent of corruption," said Fulu softly.

Winter took a sip of coffee. Considered throwing the rest in Stan-Stan's face. Took another sip instead. "Are they going to make a move on him? Are they going to try to arrest him for Gentry?"

"With the greatest respect, I must tell you I do not know. They have not arrested him so far. Not since I last checked, anyway."

"Well, they shouldn't. The most dangerous men in the country are loyal to the Recruiter. It would be like starting an intelligence community gang war."

"The river of wisdom flows past the city of madness."

"Oh, shut up," Winter said. "What the hell's wrong with you?"

"I myself cannot warn him," said Fulu in her reticent way. "It's as much as my position is worth. But if I may respectfully suggest, a warning might not go amiss." She tilted her head so that her pink hair spilled across her face in a subtly flirtatious manner. "The word of a friend is a ruby in the crown of prudence."

Winter hid his reaction behind his coffee mug. He was still chewing on the coffee when he set the mug down.

"A man tried to kill me last night," he said slowly.

"Ah, I am so sorry to hear that, my honored friend. Who would do such a thing to a man so greatly respected?"

"It was kind of strange actually," Winter went on. "He was a professional. He was waiting for me in my apartment. I was distracted. He had me dead to rights. He could have shot me as I walked in and been gone before I hit the floor. Instead, he came at me with a KA-BAR. Naked—he was naked except for a jockstrap. He tried to gut me. Like it was personal. Like he wanted to stand over me in his jockstrap and watch me die."

"Perhaps you should learn to practice the art of courtesy so as not to offend such people."

"Round-faced guy, covered in tattoos except for the middle of his face. Anyone you know?"

Winter asked because he thought he had seen something in Stan-Stan's eyes as he was describing the man. A flash of recognition maybe—maybe not. These enigmatic Asian women could be hard to read.

Fulu lifted her tall glass. The bubbles in it glimmered and danced as she drank or he drank. Whatever. Winter felt Stan-Stan was hiding behind those bubbles as he himself had hidden behind his coffee mug.

"Why would I know such an unpleasant person, honored friend?" Fulu said. She set down the glass and delicately patted her lips dry with her napkin.

Winter was about to answer, then didn't. An image had come into his mind. That frozen moment again, that moment when he had caught the assassin's wrist, when the killer's hand had hovered before him in the shadowy room. There were so many illustrations stained into the killer's skin that he could not distinguish one from another. They were just a swirl of murky shapes and colors. But in that single moment, one image had become clear, one tattoo on the back of the killer's hand: a pentagram in a circle.

Before he could check himself, Winter murmured aloud: "I knew him."

"Then he was acquainted with your personality," said Fulu in her gentle fashion. "Ah, that would explain why he might try to kill you in such a disagreeable manner."

"It was years ago. The guy knows how to hold a grudge, I'll give him that."

"Your past association had not bound you man-to-man in honorable friendship."

"I threatened to leave his head in the glove compartment of his truck. That might have put him off." Winter spoke quietly, as if to himself. "Back then, he only had the one tattoo, at least as far as I could see. A pentagram on his hand."

He fell silent. What did it all mean? He had assumed last night's attack on him had to do with the death of Owen McKay. But could it have been connected to the murder of Warren Gentry instead? Or could both stories be one story? Another memory came to him now. He remembered how he had described the assassin to the Recruiter after his first confrontation with him. He remembered how that glint of recognition had lighted and died in the Recruiter's eyes, just as it had in Stan-Stan's.

Winter narrowed his gaze at the pink-haired Chinese seductress across the table from him. "Does this guy work for us?" he asked. "For the government, I mean?"

Fulu lifted her tall glass again and drained it in a single draught. "The bonsai of infinite tattoos blossoms in the garden of mental instability," she said. She stood up from behind the table. Her green linen sheath dress showed off a sleek, elegant figure.

"How the hell do you do that?" Winter said.

"Allow me to remind you with great respect: Do not forget the Recruiter," Fulu said softly. "Our honored government is not in the most stable condition. If the Recruiter is arrested, there could be reciprocal actions by the impetuous among his friends. The result could be wailing and gnashing of teeth throughout the District of Columbia."

"All right," said Winter. "I'll make sure he's aware they're after him."

Fulu inclined her head. Then, like a swan, she glided away. Winter suppressed the urge to look over his shoulder and watch her go.

He sat where he was. He drank his coffee. He thought his dark thoughts.

# 9

The last time Winter had seen the Recruiter, the chief was stowed in a depressing little hideaway in the middle of the Arizona desert. The house was a red box nestled almost invisibly in the surrounding red rock formations, just another outcropping amid the surreal juts and crags, spurs and mesas growing up on every side of it. It had not been very many years since Winter had left the Division, but his former chief seemed to have aged a century. Rejected by the country he loved, his once-bare cinder block of a head had been coated with a patina of silver hair like moss. His formerly erect and dynamic figure had grown bent and slow. He sat in his hidden house as if on another planet, Bible on his reading table, lunch on his tray, an old man.

Now Winter traveled again through the Martian desert landscape. The red earth, the red rock, the red mesas rose all around him against the pale and cloudless sky. A dragon-toothed splash of merciless sunlight glared steadily on the windshield. Even the air-conditioning in his rented Jeep could not completely undo the baking heat. It was well over a hundred degrees outside. Every sign of life seemed to have been burned out of the landscape. Even the tumbleweed lay motionless against the saguaros. It was too hot to tumble.

The Recruiter's house was where he'd left it, hidden in plain sight, blending into the fantasias of stone. Even before Winter killed the Jeep's engine, he could see the place was empty. Not just empty; deserted. It was the difference between a sleeping man and a dead one: the life inside was gone.

Winter stepped out into the airless day. The heat bore down on him as if the sky were a slab of iron. It was a dry heat—so the Arizonans liked to say. Dry like a blowtorch or the bowels of hell, he thought.

Winter walked toward the house slowly, his shoes crunching on stone, his eyes moving across the scenery. He had brought his Glock with him. It was hooked to his belt in plain sight. But there was no one here, no one anywhere near. He could feel the vacancy. It went on for miles.

Sure enough, the unlocked door swung open when he touched it. Sure enough, the house was gutted. The chief's armchair was still there, left behind like roadkill. But there had been a sofa too, Winter remembered, and that was gone. So was the rest of the furniture—gone—what little there'd been. A week's worth of dust blew over the wooden floor. A scorpion was trying to dig its way out of a corner. Flies gathered on the windows. Some had fallen dead from the heat.

He checked the little kitchen. It was empty. The refrigerator door stood open. The fridge was empty too. He walked across the central room and checked the bedroom. The bed frame was there but the mattress was missing. There was a small lizard on one wall. More flies. Otherwise, nothing.

For a moment or two, Winter wondered whether he had come too late. Perhaps government law dogs had already hauled the Recruiter in. That would have been a disappointment to him. Winter had always idolized his chief and considered his skills almost supernatural. If the agencies had sent an army after him, he would have expected to find platoons of bodies scattered across the surrounding sand. It was, then, a pleasant relief to him when he returned to the central room and spotted the camera there. It was sitting on a windowsill: a wee beast, small enough to pinch between finger and thumb. Winter picked it up and examined it, admired it. Motion detection. Night vision. Clearly, the Recruiter had escaped and they were watching to make sure he did not return.

Winter dropped the camera on the floor and ground it to pieces under his heel. He added a curse in case anyone was listening.

He stepped out of the little house. It had been hot as an oven in there. It was hot as an oven out here too. He surveyed the empty panorama of red dust and red stone, colorless cactus and motionless weed. Nothing was moving. No glint of sunlight on metal. No suspicious shadows. Whoever had come for the Recruiter was not really expecting him to return. They'd just left the camera to see what the wind would blow in. The wind had blown in Winter.

He returned to his Jeep. Fired it up to get the air-conditioning going. But he didn't drive away at once. He sat still awhile, thinking.

The independent journalist Warren Gentry had been murdered. The Recruiter was on the run. A tattooed government assassin had gone insane, maybe still working for the federals, maybe rogue.

A man with a bug in his brain had suddenly committed murder then been killed himself while alone in a locked padded cell. The insane tattooed assassin had threatened the pathologist to keep him quiet about the details. And whatever was going on, Winter found himself in the thick of it because Gwendolyn Lord had happened to hear a story from a friend.

*Strange*, he thought. *Strange coincidence. Strange world we live in altogether.*

He put the Jeep in gear and drove away.

# 10

Tilda Bach drove to church to meet her pastor. She could not believe she was doing this. There were times these days when she could not believe who she was at all. She could not believe what she had become. It was not so very long ago, she had been a bar girl, a party girl. Reefer with her coffee in the morning, drinks with her lunch at noon, a man at bedtime and whatever drugs the man had on him and was willing to share. If you had told her she would come to Jesus, she would have laughed at you. She had not even known that she was in despair.

It was Martin who had awakened her. He had preached the word of God until she saw the light, then backed it up by putting a ring on her finger. And putting a baby inside her. Which felt to her like some kind of miracle, like it was God who put it there and not just Martin, like she was the Virgin Mary, except without the virgin part. And it was a beautiful thing. She wasn't pretending about that part at all. She loved the baby already.

It was the rest of it; the church of it, the image of herself as a Holy Roller; that was what she found so hard to believe. Sometimes, when she knelt to pray, in church or in bed when she sent her prayers into the darkness under the ceiling where God lived, sometimes—a lot of times—she felt like it was all some kind of game she was playing. Like a child believing in Santa Claus after the jig was up. Or a madman talking to some phantom he knew deep down was not really there. Did she really believe this stuff, she sometimes wondered. Who was she anyway? Where had the old Tilda gone?

These thoughts went through her mind as she turned her Toyota into the church parking lot. Who was this homemaking mama-girl tootling through town in her seven-year-old junker with a million miles on it and minus snazz? Martin had bought the ancient vehicle off a friend. Paid almost nothing for it. Brought it home so proudly. "Ta da," he sang, as he waved his hand at it. As she stood in the doorway, pretending to be overwhelmed with joy. "Wait till I fix her up," he said. And he had fixed it up. And now it was a dull-blue suburban mama car that purred like a kitten. He had fixed it up and he had fixed her up. But was she really who he'd made her? Was she really who she was or just pretending?

Pastor Mike was waiting for her at the top of the metal stairs that led down to the undercroft. He was a young man, slim and attractive in a boyish way. He wore jeans. A pink-striped shirt buttoned to the top button but one, the sleeves rolled up. It was a look: the energetic young pastor for the wives to flirt with. Trying to build a small church into a bigger one with an earnest show of enthusiasm.

He smiled as she came toward him. She had to pretend she didn't notice his eyes flick up and down her, stealing a glance at her breasts. She had to pretend it even to herself so she could have the right attitude toward him. Sometimes her whole life seemed like that, a game of pretending, as if she had been more real, more herself, when she was drugged up and easy pickings and dead to her own misery.

The undercroft—a basement wallpapered with notices and Sunday school drawings—was where the congregation gathered for coffee hour after services. Tilda brought food there sometimes. Sometimes she baked fresh cookies. What would her old friends say if they saw her? Baking cookies? Praying to God? Even now, she could not believe it was herself sitting in the pastor's closet of an office, her in the wooden chair, hand on her baby bump, him in his swivel chair with his pious pastordom, their knees about three inches apart.

"I don't know how to talk about this," she said—and immediately, just like that, she started crying. Two streams of tears ran down her cheeks. How could she tell him about the box in Martin's shed, about the picture printouts in the box and the bloody shirt?

Pastor Mike held out a box of Kleenex to her. It had been sitting right there in the mess on his desk. All he had to do was snap it up and hold it out. Of course: He was used to this, wives coming in and crying. Tilda laughed once at that and took a Kleenex and wiped her nose. But she cried even harder as she started to speak again.

"Something's the matter with Martin," she managed to say.

Pastor Mike didn't answer with anything. He just nodded to encourage her on. She could see he really was used to this sort of thing.

"I know it sounds crazy," Tilda said. "I know it does, really, believe me. But I think some kind of evil has gotten into him. Like maybe a demon or something? Are they real? Is that possible? Am I crazy? It's just I've got the baby now and all to think about . . . And I'm scared."

The pastor smiled, a practiced smile of sympathy. But Tilda could tell it was real sympathy, even if he did practice it. Even if he tried out different sympathy smiles in front of the bathroom mirror every morning, she could see he was a decent man who wanted to help her.

"You're not crazy," he told her. "We think of demons as creatures, you know. With horns or whatever. That makes them hard to believe in, because they're not that way, except in the movies. But there's evil in the world, that's for certain. There's nothing make-believe about that. What makes you think that evil's got hold of Martin?"

She sniffled. Dabbed her nose. Shook her head. "Well . . . He talks in his sleep," she said. That wasn't what she wanted to say. She wanted to tell him about the box in the shed, but the words were stuck in her throat like a bone swallowed sideways. "He says these—these filthy things in his sleep. Not like Martin at all. Not like the Martin I know. And I know he's been looking at pictures. Horrible pictures . . ."

Pastor Mike grew serious. "Pornography."

She nodded, but it felt like a lie. Because she wasn't sure the printed pictures in the box were pornography. Not regular pornography, like pictures on the internet. Was it that? Or had Martin taken those horrible pictures himself?

Pastor Mike grimaced. "That stuff, I swear, it's poison. Right there on your computer where you can barely avoid it. Like a bottle of poison just sitting in the pantry. The things it does to men's brains. There are studies about it. It ought to be against the law."

"If it were just girls," said Tilda through her tears. "Pictures of girls. I wouldn't mind that so much. I know what men are like, but . . ." She could not get the whole truth out. She could not.

"It's all right," said Pastor Mike. "I understand. It's not uncommon, this sort of thing. And I guess it is a kind of demon in a way. It's a tool of the devil, no question about that. Look, I'll have a word with Martin . . ."

Tilda shook her head sharply before she could get the word out: "No!"

Pastor Mike straightened, startled by the force of it.

"No," said Tilda again, more softly. "Don't do that. Please. Then he'd know I came here. He'd know I talked to you. Really. Don't."

Now there was concern in the pastor's eyes. "Are you afraid of Martin, Tilda? Has he said anything to you that made you worry he might hurt you?"

This was the time to tell him about the bloody shirt. But she didn't. "No. No, he's never done that," she said. "It's just . . . Well, like I said, now there's the baby to think about. I'm just . . . I've just been so worried about him, that's all. But don't talk to him. Don't talk to him, please. Please. I know Martin. That . . . that wouldn't be helpful."

There was a long moment of quiet while Pastor Mike considered. The thoughts that flashed through Tilda's mind in that moment made her wonder again about who she really was. It flashed through her mind, for instance, that she might offer Pastor Mike sex in return for his silence, offer to give him oral if he would just keep his mouth shut. Or maybe she should threaten to cry rape if he wouldn't agree. These were the sorts of things she had actually done in the old days before she found God, back when she was still the person she thought of as herself.

Luckily, before anything awful could come out of her, the pastor said, "Well, look, of course, anything you say to me here is confidential. That goes without saying. But I need you to promise me that if you feel you're in any kind of danger, you will let me know. Will you promise me that, Tilda?"

"Yes, yes," she said quickly. Relief washed through her. She could go on being this new Tilda, the pretend one. "I will. I promise."

Pastor Mike gave her a thin smile. "Good. Good. Don't cut me out, Tilda, all right? This is what I'm here for. Let me know what's going on."

"I will," she said. "I will."

But she wouldn't. She knew that. She never would.

All the way home, she prayed. She whispered through the windshield at the sky, beseeching God for help. It made her feel better. When she prayed, she knew that God was there. She could feel him listening. She didn't feel so much like she was faking it.

But whatever comfort came to her then, it vanished as she turned onto her tree-lined lane and her little house came into view. Then, her stomach dropped so violently she was afraid for the baby. She touched her bump to keep her steady in there. She pressed her lips together, staring at what she saw.

Martin's truck was in the driveway. It was not lunchtime yet, still morning. Martin never came home this early. But there the truck was, large as life.

For a moment, Tilda thought to just keep on driving. Just drive by, maybe go to the grocery and pick up a few things. Then when Martin asked her where she'd been all morning, she could say, *Just at the grocery, shopping, that's all.*

But she didn't drive by. What if he was watching through the window? What if he'd already seen her?

She pulled up behind the truck and parked and went inside.

She had another shock as she stepped through the front door. Martin was right there, sitting right there in the living room armchair. All the lights out. The sunlight spilling in through the windows, lying at his feet like a house cat, him looming in shadow. It was as if he had been waiting for her to arrive, just sitting there and waiting. And he was smiling at her, but it was not his usual smile, not his sweet Martin smile. Or it was his smile, but there was something wrong with it. There was something about his eyes that made the smile wrong.

"Hi!" she said as casually as she could. "What are you doing home at this hour?"

Martin went on sitting there, smiling that smile, not moving. "Where you been, girl?" he asked her. And again, it was his usual voice, his kind, loving voice, only not kind, not loving, sour somehow, threatening.

"I just had to drop some things off at the church," she said. She had composed the lie as she walked from the car to the house. "Some canned goods for the shelter."

He nodded slowly. "That's nice," he said. "Canned goods for the shelter. That's real nice."

Tilda tried to smile but her face felt all waxy and false. He knew, she thought. He knew she'd been in the shed. He knew she'd opened the box. He knew she had seen what she'd seen.

"That's real, real nice," he said again very slowly. Sitting there in the shadows. Smiling. Staring.

"You want anything?" she said. She had to clear her throat. "You want me to make you some lunch?"

"That'd be real nice," said Martin.

Tilda headed into the kitchen. She could feel his eyes following her.

*He's going to kill me,* she thought.

She was suddenly sure of it.

He was going to kill her and the baby both.

# PART TWO

# THE BUSINESS OF MIRACLES

*So just to remind you. An independent journalist named Warren Gentry was murdered last week, right? And I was telling you about the time the Recruiter called me in and asked me to investigate a businessman named Thaddeus Blatt. Remember? This same guy, this Gentry, had gotten hold of a story that might have embarrassed Blatt and the Recruiter thought Blatt had blackmailed Gentry into killing the story with information Blatt had gotten from our old friend Kemal Balkin, the Turk who had a bad habit of drawing powerful people into highly compromising sexual situations and then taking pictures of them. It was possible Gentry had had his picture taken in such a situation. Gentry was gay and was rumored to enjoy some kinky business of an unspecified nature. I guessed that was the Recruiter's thinking, anyway.*

*It seemed pretty flimsy. And I was worried that maybe the Recruiter was going bad on me, starting to see things that weren't there, looking to put out hits on American citizens. And when I got home and walked into my apartment, what to my wondering eyes should appear but Thaddeus Blatt himself sitting in the easy chair by my fireplace and drinking my rosé wine. And the same assassin, the one with the pentagram tattoo, the same guy who had confronted me in the parking lot concerning the whereabouts of someone named Isabella, was standing right behind him.*

*Okay, so that's where we were.*

*So I shut the door behind me. And I said to Blatt, "Help yourself to some wine."*

*"Can I pour you a glass?" said Thaddeus Blatt. I won't say he sneered at me, but he did, he sneered at me.*

*"Thanks, but no," I said. "It might slow me down if I have to rip out this creep's esophagus."*

*I was talking about the pentagram guy. I didn't look at him—I didn't want to show him that much respect—but I could feel him grinning at me. Grinning, and mentally inscribing my name on the long list of people he was going to take revenge on one day.*

*"I take it you know who I am," said Thaddeus Blatt.*

*There was a second easy chair across from Blatt, on the other side of a small coffee table. So I sat in that one, where I could keep an eye on both him and his friend.*

*"You're Thaddeus Blatt," I said. "And I take it this monkey here is your hired gun."*

*Blatt glanced up at Pentagram Boy and smiled. "What he does on his own time, I don't know. But right now, he's moonlighting as my bodyguard, that's all. Do you know why I need a bodyguard?"*

*I answered with a gesture of indifference. What did I care why he needed a bodyguard?*

*Thaddeus Blatt went on all the same: "It's because I'm told you're a very dangerous man, Mr. Winter. One of many dangerous men and women who are employed by a completely illegal intelligence division and assigned to commit murderous illegal acts at the whim of your fanatical Christian nationalist chief."*

*"Oh, he's not so bad as Christian nationalists go," I said. "As long as you don't betray Christ or the nation."*

*Blatt was one of these fifty-year-old rich boys who has a gym in each of his mansions, each one fully equipped with a personal trainer. He was smallish, but very trim, very fit. Wearing a short-sleeve polo shirt to show off his biceps and wearing it tucked into his slacks and pulled tight to show off his pecs. He had reddish hair and a handsome face from which most of the traces of corruption had been surgically removed.*

*"Have you ever heard of a woman named Isabella Gonzalez?" he asked me.*

*"Yeah, about an hour ago when your gorilla asked me where she was. Before that, never."*

*"Do I believe you?"*

*"Do I care?"*

*"Well, you might," said Thaddeus Blatt. He lifted his glass of my wine—my glass actually—and sipped it elegantly, elegantly crossing his legs at the knee. "Isabella is the daughter of Ramon Gonzalez, who heads the Gonzalez drug cartel out of Mexico. She's been kidnapped. The word on the streets is that she was kidnapped by the man called El Coba, who runs a rival drug operation. But I have reason to believe that's not what happened. I have reason to believe she was kidnapped by people working at the behest of the man you call the Recruiter. Some of your colleagues, in other words."*

*I showed him what I hoped was a carefree smile, but to be honest, I wasn't feeling all that free of care. Kidnapping the daughter of a mob boss and blaming it on another mob boss—well, it sounded like exactly the sort of thing the Recruiter would set up. Start a war between the cartels and let the gangsters slaughter each other. It was a typical Division hit.*

*"You do realize that would be insane, right?" said Thaddeus Blatt. "If that were true? An American agency kidnapping an innocent young woman in order to start a gang war? That would be completely nuts."*

*I could still feel the pentagram guy grinning at me and plotting my slow death and I still wasn't paying him the respect of looking his way. I stayed focused on the billionaire drinking my wine.*

*"What's any of this got to do with me?" I asked him. "Come to think of it, what's any of it got to do with you?"*

*"You know I have a sister who's a United States senator," he said.*

*"I know now."*

*"And a cousin in Congress."*

*"Congratulations."*

*"The smooth, legal, and democratic functioning of our government is of great concern to me. If nothing else, reliability and honesty in government are good for business."*

*Once again, I gestured my indifference. I didn't care what was good for his business either.*

*"Your chief has lost his mind, Mr. Winter," the billionaire said. "He was given a limited intelligence brief and he's allowed it to metastasize into a government murder ring. I have been working behind the scenes to have this monstrosity shut down and the people responsible punished to the full extent of the law, chief among them the Recruiter."*

*"Thank you for your service," I said—though at this point, Margaret, I have to admit, I was wishing I had let him pour me a glass of my wine. I felt like I could use it. As much as I loved the Recruiter, the things Blatt was saying did not sound all that implausible to me. I asked him: "Why are you telling me this?"*

*Thaddeus Blatt set his wineglass—my wineglass—down on the end table beside him, which was also mine. He leaned forward in his chair, his elbows on his knees. Out of the corner of my eye, I could see the pentagram guy standing behind him. Watching me. Grinning. Plotting.*

*"I'm telling you this because I believe the Recruiter is planning to have me assassinated to stop me from ending his illegal operation," said Thaddeus Blatt. "And I believe you're the man he has assigned to do the job."*

*I snorted as if to say: That's ridiculous. But was it ridiculous? Hadn't I been worried about exactly the same thing all through my long drive home? Still, it was just a worry so far. So far, I'd only been assigned to find out why Gentry had killed a story about Blatt, to find out if he was using the blackmail services of Kemal Balkin to control people in our government. So with an effort, I managed to look unconvinced.*

*"Mr. Blatt," I said, "here's one thing I can tell you for certain. If the Recruiter had assigned me to assassinate you, it would be very unlikely you'd be sitting here complaining about it, you being dead and all. Since you seem to not be dead, I think we can discount your information."*

*Thaddeus Blatt sighed. He sat back in his chair. He looked up at the man standing behind him: the pentagram guy. Finally, I deigned to raise my eyes to the pentagram guy too. I saw him look down at the billionaire, still grinning. They exchanged a meaningful glance which, for all I knew, was my death warrant.*

*But then Blatt simply folded his hands in front of himself and said: "And I suppose you're going to keep on insisting that you have no idea where Isabella Gonzalez is?"*

*"Where she is, who she is, or if she exists. And I suppose you're going to insist you have no idea who Kemal Balkin is."*

*I couldn't be certain, but it seemed to me some of the blood drained out of the billionaire's cheeks. "What's that supposed to mean?" he said tightly.*

*I tried to read his eyes. I saw no reason I should spend time trailing him around trying to find out if he was using blackmail to pull the strings of the United States government when I had him right in front of me and could simply ask him.*

*"Well," I said, "it might be that the Recruiter is a lunatic having people killed for no reason. Or it might be that some clown with too much money has teamed up with a Turkish sex trafficker in order to blackmail people into doing what he wants."*

*"I have no idea what you're talking about." This sounded unconvincing to me. But then, I was in no mood to be convinced.*

*"You know a man named Warren Gentry?" I asked him.*

*Blatt looked startled. Maybe he was startled. "The journalist? Yes. I know Warren. So what?"*

*"I understand he was going to run a story about you. Something having to do with your idiotic plan to share our weaponry with our enemies."*

*Blatt waved a hand, as if my words were mosquitoes that annoyed him.*

*"Only he didn't run the story," I said.*

*"Because there was nothing to it," said Blatt. "It was just something I had discussed."*

*So at least this part of the Recruiter's intel was good. "Maybe," I said. "Or maybe you had a crackpot plan and Gentry got hold of it and you used some information from Kemal Balkin about Gentry's private activities to blackmail Gentry and shut the story down."*

*For a moment, the room was oddly silent as Blatt sat gaping at me. Then he let out a loud laugh that sounded almost authentic. "Is that what this is about? It is, isn't it? Gentry dropped a story about me because it was a nothingburger, and your Bible-thumping boss figured it must have something to do with the fact that Gentry's gay. Right? I'll bet that's it. Along with everything else, the Recruiter is a homophobe, isn't he? So he spun this whole story up in his mind and sent you out to save the world for heterosexuality. Tell me I'm wrong."*

*Well, I smirked as if he was wrong. But was he? I really wasn't sure.*

*Thaddeus Blatt, meanwhile, rose from his chair—my chair—with an air of offended dignity. I rose from my other chair with an air of not giving a damn about his dignity.*

*"Let me tell you something, Mr. Winter," Blatt said. "This abomination you're involved in has got to be destroyed. It has to be destroyed for the sake of our democracy. Now you can help me make that happen by coming forward and telling the truth. Or you can stick with your precious Recruiter and go down with him. Because one way or another, he is going down. I'm going to make sure of it. This is absolutely disgusting."*

*I sneered again. It was the best I could do. I didn't like the man much. I thought he was probably a two-bit puppet master, far more a threat to "our democracy" than the Recruiter, who at least believed in our democracy. But I couldn't be sure. I trusted the Recruiter. I'd have followed him off a cliff. I assumed he hadn't spun up this whole conspiracy because of Gentry's homosexuality. I thought there had to be more to it than that. But maybe there wasn't. Maybe Blatt was right. And if Blatt was right about the Recruiter, then he might be right about the Division as well.*

*"Think it over," said Thaddeus Blatt. He reached into his jacket pocket. Drew out a business card. Placed it on my end table next to my wineglass. "If you change your mind, call that number. They'll know how to reach me."*

*He walked to the door. The pentagram guy also walked to the door. But along the way, the pentagram guy swung closer to me. He stopped in front of me, close enough to strike. I half hoped he would strike. It would give the situation some clarity. Also it would have cheered me up to break him in half. But all he did was grin in my face.*

*He spoke to me then, very softly, probably too softly for Blatt to hear him over there by the door.*

*"One day," he said. "One day, when I have a reason, I'm going to cut your heart out and piss on you while you die."*

*"Man, that's just unsanitary," I told him.*

*He laughed with his mouth, but his eyes weren't laughing. His eyes were looking forward to that happy future day.*

*He swaggered away from me and joined his client at the door. He went out first. Thaddeus Blatt gave me a look over his shoulder. Then he followed. Then the door shut.*

*And I was alone with my confusion.*

# 11

"So," said Margaret Whitaker. "Let's talk about Gwendolyn Lord."

"You keep saying that. You're like a broken record," Winter said.

"I want to know how your dinner went."

It seemed to her that Winter was about to answer her, about to tell her something else, something more about Turkish slave traders and pentagrammed assassins. But he didn't. He stopped himself. She was glad. She was a therapist, not a ninja. Assassins, pentagrammed or otherwise, were not within her area of expertise. Her job was—had been—to see Winter through his post-traumatic depression, to put him on track to having the life he wanted, the love he had denied himself in his guilt and alienation and confusion.

She had done all that, and done it well, thank you very much. Since passing through the crisis of the spring, Winter was full of energy and self-confidence, more confident and energetic than she had ever seen him. Their work together had restored him to the man he had once been, or maybe even lifted him to a man he had never quite been before. The only task left to Margaret was to see him established in a healthy relationship, or at least to assure herself he was capable of having one. She could do that. She knew how. But what exactly did he expect her to contribute to a battle with killers and evil Turks?

The two sat in stalemate, regarding one another in the bland, tan silence of the bland, tan room. Margaret tried on her Stern Mommy look, but she wasn't really feeling it. She was feeling wistful actually. There had always been something about her time with Winter that made her entertain daydreams about a different life, a life different from the life she had lived, her sedate marriage, her troubled son, the parade of clients with petty problems who came and went from her bland, tan room. She would miss Winter when their therapy was over. She would miss her inappropriate girlish passion for him, and that feeling it gave her of fresh possibilities, even when she knew those possibilities were never really possible at all.

"Well?" she said.

Winter surrendered. "It was nice. Dinner was nice," he said. "She's nice. Gwendolyn. More than that. There's something about her."

"Yes, you said that before," said Margaret. "Something about her. What sort of something?"

He shook his head. "It's hard to describe. I keep having this feeling that we've known each other longer than we have. It's weird because . . ."

"Because . . . ?"

"Well, we're very different sorts of people. On paper, we don't seem all that well suited to each other. She's not into literature or anything like that. She's never even been to the theater to see a play. Can you believe that? Plus she's religious. And she wants a big family."

"Well, you want a family. You want that very much, I think."

"Yes, that's all right. That part fits. But . . . I don't know. She's just a lot—different. Warmer than I am. Kinder. Softer somehow."

"Sounds like she could be a different gender. Have you explored that possibility?"

"I'm working on it. That would explain it, for sure."

"How was your conversation? At dinner. Did you tell her anything about yourself? About your past?"

"I did," he said in a tone of surprise. "I didn't mean to. It just sort of came out of me. It was kind of startling how easy it was. She's like you, Margaret. There's no false virtue in her. You can say things to her and you don't feel the sky is going to fall on you."

Margaret smiled to cover her complex feelings. She was gratified by the compliment. And she was jealous too—jealous that her time with Winter was ending and Gwendolyn's was beginning. And also sad. And also proud of the work she had done with him.

"So you're going to see her again?" she asked. She left her smile on, a neutral smile. He was a smart man, an observant man. She had to work hard to keep her feelings hidden from him.

"I am," said Winter. "I am going to see her again. And again after that, I think, if she's up for it. The whole thing seems . . ." He shook his head again.

"Seems . . . ?" said Margaret—but she already knew the word he was looking for.

"Inevitable," Winter said.

# 12

An hour later, Winter was sitting on the balcony of his apartment, gazing thoughtfully at the white dome of the Capitol Building below. It was a fine summer day, warm and breezy. Majestic summer clouds sailing across a deep-blue sky.

Wearing slacks and a red polo shirt, he sat tilted back in his patio chair, his feet up on the railing, a piece of paper held in his hand. He tried to bring his thoughts into order, but there was not much chance of that. There were just too many of them all at once.

His mind was always busy after a therapy appointment, but this was different. Usually, he was troubled by the things he and Margaret had talked about. Today, he was troubled by the things he hadn't talked about. The tattooed man and his knife attack, for instance. He had wanted to tell her about that. He almost had. He usually told her about anything that came into his head. But this time, he had thought: no. He had come to Margaret Whitaker to examine his old life, to confess his bloody sins, to win her motherly forgiveness and receive her absolution. And he had done those things, or she had done them, or they had done them together. But in any case, he felt much better than he had when he first came to her, better in fact than he ever had. But now . . .

Now the old life he'd tried to leave behind had come back to find him. Not just the tatted assassin, but the murder of Warren Gentry, the attempt to pin that murder on the Recruiter, the Recruiter's vanishing act. And Owen McKay too. And Gwendolyn too. Because it was Gwendolyn who had told him the story about McKay and it was that story that had brought the tatted assassin back into his life. Which couldn't be a coincidence, could it? And yet it made no sense that Gwendolyn was connected to any of these things.

It was all very confusing, more than he could think through. Ultimately, his instinct had been not to mention any of it to Margaret, which was also confusing. The open flow of mind between them was clouding; closing. That must mean their therapy was coming to an end.

It was sad to think about that. He had come to love Margaret during their work together. Not like a mother exactly, but sort of like. She had given him something his mother never had, that no one ever had. For the first time since he had left the Division, he felt there was a life ahead of him, a life worth living and that he was worthy of living it. And if his past was going to become part of that future life, he wanted to face it on his own. He wanted to keep Margaret out of it. He wanted to preserve their relationship as it was, in their remembered world, therapy world, a safer, kinder world than his.

He looked down at the paper he was holding. It was the paper Billy Whitefield, the pathologist, had pushed into his pocket. There was a drawing on it, a sketch Whitefield had made of the device he had removed from Owen McKay's brain. The spidery little object had disappeared from the evidence lockers and from the autopsy report. Whitefield had had to draw it from memory. He had sketched a marking on the side of the device. A series of lines and crosses suggestive of a sparkling star. Winter had tried to feed the image into a brand logo database but had not come up with anything. He suspected the pathologist's drawing wasn't exact enough to make the right connection.

His phone buzzed where it was lying on the small glass table beside him on the balcony. Winter glanced at it. It was Dean Copely calling. Odd to have him call in the middle of summer. Winter dug his earbuds out of his shirt pocket and put them in.

"Oh, Winter," Copely sighed. No hello. No bluff, friendly chit-chat. This was where he started, sighing out his name like a princess locked in a tower yearning for her hero knight.

Winter smiled with one side of his mouth. Well, the dean was a hysteric, not to mention a moral coward. And Winter, with his outlook and values rooted firmly in the eighteenth century or thereabouts, was always a political problem for him. Students complained about him. Other professors complained. And Lori Lesser was constantly trying to terrorize the dean into firing him for one or another offense against her modern sensitivities. But while the dean was a coward, he was also a Machiavel. He had a deep understanding of the intricacies of university politics. He couldn't fire Winter, or thought he couldn't. Winter did not have tenure, but he had something better. He had Copely's darkest secret. A little problem about an underage Thai prostitute who had tried to extort him—sextort him, as it was called in the business. Winter had made the problem go away. That was more or less his job interview. And while he would never have used this secret to retaliate against the dean if the dean did fire him, the dean didn't know that. Like most corrupt men, he assumed everyone was as corrupt as he was. Which suited Winter fine. He liked his job and, given the state of American education, he felt it would be difficult for someone like him to secure a position at a university where the dean was not being sextorted by an underage Thai prostitute. So he preferred not to get fired.

"I'm guessing this is about Lori," he said.

"The woman is like a Fury," Copely whined. "It's like she rises out of the earth just to plague me."

"This is the business where she wants me to rejigger my 101 poetry class next year?"

"There's got to be a black Romantic somewhere. Maybe in one of the colonies. She says you're a racist now. You know what that means. That means she'll be calling me a racist next."

Winter laughed.

"That's the other thing. She says you laughed at her concerns."

"I did laugh at her concerns. She's becoming ridiculous. She went to some sort of conference."

"I know, I know. The conference. She's going to kill me with that conference."

"Ignore her. The president considers me a hero nowadays. That thing with the girl and the gun and all that—that must have saved the university zillions in lawsuits and bad publicity. The last I heard she was talking about giving me early tenure."

"She was. She is. Computer Sciences wants to build a freaking statue to you. It's just Lori who hates you. But she's obsessed. Why'd you have to laugh at her? You know how that sets her off."

Winter didn't answer. Copely's mention of Computer Sciences had given him an idea.

"Listen, I have to go," he said.

"She's killing me, Winter," said the dean.

Winter cut the connection and called Roger Sexton, his friend in Computer Sciences. Like the dean, Sexton owed him. Winter's little act of heroism—the girl and the gun and all that, as he called it—had saved him a lot of trouble and pain.

Sexton answered on the first ring, eager to please.

"My friend!" he said with what sounded like real enthusiasm.

"I'm looking at a little gizmo that was planted in a man's brain," Winter said. "It has a logo on it. A series of lines that sort of looks like a star with sparkles around it or something."

"Thaumatix," Roger Sexton answered at once. He made his voice deeper, louder, like the voice of an announcer in a TV commercial. "'We're in the business of miracles!'" he said.

# 13

*The Business of Miracles.*

The words appeared on windows everywhere around the Thaumatix office park. They floated amid fantastic scenes and swirling swaths of color. They hung like smoke over the spires of imagined cities, vanished into digital designs, and reappeared in the flowering depths of three-dimensional gardens that seemed to rise into being out of bright nothingness and fall away to nothingness again.

Winter had never seen anything like this place. It was something new in the world, a world in itself. A kingdom of sparkling glass and flowing imagery. A city that had appeared like a conjuring trick amid the cornfields of Nowhere, Indiana.

From a distance, as the jitney approached, the office park looked like a portal of sunlight, a dazzling passage out of reality. Then, as the little bus drew near, the brilliance resolved itself into temples and towers that seemed alive, evolving, dying, born again. The others with him on the jitney oohed and aahed at the first sight of it and even Winter held his breath with parted lips. The bus had picked them up at a little airstrip forty miles away. For forty miles, they had traveled past nothing but tall summer cornstalks under a vastness of cloud-riffled sky. They could have stared into the distance up ahead until their heads ached and seen only more of the same. So when the office park was suddenly there in front of them, it seemed it must have risen like a dream from the sleeping earth or fallen from the sky like alien fire.

As the jitney passed through the security checkpoint, Winter could begin to see how the effect was created, or some of it at least. On buildings all of glass, weirdly lifelike holograms were somehow projected from within. The images moved and morphed, folded in on themselves or drained into some internal vortex, transforming from works of art to scenes of seasons, and even cornfields sometimes, which made the buildings seem to vanish into their surroundings.

And every now and then, in the midst of these living murals, those words floated by again: *The Business of Miracles*.

With the help of Roger Sexton and his contacts in the world of tech, Winter had had himself inserted in a VIP tour of the company headquarters. There were ten visitors in all: a congresswoman, two CEOs from Silicon Valley, a Hollywood actor, the representatives of several investment firms, a female personal advisor to a famous billionaire, and Winter. Winter had joined as a representative of Winter Investments. That was the actual name of his father's company. A friend there had agreed to handle any calls that came in checking on his identity.

As the group alit from the bus, they were greeted one by one by a woman who introduced herself as Bethany Day. She was strikingly tall, strikingly beautiful, crisp, and intelligent, with an admirable talent for walking gracefully on impossibly high heels. Flanked by po-faced security guards, the little group followed the mesmerizing motion of her flowing royal-blue A-line dress and likewise flowing auburn hair until she and they all passed into the holograms within the glass structures as if into a vision writ on water.

The building they entered was even more spectacular within than it had been without. Fabulous scenes of stars and planets, fairy-tale cities, jungles, savannahs, and ocean depths sprang to full-blown life on every side of them. Meditative music played low. Office staff went by, absurdly real, absurdly young. The men wore tattered jeans and branded T-shirts. One rode a skateboard, one a scooter. The women—as if they worked for an entirely different company—were tenderly draped in pastel dresses or fitted slacks and blouses. The click of their heels was audible beneath the ambient soundscape.

"When Isaiah Kahn began this company, brain–computer interface was a science fiction fantasy whispered about by basement-dwelling nerds on obscure internet forums." So said Bethany Day. She spoke without turning, marching ahead of them through the manufactured hallucinations so that it seemed as if the holographic world parted at her approach. Her certain stride on those amazing heels of hers gave her movement a sinuous eroticism that seemed to Winter a science fiction fantasy in itself. "But Isaiah recognized it at once for what it was," her spiel went on. "The next stage of human evolution. It's a tragedy he did not live to see his vision become reality."

Isaiah Kahn had died in a motorcycle accident five years before at the age of fifty-two. Happily, that did not stop him from appearing suddenly on a podium before them, an animated hologram as realistic as the living man.

"Humans have enhanced their bodies through technology since the invention of clothing," he told them all boldly. He was spindly and spike-haired, goggle-eyed and narrow-lipped, just as he had been before his Harley cruiser skidded through a railing near the Donner Pass. "If you think about it, eyeglasses, pacemakers, birth control—they're all forms of cybernetics. The brain–computer interface is simply another step toward taking human development into our own hands. Welcome to Thaumatix. We're in the business of miracles."

Having said which, Isaiah Kahn disintegrated into particles of light that flew off every which way like fireflies.

"Wow," said the Hollywood actor walking just ahead of Winter. Until this, nothing in the morphing fantasia around them had been able to draw his eyes from the rear view of Bethany Day. Even now, as he gaped at the vanishing sparks that had been the late Isaiah Kahn, he stumbled after their guide as if dragged on a leash.

Winter lingered behind the group a moment. He was beginning to find the light show and the music and even the slithering Day distracting; overwhelming. How did people think in a place like this? How did they get any work done? A man accustomed to focused intellectual labor, he rested his attention for a moment by examining what seemed a framed video hanging in midair. It was a movie of two monkeys standing at either end of a table.

"That's Lola and Cola." One of the security guards, an enormous man with red-brown skin, had stopped beside him. "One of the company's earliest experiments. Kahn taught them to play the video game *Pong*. Then he gave them implants that linked their brains to the machine so they could play the game with their minds."

"Monkeys can play *Pong*?" said Winter.

"With their minds," said the guard.

"I'll be damned."

"Right?"

With a friendly smile to gentle the gesture, the guard shepherded Winter back into the group. Just as he rejoined them, Bethany Day finally stopped beside a waterfall. She turned to face them with balletic grace. The others pulled up short, collecting around her.

"When you were selected for this tour, each of you signed a nondisclosure agreement," she said. Even the movement of her lips was hypnotic. Winter had begun to suspect she, too, was a manufactured image, a hologram concocted out of calculated attractions. "You promised not to reveal what you saw here. Every one of you is going to break that promise. Once you pass through this door, you're going to see things you simply have to talk about. Our slogan at Thaumatix is 'We're in the business of miracles.' As you're about to see, it's not just a slogan."

Beside her, the waterfall whirlpooled into a funnel of stars. Bethany Day walked into it in her inimitable Bethany Day–like way. The tourists followed helplessly. Winter too. There was darkness. Motion. They were rising through starlit emptiness. A moment later, two doors slid open and they emerged from infinite space onto a glass walkway about four stories above the ground. For the first time since they had entered the building, there were no holographic displays. The windows were clear. They could see the surrounding cornfields beneath the endless sky. Winter found this dose of the natural world a tremendous relief to his overworked senses. As the group crossed over the walkway to the next building, his gaze lingered on the slowly drifting clouds. *Monkeys can play* Pong, he thought, not without wonder. The world, it seemed, was stranger than he knew.

Then, as far as he was concerned, it grew even stranger.

They came into a vast, windowless room, the walls white. There was no music here. There was instead a murmurous quiet, like voices borne on the wind. There were wide swaths of open space. People gathered in clusters at various stations. It made Winter think of a medieval fair, but that may have been because his mind was full of antiquated literary references. Another observer might have been reminded of a trade show.

Bethany Day's movements had acquired a new solemnity. She walked with stately, measured steps, not wholly real, like a toy soldier marching in *The Nutcracker.*

"This is Ted," she said. "He was injured in the war."

Ted was in his mid-twenties. Winter thought he must have been a handsome lad and strapping once. His limbs were mostly gone now; only one arm fully remained. The other arm and his two legs were prosthetics. His face was slack and scarred with burns. His hair was only wispy traces of the hair he'd had.

On his head, he wore a golden mechanism. It ran from the back of his neck to his head's crown, with a solid metal strap locking it in place at his chin. Two young men and a young woman stood around his wheelchair, gazing down at him proudly as if he were their creation.

"Hello, everyone," said Ted. "Thank you for coming." But his mouth didn't move when he spoke. His voice came from a speaker beside him. "When I was blown up by an explosive device, I suffered brain injuries that left me unable to speak. This Thaumatix helmet you see on my head can read my thoughts and translate them to a computer that translates them into speech. My voice has been reconstructed from old videos. As you can hear, it doesn't sound mechanical at all. And I can do this."

As if by magic, a computer on a stand before him turned on. A conferencing platform appeared on the monitor. A cursor responded to invisible, silent commands. A man in uniform came into view on the conference screen.

“Hi, Ted,” the man in uniform said.

“The device also allows me to connect with the computer,” Ted told the tourists. “This has allowed me to participate in online meetings, where I can continue to contribute my technical expertise in guided weapons systems.”

Standing next to Winter in their little group, the congresswoman let out a gasp. She covered her mouth with her two hands and started to cry. Winter choked up too, pressing his lips together hard, his vision blurring. He had read about such technology but that was not like this, seeing it give voice and power to the broken soldier right there before him.

*And those stupid monkeys were wasting their lives on* Pong, he thought.

“Now this is very cool,” said Bethany Day. Moving in that dancing march to the next station, she led the group to gather around two sinewy young men in their early twenties. There was a metal ball sitting on a stand between them. “Show ’em what you can do, boys,” said Bethany Day.

One of the young men gestured. The ball rose into the air. The people in Winter’s tour gasped. The boy flicked his hand and the ball sailed over to the other young man. The second young man raised his hand but did not touch the ball. Nonetheless, the ball stopped in the air. Turning his hand, he made the ball orbit his head and zigzag in the air before him. Then he made it fly back to the first young man.

“The hand gestures are extra,” said Bethany Day in a confidential tone. “I think they do it because it makes them feel like wizards.”

The visitors laughed as the young men clasped their hands behind their backs and continued to control the ball between them with their minds.

"Leonard here is one of our masterpieces," Bethany Day said, gliding on her high heels to the next station. "A swimming accident left him a quadriplegic three years ago. He was completely paralyzed from the neck down."

Winter, already dazzled, looked on open-mouthed as Leonard, strapped into a wheelchair, raised his right arm, opened and shut his fingers, then raised his left arm and clasped his hands together. There were murmured words of astonishment all around him. Both the women in the tour were crying now. Some of the men were discreetly dabbing at the corners of their eyes.

"I couldn't do this a month ago," Leonard told them. He was an open-faced kid with corn-yellow hair. "My implant has formed a line of communication with my nervous system, circumventing my broken spine. The techs think I'll be able to walk sometime in the next six months."

"Son of a bitch," Winter whispered.

"Now over here . . ." Bethany Day began.

"Mr. Winter."

The voice came from directly behind him. Startled out of his awestruck gaze, Winter turned. A man was standing close to him. He was in his late thirties or early forties, tall and fit. Handsome in an unpleasant sort of way. Styled hair, classic features. The sort of good looks men have when they care too much about how they look. He was dressed just a little more formally than the other men Winter had seen here. He wore jeans like the others but had a sports jacket on over a polo shirt. He was flanked by two uniformed security guards, large, pale-faced men of military bearing, grim with purpose.

"Would you come with me please?" the tall man said.

Winter glanced at the tour, already moving away from him to the next miracle. He glanced back at the tall man, who raised a hand in the opposite direction: *this way.*

What could he do? Winter walked that way. The tall man walked beside him, saying nothing. The security guards were behind him, one on either side.

"I was enjoying the tour," Winter said to the tall man.

"Too bad. Now it's over," the tall man said curtly.

They reached a wall—what seemed, at first, to be a blank wall. But the tall man pressed his index finger to an unseen sensor, and a door slid open. The tall man gestured again, his expression harsh: *this way.* Winter walked through the exit with the tall man and the security guards right behind him.

They were in a stairwell. All embellishments were gone. All the holograms, the music, and the dazzling show. The walls here were made of cinder block, painted pale yellow. The metal stairs went up and down. There was an elevator too, a service elevator with stainless steel doors. The tall man pressed the call button on the wall.

"My name is Arthur Dimmerman," he said. He had a slightly nasal voice, pinched and snide. His tone was perfunctory, as if this conversation, though necessary, bored him. "You might want to look me up. Spoiler alert: You'll find out I'm an attorney. You'll find I specialize in ruining people's lives. Some of those people were rich and powerful when they first crossed my path. When I finished with them, they were poor and weak and sorry we had ever met."

The elevator doors parted. Arthur Dimmerman made the same gesture as before: *this way.*

"You sound like a fun guy," Winter told him.

He stepped into the elevator. Dimmerman stepped in after him. Then the two guards entered and stood just within, hulking, their backs to the doors. Their dead, unpleasant stares were aimed steadily at Winter, yet they seemed somehow sightless, as if he weren't worth the trouble it would take to see him. The elevator doors closed. The elevator descended.

"Your cover story slipped past our security team," Dimmerman went on. "But it didn't slip past me. I know who you are. I know why you came here. I know where you work. I know what you used to do. I even know about your trust fund and the details of your investments. If one word of what you saw here today escapes your lips, even if you're alone, even if you're just dreaming and talking in your sleep, I will initiate a series of legal actions against you that will seem to go on forever, but in fact will end brutally fast with you bankrupt and unemployed and possibly facing criminal charges."

"Golly gee, Mr. Dimmerman," Winter replied. "You don't seem like a very nice person at all."

Dimmerman did not respond to that. He did not laugh or smile or frown. The only sign he'd even heard what Winter said was a sort of flicker of fire in the depths of his steely blue eyes. Winter interpreted this as a sign of sadistic anticipation. He thought Dimmerman was hoping Winter would give him an excuse to unleash his legal powers on the task of his destruction.

The elevator doors slid open. There was that gesture again: *this way*. Winter stepped out into a cinder block alcove with an exit door of heavy metal. The two security guards got out with him, but Dimmerman stayed on board the elevator. For a moment, he and Winter exchanged baleful glares through the elevator's opening.

"What did you guys do to Owen McKay?" Winter said.

One small corner of Dimmerman's mouth turned upward. It was a smile of sorts, but not a friendly how-do-you-do smile, more of an I'm-going-to-roast-you-in-the-firepit-of-my-flaming-disregard type of smile.

“One word,” Dimmerman said. “That’s all it will take, Winter. One.”

The elevator doors slid shut in Winter’s face. There was a loud *clank* behind him. He turned to find that one of the large, pale-faced security guards had opened the exit door and was holding it for Winter. The other large, pale-faced guard looked on grimly.

Winter walked out into a drab parking lot, its pavement baked warm by the late morning sun. The jitney was there, not ten steps away, motor running, door open, driver in his seat, waiting. Winter walked to it with one security guard on his left and another on his right.

“I hear you guys can be taught to play *Pong*,” he said to one of them.

They stood watching with expressionless stolidity as he boarded the bus and was carried away.

# 14

Winter did not go home, not directly. He went instead to a little town named Hilltop in Arkansas. This was no small journey. There were no flights out of Indianapolis that went anywhere near his destination. The best he could do was stop over for fifty minutes in Atlanta, then fly to Little Rock, then drive from there. By the time he reached the rental car place, there was nothing available but a sad little black Camry, which depressed him. By the time he drove the sad little Camry anywhere near Hilltop, it was dark of night. He was forced to take a room in a roadside motel so dingy his only consolation was that he thought even bedbugs would prefer to stay elsewhere. He wished he had not come.

The fact was, he might not have bothered if Arthur Dimmerman had not threatened him. Winter was a man well able to control his temper, but he had a temper, a good one, and he disliked being threatened. He disliked it only a little less than being attacked and he was already annoyed to have had a naked tattooed man try to gut him in his own apartment. To be forced to listen to Dimmerman's snarling threats of legal action on top of that had turned his determination to stone.

He had been at his computer, trying to find out more about Owen McKay, but there wasn't much to find. McKay had been living in Oklahoma for a little more than three years before he murdered his wife and son and then somehow died inside that locked cell. Where had he been before that? It seemed impossible to find out. He seemed to have left no traces anywhere. Winter had hunted down some business records that gave his place of birth as Hilltop, Arkansas. He had found a single page of information on Hilltop. Nine hundred seventy-three people lived there, nine hundred sixty-two of them white, eleven black. He called the Hilltop city hall several times. Only voice mail answered. *Leave a message*, a man's voice said. Winter had left several messages, but no one had returned his calls.

He spent an all but sleepless night in his motel, tossing and turning under a sheet like sandpaper that scraped against his skin. He fell asleep shortly before dawn and woke up shortly after. Weary, he dawdled in the motel coffee nook, feeling lonesome and sorry for himself. The coffee tasted like it had come from a pot in which a rat had died.

Away from his depressing hotel he drove in his depressing Camry. It was many a mile through wooded emptiness before he reached the town-o. He might have missed the town-o had he not been watching for it. A gas station went by. A general store. A cabin among the trees and then another. The moment he arrived at Hilltop's city hall, he understood why he had been unable to get through to anyone.

*City of Hilltop Municipal Building*—those were the words painted sloppily on the green awning over the door. The building itself was a little stucco box with some brick facing on the sides and a peaked roof that looked like it was made out of plastic desperately yearning to be wood. Winter parked in a little patch of dust out front. He got out and tried the building's door. It was locked. The windows were dark. Winter pressed his face to the glass pane in the door and peered into the shadows within. He saw Christmas streamers hanging on the walls inside. He saw a metal Christmas tree and a wreath. It was July, and already eighty-five degrees and humid here. But that was the whole point: There was no here. He had already seen everything there was to see. Isolated cabins in a widespread forest of oak and pines. A general store. A gas station up the road. No reason to staff a municipal building. No reason to update its decorations from Christmas to Independence Day.

Winter turned away from the building. He figured he'd head back to the general store and find out whatever he could from whomever was there. But before he took a single step toward his pathetic Camry, up sidled a state police car. This did not surprise Winter much. A stranger peering into the municipal building was probably big news in this nowhere of a place. Maybe somebody called the statie or maybe the statie was already hanging around the general store having a cup of coffee with the locals.

In any case, the car pulled up behind his Camry and idled there. The trooper rose out of his car, a tall, big-bellied fellow who looked to be near sixty. He called out over the roof, "How you doing this morning?"

Winter began walking toward him. "Good morning, trooper, how are you?"

The trooper had a large face pasted on a large head with an easy smile pasted on the face. But the eyes were a cop's eyes. They watched Winter closely as he approached. By the time Winter reached the opposite side of the patrol car, he could tell the trooper had decided he was okay, or at least not a felon. The smile grew more authentic as they faced each other over the roof.

"Well, I'm doing pretty good, given the weather," the trooper said. "If you're looking for Curtis—the mayor—he's on a run with the flatbed. I don't think he's likely to get back here before nightfall. Is there anything I can help you with?"

"There is actually. I'm trying to find out about a man named Owen McKay. He passed away not long ago in Tulsa, Oklahoma, and I was told he was born here about thirty-seven years ago."

The trooper gave his big head a big shake. "Well, no, he was not, I can tell you that much for certain."

"Really."

"Lived here all my life. Population has never topped a thousand and not one of them is named McKay and never has been. Plus if you want to get yourself born someplace antiseptic, you got to go on over to the medical center in White River. So really no one's actually born here when you come right down to it. You might want to check over at the center to see if they have any record of him. What is this, about some legacy?"

"Yes, that's it. Not enough to worry about but too much to ignore," Winter said. "Well, thank you. Thank you, trooper, very much." He moved to his Camry. "I'll head over to White River and check the records there."

And he would. He would do that very thing. But he already knew he wasn't going to find any Owen McKay in White River either. Or at least not his Owen McKay. He did not think his Owen McKay was Owen McKay. In fact, he was just about certain that, before his Owen McKay arrived in Tulsa, Oklahoma, some three years ago, his Owen McKay had not existed at all.

# 15

It was a long way home, a long week altogether. He was glad when Saturday came. It was a pleasure to sit next to Gwendolyn in Chicago's vast and magnificent old Nederlander Theatre with its sky-high ceilings and its niche sculptures and elaborate designs. Winter even had to admit to himself that *Phantom of the Opera* was not entirely intolerable. He wasn't completely sure whether he was enjoying the show itself or only Gwendolyn, but in either case, he was content—happy even—because Gwendolyn was absolutely rapt. Every time he glanced at her, she seemed to be in an ecstasy of wonder. She was gazing up at the stage with childlike awe. He found himself watching the performance through her eyes. The ghostly graveyard scene, the river beneath the opera house, the masked phantom passing through mirrors, the chandelier dropping from the theater ceiling so that the audience screamed, then laughed. And all those swelling, meltingly romantic tunes—despite his firmly held prejudice against all modern music, he could not help but enjoy them on Gwendolyn's behalf. He could only maintain his self-respect by assuring himself that, had he been there alone, he surely would have detested them.

Afterward, at their late dinner in a corner of a small Italian restaurant in the West Loop, Gwendolyn went on and on about the show with an enthusiasm he found delightful. *Oh, the music! Oh, the romance! Oh, the magical entrances and exits!* Winter thought the light in her eyes might strike him senseless.

"Do you know what I really liked?" she said.

Winter had once again chased the waiters away so they could drink a glass of wine in peace.

"Tell me," he said.

"I like that you took me to it even though you must have despised it."

He laughed. "I'm a bit of a snob about these things. I didn't know it showed."

"It showed. What did you do? Buy tickets for something else and then change them when I told you I'd never been to the theater before?"

"Now how on earth did you know that?"

"I could hear the panic in your voice when I told you. What did you buy at first?"

"Chekhov."

"Ooh, yes." She shuddered. "I've heard of him. He sounds very Russian."

"His friends used to complain of it," said Winter.

"How did you know I would like this one so much?"

"It's been running since 1492. Everyone must like it."

"No," she said. She looked fondly at him across the surface of her merlot. "I don't think that's what it was."

Winter smiled down at the tablecloth. He could not bear that look of hers for long.

"Cameron," she said. She reached across the checkered tablecloth and touched the back of his hand. "Recite some more poetry."

"Oh. No. That's kind of you, but you don't have to make it up to me. The show was fine."

"No, I mean it, though. I loved when you did that."

He raised his eyes to her, surprised. "Really. You want me to recite."

"I really do."

"Well . . . what?"

"I don't know. I don't know much poetry. Something you like."

Winter's lips parted and closed without a sound. What he felt wasn't panic, but it was something awfully like panic. He felt if he hesitated long enough to choose wisely, he would forget every poem he'd ever known. So he said the first thing that came to him.

"'She walks in beauty like the night / Of cloudless climes and starry skies / And all that's best of dark and bright / Meet in her aspect and her eyes / Thus mellowed to that tender light / Which heaven to gaudy day denies . . .'"

She still had her hand on his and when he found the courage to look at her, he saw her eyes had misted. Now he did panic.

"Too much?" he said.

She shook her head. "No," she told him. "No. Right on the button. Full prizes. It's wonderful. It's like you have a whole world in your head."

"A lost world," Winter said.

"Not altogether lost," said Gwendolyn Lord. "Not as long as you have it."

They both withdrew into their menus like boxers pulling back from an exchange. *Lord Byron*, Winter thought. *A bastard and a half, but he had his uses.* He summoned the waiter urgently before either of them felt compelled to speak again.

The moment they were alone though, Gwendolyn went on. "Why do you like it so much? Poetry. I always hated it when I was in school. I could never understand it. What does it do for you?"

What astonished Winter was how readily he answered her, how easily the words came. He was certain he would have ducked the question from almost anyone else.

"I don't know, not exactly. But I think—I think at any given time and place, most of the things people believe are false. Most of what they admire is trash. Most of what they desire is worthless. But every now and then, not that often really, but now and then, someone sees the beauty in something and has the ability to write it down. And there's a truth in that that's real somehow, that you can depend on—in the night or in trouble or whenever it really matters. It's like the nugget of gold a prospector picks out of the mud and stones. If you gather enough of them, you have something of genuine value. That's how it seems to me anyway."

Gwendolyn made a soft noise. She lifted his hand and drew it to her cheek. Then she kissed it.

Winter's face grew warm. More words came out of him before he thought them or willed them. "You are uncannily beautiful," he said.

She laughed. "I'm not. I'm moderately cute at best."

"How would you know? I'm the one who's looking at you."

She kept his hand. She toyed with it. "If I ask you something, will you promise to tell me the truth?"

He, who had lived so much in secret, drew a long breath, considering. "No," he said finally. "But I promise not to lie."

"All right," said Gwendolyn. "When we came in here, the maître d' pulled that seat out for me, the seat you're sitting in. But you took it. Which was very un-Cameron of you from what I've seen so far. I'm guessing it was because that chair is against the wall and gives you a view of the restaurant. All the time we've been talking, your eyes keep lifting up and checking around, watching the door."

Winter drew his hand back, bringing her hand with it. He pressed her hand to his lips and kissed it, then let her go.

"I guess what I want to know," she said, "is: Have I gotten you into some kind of trouble? Telling you that story about the man who died in the cell? Have I put you in some kind of danger?"

He had known she was like this. Observant. Smart about the ways people were. Almost a mind reader. That day she had told him she was a widow—it was because she had caught him glancing at her wedding ring and knew what he was thinking and wanted him to call. He had known since then that she was like this. So it was no wonder to him she understood him now. In that place in his mind that was trained for violence, the tattooed man never left him. Not when they watched the show together, not when her eyes gleamed with enthusiasm, not when they misted over, and not now. He did not think the tatted killer would return, not this way, out here, in the open. The assassin was obviously not working on his own. He had an employer. A master. And judging by the way the tattooed man had acted with Whitefield, judging by the way Dimmerman had acted with Winter himself, what that master wanted was silence, people scared into silence about whatever it was that had happened to Owen McKay. What the master did not want was a trail of murders and bodies that could be followed back to the truth. Winter suspected the tattooed man had been sent only to frighten him but that his thirst for revenge had carried him away. He would not return to kill him simply for his own pleasure. All the same. He had seen the killer up close in his apartment. The tattooed man was insane. He had remembered every one of Winter's old insults from their first meetings. He hated him for them. He had promised him a slow, humiliating death, and he meant to deliver it. For now, he would be restrained by his employer. But Winter felt pretty sure his goodwill and self-control would not last forever.

"Well, a little," he said to Gwendolyn. "You've gotten me into a little trouble."

"Oh, I am so sorry. I wish I'd never said anything. I was just trying to make conversation."

"No. Don't be ridiculous. I was the one who chose to look into it. I wanted to impress you."

"You should have skipped right to that poem. Really."

"Let me ask you something," Winter said. "Your friend Livy. Livy Swain. She said she visited you and you had a girls' night out. That you had too many drinks, and she told you what she knew she was not supposed to tell you . . ."

"Yes." Gwendolyn nodded eagerly, eager to help him and make things right. "She said she had overheard someone say something in a coffee shop and it had gotten under her skin. This was right before we had our night out. At her hotel. She overheard some random conversation this couple was having."

Winter lifted his chin. "Ah," he said.

"They were talking about not letting yourself get pushed around in life. Not letting people bully you and stop you from telling the truth. They were saying how it could ruin your life to hold back the truth when you knew you should tell it. She was already feeling bad about being intimidated into silence by her bosses. And I guess after she had a few drinks, the story just sort of came out of her. Why? Why are you smiling like that?"

They fell silent as the waiter brought them their pasta. But when the waiter was gone, as they began to eat, Winter said, "When I was in the service, we were trained to manipulate people. Mostly that's what we did. Manipulate them to get them to do what we wanted. They made choices they thought were their own, but actually we had maneuvered them into a position where that was their most likely option."

"I don't think I understand."

"It's like a magician forcing a card on you. He says, 'Pick a card, any card,' and you think you choose randomly, but really the way the magician holds the deck has made it all but impossible for you to pick anything but the ace of spades or whatever it is he wants. Magician's choice—that's what it's called. So, for instance, if we thought it was important for, let's say, a drug dealer's wife to find out her husband was cheating on her. We might just tell her and send her pictures of her husband with another woman. But if we wanted to remain completely invisible, that would give us away, you see? Instead, we would want her to think she had found out about the affair on her own. So we would do something like, we would place two women agents next to her—maybe in a coffee shop, just like with your friend. Our two women would pretend to have a casual conversation. One of them would tell a story to the other about why she suspected her husband and how she exposed his infidelity. And there would be all these details that were similar to things we knew our target, the drug dealer's wife, would have experienced with her husband. Our agent might even explain the best way to get the information that would confirm her suspicions . . ."

"Oh, I get it," said Gwendolyn. "You would plant ideas in her head." She had a forkful of penne lifted in front of her and was about to put it in her mouth when the whole picture struck her, and the fork clattered back onto her plate. "Wait. You're saying someone did that to Livy so she would tell me."

"She would tell you and you would tell me."

Gwendolyn sat up straight and gasped. "No! Who would do that? Who *could* do it? They would have to know that she knew me and I knew you and that I would tell you . . . I mean, who could arrange all that?"

Winter made a face and shook his head. "I can't answer that. I'd have to lie to you, and I promised I wouldn't. But trust me, he's a better spy than me and a better psychologist than you, and perfectly capable of pulling it off."

Gwendolyn was about to respond, then checked herself, then said, "All right. All right, but you do have to promise me you won't get hurt looking into all this. I would never forgive myself. Also, who would teach me about poetry and the theater?"

"Well. I'll try not to get killed, I'll promise that much," Winter said. "But I might get hurt. You might have to nurse me back to health and say 'Poor thing,' a lot. I'd enjoy that. I'm a sucker for maternal care. I had a very neglectful mother."

"Oh. Poor thing."

"There you go."

By the time their dinner was over, Winter's crowded mind was empty of almost everything except for her. He had been in love before. With Charlotte. With Madeleine. This was not like that. Not at all. With those other women, some passionate connection had stolen over him over time like a flame steals over a fuse. There was no mistaking the explosion of desire when it came. This, though—this was a mysteriously quiet business. The things he was suddenly saying to her, the questions he answered without pause, the words that came out of his mouth unbidden—when had this intimacy grown up between them? When had he started to include her within the guarded circle of his confidence?

And wondering that, he began to wonder also: What would happen if he asked to stay with her tonight? What would happen if she said yes? Because he thought he might, and he thought she might, and he thought they shouldn't, because once he stayed, even for a single night, there would be no leaving, not ever, and he could not imagine he was ready for that. After so long a period of depression and confusion, he could not believe he was ready to begin the rest of his life.

He was thinking about this when the waiter brought the check to him. Gwendolyn made a motion toward her purse.

"Now, now," he said, "don't try any of that twenty-first-century stuff with me."

"You're right," she said. "It's a rotten century. I only stay for the antibiotics."

"Fair enough."

"Well, in that case, excuse me."

He rose from his chair and watched the swing of her pink slip dress as she walked to the ladies' room. For a woman who'd never been to the theater, she'd known exactly how to dress. Elegant but not quite formal. A lighter color for summer. He found this wisdom womanly, and admired it very much.

He sat back down. He continued wondering how he should end the evening. The waiter came and collected his credit card, and he went on wondering. To distract himself, he drew his phone from his pocket and scrolled through his news feed.

Just as Gwendolyn came back into the room, he saw the story out of Connecticut: "GREAT NEIGHBOR" WANTED IN RAPE-MURDER.

His eyes went over the lede paragraph quickly.

"A man Riverbend residents referred to as a 'great guy and a great neighbor' is wanted in the kidnap, rape, and murder of a

16-year-old girl. The victim's friend, who witnessed the abduction, said local carpenter Harris Turner repeatedly shouted, 'It's still inside me,' as he forced Northwood High School student Nancy Franklin into his car at knifepoint and drove away with her . . ."

"Cameron?"

Startled back to himself by the sound of her voice, Winter leapt to his feet and forced a smile. But there was no chance of escaping Gwendolyn's talent for observation.

"What's wrong?" she asked him.

He gestured as if to say it was nothing, but she went on gazing at him with concern.

"You look as if you'd seen a ghost," she said.

# 16

It was another wearying zigzag of a journey to get to Northwood, Connecticut. He took a plane to New York City, then rented a car, and started driving.

All through the flight, he replayed the end of his evening with Gwendolyn in his mind. How he had parked with her outside her building. How he had turned to her in the driver's seat to take her into his arms and how she had come into his arms on her own and with a force of passion that had caught him by surprise. Long kisses later, she was lying across him and he was pressing her to his chest, breathless and still confused and too hungry for her to care anymore about his confusion.

He still was not sure what exactly had happened after that, who had said what and what they had meant by it, and whether he had been a fool or a wise man. The only thing that was clear was that they both knew something strange was happening to them, that they were not deciding on a night together but on a lifetime. He thought it was she who had stopped them. That is, he knew it was she who had said the words but was not sure whether or not she had acted on some silent signal from himself. He felt like a coward when he left her there. As he drove home, he explained to himself that he had not been a coward, but he still felt he was. Yes, they'd only been to dinner twice. So yes, they had not known each other halfway long enough to play for such high stakes. But so what? These were easy times. And for all her religion she did not seem unwilling. So what if it turned out to be a mistake? It did not have to mean anything, even though it felt like it would. Couldn't they just admit the error and part as friends?

So then maybe it really was his fear that had stopped them even though it was she who had said the words. Or maybe it was her fear and he just felt bad because he'd wanted her to stop them and, being a man and hot for her as he was, he was supposed to want them to go right on, regardless of the consequences. He didn't know. He went over it and over it and he still didn't know.

As the jet descended through the summer haze and as the jagged magnitude of the Manhattan skyline rose into clarity with all its blunt power and indifference, the craziest thought came into his head seemingly out of nowhere: *It's not that I love her. It's that I've always loved her.* Which only confused him more.

He was glad as he drove north . . . well, glad first of all that he had managed to score a brash maroon four-door Chrysler with a monstrous V-8 so he felt like a person of substance instead of a meaningless loser in a dusty black Camry in the Arkansas back-country. But he was gladder still to be able to train his mind on this new murder case, thus breaking off the looping replay of that long kiss good night and its unsatisfying conclusion.

The suspect in the case, Harris Turner, was still on the run. The police had found his car—and the body of the girl near the car—but the man himself had vanished into the forest. Eventually, they had brought out the dogs, but it was too late. Turner had made it to the edge of the Deep Pine reservoir and that's where the trail ended. The police conjectured he had swum to another shore, but which? They were looking at more than eight hundred acres of water with two islands in the middle and maybe fifteen miles or so of shoreline bordering on forests and roads and a couple of towns. The murder had taken place three days before. The fugitive could be just about anywhere by now.

But never mind all that, Winter had to get there as quickly as he could. The similarities between this murder and Owen McKay's murder of his wife and child were just too many and just too stark.

On the surface, McKay and Turner were different. Turner was black. Younger than McKay by a decade, only twenty-six. He was not a tech guy, like McKay, but a simple handyman, although apparently such a talented carpenter, he was a favorite among the local contractors. He was married like McKay, but had no children. And he did not seem to be a churchgoer; at least there was no mention of any church in the news stories.

In deeper ways, though, the two situations were much the same. Like McKay, Turner was considered by all who knew him to be a good man. Devoted as a husband, honest in business, helpful as a neighbor, always friendly and so on. He had no criminal record, no history of violence. He had given no signs that he was going mad. And that cry as he'd abducted his victim: *It's still inside me.* Wasn't that almost exactly what McKay had said as the police carried him away? *It's still in there?* Didn't it hint that one of those spidery devices from the miraculous folks at Thaumatix would be found inside his head? That is, if there was an autopsy. That is, if he died mysteriously in custody as McKay had.

That scenario was what ignited the sense of urgency in Winter, why he'd left for Connecticut the morning after his date with Gwendolyn. He wanted to try to get to Turner before anyone else could. He wanted to find him still alive, to ask him what was inside him, and how exactly it had gotten there.

Winter hadn't called the police. He didn't want to alert them to his intentions. He didn't want them to get in his way. Instead, he had tracked down Turner's wife—Vanessa—and phoned her from the airport. He had told her about the McKay case in Oklahoma.

"That's just like Harris!" she had cried out.

She had agreed to talk to him as soon as he arrived.

Northwood was a town of about four thousand people, in the northeast corner of the state, near the New York border. It had a tidy, prosperous New England air about it. A steepled church at the center. A library building of stone. Houses of stone or of white clapboard lined up one after another. In the heat of summer, there were young people all around, college students and campers strolling the sidewalks in T-shirts and shorts. Old folks too, haunting the antique stores clustered on the main road.

Winter sensed the tension as he drove through. Why were the young folks on the street instead of down by the water or off in the woods? They were afraid, that's why, he thought. And look at the state police cars—he counted three of them—no, four. One parked in the mini-mall and one in the library lot. Two more patrolling the side streets. Winter was willing to bet they weren't hunting for Harris. They were just there to make the locals and tourists feel safe. All of whom were white, he noticed. White or Asian or tan. There wasn't a black face to be seen among them. The police had come out in force to reassure them they would be protected from the black rapist-murderer running loose in the surrounding forests.

The part of town where the black people lived—all two hundred of them—wasn't actually part of the town at all. It was a collection of streets beyond the Northwood limits known as Riverbend. The houses there were old and small, some of them with one room only, wooden and painted white but with the white yellowing and the paint chipping away. The grass on many of the lawns was overgrown and threaded with weeds. There was another church here, a fine little neoclassical building with gray shingles and a pedimented portico with four white columns and a cupola up top. When Winter drove past, the congregation was just emerging into the misty daylight, the late service over. Black folks, all of them. He drove on by, as Mrs. Turner had instructed him, and found her house in a nearby grove of pines.

The Turner home was different from the others. He could see the house had started small like the rest, but Turner the carpenter had added rooms and a second-floor balcony. The paint was new on the old clapboard, and the new siding was bright white. The lawn was trim and neat. Trees had been cut down to create a yard.

"He's always working on the place," Vanessa Turner told him.

She was a tiny, delicately shaped woman. Very dark-skinned, with her hair pulled tight against her scalp. Winter thought she would be pretty in a homey way when she was happy. But as she was now, fretful and grieving, she looked sunken and worn. Her cheeks were slack. Her eyes were puffy. Her presence was dulled by her black slacks and T-shirt. When he'd first arrived, there had been two other women with her, older women, helping her keep watch during the emergency. The women had left as if on cue when she let Winter in. They had given him suspicious looks as they passed him on their way out the door.

Winter sat with Vanessa Turner at the small kitchen table. There were plates and pans of food on the counter and on the stove, all wrapped in plastic. Mrs. Turner had brought him lemonade from the half-empty fridge. Which he was grateful for. It was humid and hot, even indoors with the air-conditioning on.

"I mean, Harris, he works hard," she said. "Always making things better for us, nicer. He has plans, that man. Plans for good things."

She did not meet Winter's eyes as she spoke. Her voice was weak and hollow. As it trailed away to silence, her gaze sank down and sideways until she was staring blankly at the kitchen floor.

"Mrs. Turner," Winter said, as gently as he knew how. "How long did Harris live here in Riverbend?"

She lifted her shoulders as if they were a great weight. "Three years about, I guess. I met him pretty soon after he came."

"Do you know where he came from?"

"Texas. Dallas some of the time. Says he's originally from a little town called Apple Orchard. That's where he was born. He says wasn't but eight hundred people lived there."

"He ever go back for a visit? Ever get a call from his family there? Anyone in Texas?"

"He doesn't have no family. Mother and father both gone. No brothers or sisters."

Winter nodded. He glanced out the window. A pleasant view of grass and hickories. Lawn chairs in the shade. A pleasant place for husband and wife to pass the evening together while the summer light lingered.

"You know," he said. "I hope this won't sound unkind, but . . . Well, there's something you haven't said to me. Something I expected you to say, but you haven't, so it surprises me."

When she lifted her eyes to him, he saw the fear in them. They were pools of fear. It made him hurt for her.

"You haven't said, 'It's all a mistake.' You haven't said, 'My Harris couldn't have done such a thing.' I expected you to say something like that."

"I told the police . . ." she said weakly. But then again, her voice trailed off.

"Right. You said it to them, to the police. But not to me. Because I told you about Owen McKay, and you recognized the similarities to your husband."

Again, she looked down miserably at the floor. She had poured herself a glass of lemonade too, but she hadn't touched it. Fear and grief had sapped her of all appetite and energy. Lassitude draped over her like a shroud.

"You saw signs," Winter said. "Signs he was changing."

She nodded—nodded down at the floor. "I grew up in the church," she told him. "Sang in the choir. I still go sometimes. I find it a comfort. But Harris—he laughs at all that. He says, 'Nothing in the sky but clouds, baby. Nothing in the ground but dirt and that's where we heading.'" She bit her lip. Then quickly, she added, "He's a good man. Don't get me wrong. He always has been. A good, good husband. Took good care of me, never ran after women. Didn't drink at all, not at all, and none of the dope they all smoke neither. Anyone who needs help in this neighborhood, they know to come to Harris, even in the middle of the night sometimes. Whatever it is. Broken dishwasher, car won't run. Some money to tide them over . . ."

She drifted into silence—like an old woman drifting into sleep, Winter thought. He found it painful to watch her. The grief was like a great beast crouching on her shoulder, claws in her flesh, teeth in her neck, sucking the life out of her.

"But you saw signs," he repeated gently.

She hoisted her heavy gaze to him, her hollow gaze. "If he had been with the Lord, I don't think the demon could have gotten into him. Making him talk in his sleep, saying things, awful, awful things. He never talked like that before. Muttering to himself. His eyes on the women as we drove by. The look in his eyes. It was awful. And sometimes even . . ."

She sat slumped in the wooden kitchen chair, shaking her head.

"He was even rough with you sometimes," Winter said.

"He never was before. He was always such a loving man. It was a demon in him. It had to be. I can't think of no other explanation."

Winter left her alone in her long silence. Let her rest there. He drank his lemonade. Glad of it. His mouth was dry and bitter.

"One night," she suddenly said—still speaking to the floor. "Just before . . . just before this all happened. Him and me were watching a movie together on the TV. It was about a man in prison, on death row, and this preacher came to see him. *The Midnight Hour*, that's what it was called. And soon as that preacher in the movie drove up, soon as he got out of his car, Harris made a noise like I never heard him make before. Like he was strangling almost. And he jumped up. Ran out of the room. And I was like, 'Harris, honey, what's the matter?' But I went on watching the movie. Then I heard him, in the back room. Making a noise like he was crying. Harris never cried, never. That wasn't his way at all. I went back there to see him, quiet like, so he wouldn't hear. And the door was part open and I saw him in there. On his knees at the window, like he was praying. He didn't even believe, but he was praying, like for dear life. I guess the sight of that preacher in the movie made him recognize the evil that had gotten inside him. He kept saying just what that girl said he said. He kept saying, 'Oh Lord, please, it's still inside me.'"

This time, when she made the effort to lift her head and meet Winter's gaze, he saw—along with her fear and her grief and her lassitude—he saw a depth of wild desperation. She was desperate to know, to know anything he could tell her, anything that would solve the mystery of why this terrible thing had happened to her, to her and her loving husband. The sight made Winter ache to help her.

"Mrs. Turner," he said. "I don't think it was a demon that got into your husband. I think it was some sort of implant. Like, a machine. Something that someone put inside his head."

She stared at him a long moment. "What do you mean?"

"I don't know exactly. When the coroner in Tulsa did an autopsy on this man Owen McKay I told you about, he found some sort of device in his brain. I think there may have been a similar device implanted in your husband."

"Why would anyone do that? Put something in a man's head to make him do evil?"

"I . . . I don't know." It made him feel weak and useless to say so. To be a man unable to help a woman in such distress. "Maybe it was just that. To control him. Make him do things he didn't want to do. I don't know. I'm just saying, if someone did do it, they did it to Owen McKay too. And I think they killed McKay to keep anyone from finding out."

Vanessa Turner's mouth opened and closed twice, before she could say, "Oh my God. Oh my God. They gonna kill my Harris?"

"I don't know. But I'm afraid they might, yes."

"You mean the police? The police will kill them?"

"No, no, I don't think the police but . . ."

"Because it was a white girl?"

"No. No. It's not that. It's this machine. Someone is trying to keep people from finding out about it. And . . . Again, I'm sorry, I don't know."

A violent shudder went through her. She clutched her face in her two hands and sobbed. Winter grimaced at the force of the pain in her, at his own helplessness. He leaned toward her.

"Mrs. Turner," he said. "I want to get to your husband before they do. To try to keep him alive so we can find out the truth. If someone put a machine in him that made him do this, then he can't be held accountable. If I could find him . . ."

She sobbed again, her whole body trembling.

"Your neighbors and friends have been bringing you food," Winter said. He gestured at the kitchen counters. "I see the plates all around. Friends have been bringing you food, right? But the refrigerator—the refrigerator is half empty."

"Oh, my God," she cried. "Oh, my God, help me. I don't know what's happening. God Almighty, I don't know what to do."

Winter's throat tightened. He had to force the words out. "Mrs. Turner, I think you've been bringing food to your husband where he's hiding out."

Her hands dropped to her lap as if they were weighted. Her face was twisted, wet with tears. Her eyes were all desperation.

"I think you know where he is," Winter said.

# 17

Winter had not dressed for hiking, but he'd tossed some workout clothes in his overnight bag in case he found time to get to the gym in his hotel. He put on the sneakers and the T-shirt and headed into the woods.

The police were still beating the duff around the reservoir where they'd lost the fugitive's trail, but Winter knew now it was the wrong body of water. There was a much smaller pond about twenty miles away, a fishing hole where a brook collected. Harris Turner had made his way there, knowing his wife would figure it out and come to him.

Winter parked by the side of a small road and found the trail-head buried in brush. He pushed his way into the forest and soon found the brook and followed alongside the running water to the fishing hole. He was at the bottom of a gorge here. The trail wound up to a ridge. He began climbing. He'd brought a bottle of water with him, but the humidity was thick. The bottle was soon empty and he was soon breathless, his T-shirt dark with sweat.

For a while, he could see very little up ahead of him. The trees were thick, their leaf-laden branches intertwined. They blocked his view up the rise. The frog song from the water and the birdsong from the trees and the cricket song all around him and his own heavy panting filled his ears. The close forest and its noises gave him a deep sense of solitude, as if he were wholly cut off from the town around him, though the town was really very near.

He kept climbing. The narrow trail grew more narrow still. But now he began to catch glimpses of a structure through the leaves up ahead. He was nearing the top of the hill.

Then something snapped loudly. A branch nearby. Something—someone—had stepped on it. Winter stopped. He peered into the bright green of the forest. The intertangled leaves. The twisting vines. That noise—it could have been an animal walking, a dead limb falling. But Winter didn't think so. It could have been Harris Turner, waiting for him, still holding the knife with which he'd killed the girl. But Winter didn't think it was Harris Turner either.

He stood still, second after second. Listening to the forest. To the air moving in the thick leaves and to the birdsong. He didn't hear another footstep, but he sensed a presence somewhere on the ridge above him. Not Harris Turner. But someone. Waiting for him.

He began moving again. More slowly, more softly, his eyes panning over the territory ten degrees at a time. But the lush summer woods were a voluptuous chaos. Easy for a person to blend into the twisting shapes, the emerald depths. Easy to become invisible in there and wait for him. Still he climbed, and the structure on the ridge began to emerge for him in full. It was a half-finished house—the house Harris Turner had been building for a wealthy client who lived overseas. It stood in a clearing at the top of the hill with views in all directions, views of lake and forest and of the church steeple in the town below.

Winter stepped out of the trees and stood at the base of the building. A half-made house. A weekend retreat for a lover of solitude. The ground floor had a layer of wall made of some kind of composite material. The second floor was only a naked framework of wood. The front door stood open.

Now, across the open space, a small wind blew and the green leaves whispered. Again, Winter moved his gaze in small arcs across the line of trees enclosing the near horizon.

He stopped and stiffened when he spotted the assassin.

The tattooed man. He stood motionless, a shadowy shape amid the forest shapes and shadows. With his face darkened by all those tattoos, he might have been mistaken for a piece of the scenery, a tree trunk or a boulder. But then he grinned—a long, slow grin. Winter saw the white of his teeth. The two men stared at one another across the little distance.

Then the killer turned away. Walked away—slowly. Descended slowly, deliberately, down the far slope. He melted—slowly, deliberately—into the trees. Winter remembered what Whitefield had told him. How the naked assassin had strolled away from his bedside in his own sweet time, as if he owned the place. As if he were death itself and the whole earth belonged to him.

For a moment, Winter thought to race after the tattooed killer, to try to bring him down. But the wind stirred again, and a smell—a tart, coppery smell—reached him. He realized what it was at once. He started running.

He knew he was too late before he came through the door of the house and saw the body.

Harris Turner lay flat on the floor, his arms splayed, the monster pistol flung away from him. There was blood everywhere. Blood and flies and the hellish buzz of flies. Turner's head was all but gone.

Winter stopped in his tracks just over the threshold. There was no point in running to the man. He was finished. Furious and sick at heart, Winter walked out of the house. Stood with his shoulders slumped at the edge of the clearing. He brought his phone out of his pocket. He thought of Mrs. Turner, of her desperate eyes. A woman in such distress and he hadn't been able to help her. He felt like the greatest failure in all the world.

He called the police.

# 18

"An English professor," the detective said.

Winter rubbed his eyes and sighed. "It's a long story."

The detective was named Tom Shaw. He was a man in his forties, small and trim, with hawklike features and a full head of sandy hair. He had been sent from the state's Major Crime Squad to oversee the case. He had very pale gray eyes. Winter thought he discerned considerable intelligence in them.

"Well," he said. "A long story's no problem. We've got nothing but time, Mr. Winter. Since it seems my fugitive has brought himself to justice."

There was no local police force in Northwood. The state cops covered it. Normally, a resident trooper patrolled the place. He had an office in the town hall. The town hall was another fine old neoclassical building, almost a replica of the church in Riverbend, except about four times larger. Shaw had set up shop in there: a corner cubicle with a view of the main street. There was a desk here, a couple of chairs, a small sofa, and a mini-fridge. There was an American flag and a state flag bearing a white shield with grape vines on it and the motto QUI TRANSTULIT SUSTINET, or HE WHO

TRANSPLANTED STILL SUSTAINS, as Winter translated it—whatever that meant.

Shaw, in a white shirt and slacks, was in the swivel chair behind the desk, tilted back, his hands laced together on his flat stomach, his jacket draped over the chair back. Winter was in the metal chair beside the desk. Slumped, dispirited with failure.

"It wasn't a suicide," he told the detective. "It was murder."

"You keep saying that."

"It was well done."

"It was perfectly done," said Detective Shaw. "If it was a setup, it sure didn't look like one. Whoever did it got the recoil right and everything. An amateur would have left the gun in the victim's hands."

"He's no amateur."

"So you said. An insane muscleman covered in tattoos, about . . ." He checked the slender notebook open on the desk. "Two inches taller than you. Which you know because . . . ?"

"He tried to kill me. We were face-to-face."

"Right. That happen a lot in the English professor business?"

Winter laughed once mirthlessly. Shook his head, frustrated. He thought it best to refrain from making any smart-ass responses.

"I called Tulsa," Detective Shaw said. "They didn't know anything about any gizmo in this Owen McKay's head or anything like that."

"No," said Winter. "They wouldn't. They've been terrorized into silence."

"All of them."

"Enough, I guess. How many would it take?"

"All right. So you think Turner had this thing in his head too."

"I'm guessing that's how the killer tracked him," Winter said. "That's why he knew where Turner was and got there before I did.

I'm willing to bet the autopsy is going to show Turner's been dead since at least last night, maybe longer. I think the killer only stayed there to make sure I understood what had happened, what would happen to me if I talked."

"So you think he has some kind of grudge against English literature."

Winter managed to let this pass. "The problem in Tulsa was the cops were too quick on the scene. They got their hands on McKay before the killer could get to him. That made it a lot harder to stage a suicide. Especially with him locked up in a safety cell. I still can't figure out how they did it."

"This was easier though," said Shaw. "The killer just had to trace Turner to the house in the woods and shoot him."

"Right," Winter said. "With . . . what was that? A Desert Eagle, it looked like."

"Very good. You know your weapons."

"That's a .44 Magnum."

"Your specialty is poetry, you said?"

Again, Winter ignored this. "He used the big bore to make sure Turner's brains were turned to mush. Practically blew his head clean off. That way, he could take the gizmo and leave no trace."

"We're checking to see if Harris owned a Desert Eagle. It's not that common."

"I'm sure there'll be a record of him buying one."

"Because it's all a big conspiracy, you mean."

"Yes," said Winter. "That's what I mean."

Detective Shaw gave him a droll look, swiveling.

"Check out Turner's place of birth, if you can," Winter said. "Apple Orchard, Texas. They choose places that are hard to get to, hard to reach. But if you do get through, you'll find there's no record of him there. There'll be no record of him anywhere before three years ago."

"Because . . . ?"

Winter gave a helpless gesture. "Because there is no Harris Turner. I don't know the whole story. I think a company called Thaumatix is involved. They make brain implants. They told me if I mentioned them to anyone, they'd sue me into bankruptcy."

"And if that doesn't work, they'll send this tattoo guy after you."

"Something like that. Yes."

Detective Shaw frowned thoughtfully.

"You know what bothers me?" he said. "I mean, you know what really bothers me?"

Winter gestured: he did not know.

Shaw said, "What bothers me is: You sound crazy."

Winter gave another sigh.

"You sound crazy," Shaw said. "But I'm looking at you, and you don't look crazy."

"No?"

"No. Not to me anyway. I mean, you don't look like an English professor either. It's a good imitation but . . . Those big knuckles of yours. That's serious martial arts training. Punching a post. Fist push-ups on concrete. And the military bearing. If I took a wild guess and said you were some sort of intelligence agent, would you have to kill me?"

"You. Your family. Your friends. It'd be a bloodbath."

Detective Shaw smiled with one side of his face. "Right. So you think these Thaumatix people are putting gizmos in people's heads and then controlling them? Is that it? Making them kill people?"

"No," Winter said slowly. "Or maybe. I don't know. I don't know why they would do it. As an experiment maybe? The whole thing doesn't really make sense to me."

"I'm glad to hear it. If it did make sense to you, I'd think you really were crazy." Detective Shaw faced forward and slapped the top of the desk. "Well, here's where we are. The ME's office hasn't done the postmortem yet, but right now they're saying it was suicide for sure. No other possible explanation. To be honest with you, if it turns out to be anything else, I'm pretty sure it'll be something beyond my pay grade. I'll make some calls, but . . . there's nothing my bosses like better than a closed case all tied up with ribbons. Which as of right now is exactly what this is."

Winter left the town hall feeling at once hollowed with exhaustion and weighted down with his failure. But that was nowhere near as hollow and weighted down as he felt after he drove back out to Riverbend. He wanted to talk to Mrs. Turner again, to tell her how sorry he was that he had not been in time to save her husband. He'd never had a chance really. Harris Turner was probably dead before he got to town.

*So why bother the grieving woman?* he asked himself. *Do you want her forgiveness? Her blessing? Is there anything you can say to her that will make her grief any less?*

In the end, it didn't matter why he was going to see her. As soon as he drove past the church in Riverbend, he caught sight of her. She was surrounded by friends and neighbors. She was weeping with painful violence. Two women were supporting her by the elbows as the sad gathering moved along the sidewalk. They traveled as one to the church door, then passed inside out of sight.

Winter thought of Gwendolyn. How she believed in God and in demons, like Mrs. Turner did. He hoped Mrs. Turner would find some comfort in the church.

But the words that came into his mind were not from the Bible. They were English poetry. Of course. Tennyson, in this case. Who imagined that his death would be like sailing over the sandbar near the coast and out into the greater ocean.

Twilight and evening bell,
And after that the dark!
And may there be no sadness of farewell,
When I embark;

For tho' from out our bourne of Time and Place
The flood may bear me far,
I hope to see my Pilot face to face
When I have crost the bar.

Well, Winter thought, there was no harm in hoping. He drove past the church without slowing down.

# 19

He didn't want to stay the night. He called his hotel, canceled his reservation, and made the long drive back to the city. He caught the last flight out and did not make it all the way home until ten that night. He felt beaten down in mind and body as he moved down the hallway to his apartment. But as he approached the door, he came awake with caution.

Before this, Winter had never used a lot of security measures to keep himself safe. Detective Shaw might have been right about him: He might have just been playing at being an English professor. But if he was playing, he had put his heart and soul into the role. He had wanted a new life, this life, the life he thought he would have had if things had gone the way they were supposed to with him. But now it seemed that the life he had left behind was not through with him. So now he had his apartment wired.

He'd put alarms on the door and the balcony. They would have lit up his phone if anyone tried to enter. He had a couple of motion-sensitive cameras in place that would feed video into his phone. Plus he had a second layer of alarms and cameras that were set on delay, so if an intruder managed to scan the first layer and shut it down, the second would go on afterward, after the intruder felt he was in the clear.

But Winter had never put much trust in such gizmos. He did not feel certain the apartment was empty until he checked the door. He had planted one of his own hairs there in the crack of the jamb so it would fall to the floor if anyone came in. He had planted a second hair in the hinge in case anyone was smart enough to find the first. Both hairs were undisturbed. He felt sure there was no one in the apartment. The tattooed man had not returned. He used his phone to shut off all the cameras and alarms. Then he went inside.

He had slept on the plane so he was now both exhausted and wide-awake at the same time. He poured himself a glass of whiskey and planted himself in his living room reading chair.

He wangled his laptop out of the case on the table beside him. He opened the computer on his lap. He called up one of the streaming services and searched for the movie *The Midnight Hour.* He sipped his drink and stared glumly at the screen as the film began to play.

It was as Vanessa Turner had told him. The story was about a man on death row. Apparently the man was innocent. A reporter was trying to clear his name before the midnight hour of his execution. Winter watched the screen, but he couldn't really pay attention. He was too busy ruminating over what a poor excuse for a knight in shining armor he was. How the tattooed man had beaten him to Harris Turner. Of course he had. Because he could track the device in his brain. And Winter hadn't even thought of that. Of course.

He blinked out of these gloomy meditations as the scene he was waiting for began to play on his monitor. This was the scene in the movie Mrs. Turner had told him about, the scene between the condemned man and the preacher. He watched and listened.

The preacher and the prisoner were discussing why a good God would allow an innocent man to go to his death for a murder he didn't commit. Winter watched for a few moments, then paused the movie. What was it Mrs. Turner had told him? It was not the conversation in the prison cell that had upset her husband. As soon as the preacher drove up and got out of his car, she said, Harris had run out of the room. He had fallen on his knees, praying for help. He who did not believe in God. What was it that had upset him then?

Winter rewound the movie. He reached that earlier scene, the scene where the preacher drove up to the prison. There was an overhead shot, taking in the entire prison, a grim, gray stone fortress with castlelike watchtowers above the barbed-wire perimeter. The preacher's car drove into the surrounding lot. There was a cut to a close-up: the preacher getting out from behind the wheel. He was a middle-aged black man in a black suit and tie. He had gray hair and distinguished features. He looked around sorrowfully. Then there was a cut to a new scene. He was walking down a prison hallway with the warden.

Winter paused the movie again. He sat there with the laptop on his lap and the drink in his hand. He sipped some more whiskey. It was good whiskey. Smooth. It dulled the pain he felt at what a miserable Galahad he'd been. It dulled the memory of Vanessa Turner being shepherded into church, her body wracked with grief.

What was it that had set Harris Turner off when he watched this movie? he wondered. What was it that made the atheist sob and pray? Was it the shot of the preacher that had affected him? No, that couldn't be right. There was nothing particular about him that would have been the trigger. The preacher wasn't even wearing clerical garb. You couldn't know he was a preacher until he came into the condemned man's cell. The only other feature of the scene was the wide shot, the overhead shot of the prison.

Winter rested his head against the back of the chair. He stared up at the ceiling and thought about that for a while. Then he looked down at his laptop again. He clicked away from the movie. He went on a film site and typed in the movie's title. According to the production notes, *The Midnight Hour* had been partly shot on location at Osage Prison near St. Louis.

Thinking that over, Winter lifted his whiskey to his lips again.

A floorboard creaked behind him.

The laptop tumbled to his left and his glass went flying to his right, spitting whiskey, as Winter spun out of his chair. He landed crouched on the floor, ready to spring and fight.

By then, of course, the man who had snuck up behind him could have easily killed him.

Luckily for Winter, it was the Recruiter.

# 20

Winter collapsed to his knees, breathing hard, his head hung down, his heart thumping.

"That's a very expensive single malt you just sprayed all over your rug," the Recruiter said mildly. "Not to mention the laptop."

"How did you do that?" said Winter. "Get in here like that. You almost gave me a heart attack." He grabbed hold of the chair arm and laboriously pulled himself to his feet.

"Then you would have seen face-to-face what you mindlessly deny through a glass darkly. So you're welcome, Poetry Boy. I almost cured the faithlessness that makes your life the slow slog into damnation that it obviously is. Have you got any coffee?"

Winter collected his laptop, relieved to see it was still working. He set it on the table. "I'll make some." He scooped up his glass and carried it into the kitchen.

From there, as he loaded up the coffee machine, he could steal glimpses at the Recruiter in the living room. He had not changed since the last time he'd seen him. The once-vigorous man looked old. Dressed in a colorless windbreaker and saggy slacks, he shuffled stiffly to the sofa. He dragged the brown-leather newsboy cap off his head as he went. His blocky head, once shaved, was covered with a thin mossy layer of gray hair. His walk, once bold, was bent and slow. He sank into the sofa with a sigh.

The jacket, the hat. It was a lot of clothing to be wearing for such a warm night. Winter guessed the Recruiter had a gun hidden beneath the windbreaker. He also suspected he was carrying a lot of his clothes on his back, and a lot of his possessions in his pockets. He was traveling light. Traveling fast.

Winter moved into the doorway and leaned there as the coffee perked. He studied the Recruiter from the side, his profile. He looked weary.

"You want something to eat?" he asked.

"That would be surprisingly charitable of you given your godless and therefore morally inchoate state."

"I'll make you a sandwich."

Winter had reassembled the apartment after his fight with the tattooed man. He had returned the books to their bookshelf. He had returned the bookshelf to its place against the wall. When he set the coffee and sandwich down on the low coffee table, the Recruiter was turned away from him, studying the book bindings.

"No Bible?" the Recruiter said.

Winter went to the bar to refill his whiskey glass. "There's one around here someplace. I have read it, you know."

"Then you have no excuse."

Pouring from the bottle, Winter smiled. He was glad to see his old chief. He'd been worried about him. He only realized now how much. His respect for the man was such that he didn't like to think of him in trouble. He liked to believe he could handle anything. If a vastly corrupt intelligence bureaucracy had dispatched the American military to bring him to ground, well, pity the military. But deep down, he knew this was sentimental. No one is invulnerable. Everyone can be taken down.

He dropped heavily into the chair across from him, clutching his fresh whiskey. He raised it in a toast. The Recruiter tore hungrily into his sandwich.

"Stan-Stan tells me some of our old paymasters want to pin Warren Gentry's murder on you," Winter said.

The Recruiter dabbed mustard off his face with a paper napkin. "Do they? If they do, they haven't said anything to me about it."

"Because they can't find you."

The Recruiter shrugged. "'The wind blows wherever it pleases. You hear its sound, but you cannot tell where it comes from or where it is going. So it is with everyone born of the Spirit.'" he said.

"Uh-huh. You didn't happen to actually kill Gentry, did you?"

"If I had, Poetry Boy, I would tell you no so you wouldn't have to lie for me."

Winter nodded. "But did you?"

"No."

"He wasn't killed in a mugging gone wrong though, was he?"

"I wouldn't know. I wasn't there."

With his sandwich half finished on its plate—half devoured in what seemed to Winter a fit of serious hunger—the Recruiter sat back in the sofa with his coffee mug in his hand. He drew in the steam of it. Like a homeless man drawing the heat off a trash can fire, Winter thought.

"Here's what I do know. Warren Gentry found Jesus," the Recruiter said. "Do you know what that means?"

"I have a vague idea."

"You might want to consider it. The man is a journalist, a homosexual, and a sadist. He is three times damned. And yet now, he will be resting in the heavenly bosom of Abraham while you beg him to dip his finger in water and bring you a droplet to cool your tongue as you writhe in agony in the fires of hell."

"Well, if he's a homosexual sadist, I could see why that would be heaven for him."

It was always hard to read the Recruiter's expression. His face was a dark, dark brown and forever deadpan. So Winter could not be entirely sure, but it seemed to him his chief sipped his coffee with an almost dreamy pleasure. No matter how much he wanted to elevate the man to mythic status, it was plain to see it was rough on him, living on the run like this.

"The point is," the Recruiter went on, "Mr. Gentry had a change of heart, and he was therefore baptized into the death of our amazing all-American Lord and Savior Jesus Christ. This in turn made him hopeful of partaking in his triumphant resurrection, so that he repented of his sins. One of which was spiking a story that would have embarrassed Thaddeus Blatt back in the day. Which he did because he feared Blatt would release Kemal Balkin's pictures of him practicing his damnable perversions."

"That's not the way Gentry told it to me. He said there was no blackmail involved at all."

"It's possible he told you the truth, or it's possible I am telling it to you now," said the Recruiter. "But in either case, since the days when I sent you to find out what happened, Gentry—perhaps in an appropriate inner misery of self-disgust at his own moral cowardice—plunged deeper and deeper into an orgy of suicidal indulgence in drugs and did I mention damnable perversions."

"Until Jesus saved him," I drawled.

"That's right. And be careful of the tone in which you speak of the Prince of Heaven," the Recruiter said. "Because if annoyed, he will kick your sorry backside and all its irony down a flight of stairs of cosmic proportions, all-loving though he may otherwise be."

The Recruiter set down his coffee mug, parting with it regretfully, or so it seemed to Winter. He then set to work devouring the other half of his sandwich.

"Let me guess," Winter said, while the chief ate. "Gentry decided to redeem himself by going after Thaddeus Blatt again."

His mouth full, the Recruiter could only nod.

"Was he going to print the story he spiked?" Winter asked. "Or had he come up with something fresh?"

After another moment or two, the Recruiter swallowed. "New," he managed to say. He dabbed at his lips with a paper napkin. "It had to do with Blatt's enormous investment in a biotech firm. It's fascinating how many men who reject God because they don't believe in miracles, believe in the miracles promised them by other men. When Jesus Christ returns in clouds of glory to create a new heaven and a new earth because the old heaven and earth will have passed away? Thaddeus Blatt will be taken completely by surprise because he thought the future would be all about transhumanism."

Winter opened his mouth to respond, but he did not respond. He just sat there with his mouth open. What was happening in Winter's mind at that moment felt to him something like a strangely backward animation: building blocks lying scattered on the nursery floor suddenly rising in air and assembling themselves into a complex castle. Where before there had been a jumble of bricks and nothingness, there was now suddenly a structure that looked as if it might make some kind of sense.

"Thaddeus Blatt invested in Thaumatix," he said.

"According to Warren Gentry, Blatt secretly invested tens of millions and maybe as much as a hundred million dollars in Isaiah Kahn's projects," the Recruiter said. "Have I ever warned you not to put your faith in princes, Poetry Boy, or in any other human being who cannot save you?"

"You may have. I probably wasn't listening."

"Probably not. But Thaddeus Blatt was suddenly made aware of the error of his ways when Isaiah Kahn rode his motorcycle off a cliff to land at the foot of the throne of judgment. Then it came to pass that many of the miraculous outcomes that he had been declaring were on the verge of fruition at Thaumatix were instead on the verge of the fantastical."

This may have been as close to making an actual joke as Winter had ever heard the Recruiter come, although he sometimes suspected that everything the Recruiter said was a joke in some sense.

"I visited Thaumatix," Winter told him. "I saw demonstrations of their work. It was very impressive."

"I saw a magician cut a woman in half once," said the Recruiter. "He passed a sword right through the middle of her. It gave me a shudder of delicious horror."

Winter just managed to stop himself from cursing. The Recruiter did not approve of cursing.

"You're saying it's all fake?" Winter asked.

"No," said the Recruiter. "Not all of it. Not fake really. The work Kahn was doing at Thaumatix showed tremendous promise, in fact. It simply wasn't complete when he died and wasn't likely to get complete without Kahn's genius working out the problems. So after Kahn's death, Thaddeus Blatt discovered he had made a tremendous investment in a company of almost no discernible value."

Winter had forgotten the drink in his hand. He remembered it now. "So what did Thaddeus do?" he asked, and drank.

"That is the question Gentry asked himself," said the Recruiter. He had finished his sandwich. He was luxuriating in his coffee mug again, inhaling deeply from the remaining steam. "A man of Blatt's wealth can afford to drop a hundred million dollars here and there, but it hurts his pride, and will hurt his reputation too when the secret comes to light. In any case, Gentry figured he must have done something. Because the company was apparently thriving when it should have been collapsing into itself. The question was why. So Gentry asked around. And he finally asked around enough that the fact that he was asking around came to my attention. And I was curious enough to have some of your old colleagues start looking into it."

"The Invisibles."

The Recruiter did not laugh out loud, of course, but Winter thought he saw in his eyes what would have been laughter if he had been the laughing type. "Is that what you call them?"

"Yes. What you're telling me is: You've always suspected Thaddeus Blatt of being a corrupting element in our government and you smelled a chance of destroying him. So you set the Invisibles on the case. And somehow this led you to find out about the impossible murder of Owen McKay and the Thaumatix gizmo the pathologist found in his brain."

The Recruiter inclined his chin with what Winter hoped was approval. "You were always the smartest of my agents, Poetry Boy."

"Which is why you arranged to have me investigate McKay's death by getting Livy to tell the story to Gwendolyn. I knew that had to be you. The psychology was too precise for any mere mortal. You know, you could have just come right out and asked me to look into it."

"I'm at a time in my life when I consider it wiser not to exist."

"I should probably be annoyed you sent me on such a dangerous assignment without letting me know."

"I would be, if I were you."

"I mean, that tattooed clown showed up here, you know. The killer. He came within an inch of disemboweling me. It would have been nice if you'd warned me something like that might happen."

"Just one more effort I made to bring you to the truth of Christ by bringing the two of you face-to-face. My evangelical persistence astonishes even me."

"Who is that asshole anyway? With the tattoos. Does he work for Blatt exclusively? He doesn't, does he."

The Recruiter made what for him was an expressive gesture. He tilted his head. Raised an eyebrow. "Who knows? As I understand it, he was a freelancer back when I knew him. I'm told he worked for our government from time to time. I never used him myself. The way I heard it, he ultimately became so unreliable even our intelligence community wouldn't hire him. But I believe Blatt still calls on him from time to time."

"You know his name?"

"I know some of the names he's used now and then, but I don't think they matter much. He changes them at will, as I understand it. Usually people just call him by some nickname or other. Pentagram or the Illustrated Man or Tattoo. Something of the sort."

"He's probably the one who killed Gentry, isn't he? To keep him from getting at Thaumatix."

"I think that's a reasonable supposition. As I say, I wasn't there."

The two men fell silent. Winter brought his glass to his lips. He drew in the aroma of the malt without drinking. He watched the Recruiter over the glass's rim. The Recruiter sat so still that Winter wondered whether he might be sleeping. It would be like him to have developed some magical way of getting his sleep while remaining wide-awake. But he knew this too was sentimentality. Clearly, the man was exhausted—more exhausted than he himself—exhausted and on the run, hunted by unseen agents far more powerful than he was. And why? Why did they want to crush him so badly? And why did he want to go on inciting their anger? He was retired. Forced into retirement. There was nothing for him to do. He could have kept his head down and stayed safe.

Winter had no answers. He did not even know what side the Recruiter was on anymore or what he was fighting for or what he stood for. Was it just some fanciful idea of what this country was or was meant to be or used to be? Some antiquated faith in a God who gave a damn about that or anything? Would he die for those beliefs? Would he kill for them? Would he lie, even to Winter? Winter thought he would. He thought he would do all that. Yet Winter had to admit it to himself: None of this changed anything, as far as he was concerned. The Recruiter was still a hero to him. A man who took on his own soul the black weight of murder so that his fellow citizens could tell themselves they were living in peace. He was the only mentor Winter had ever had, and Winter would have died for him. He was not sure why he would but he would. Still. Today.

"All right. I'll find out what I can," he said.

"I know you will, son," said the Recruiter. And then, because the Recruiter could always read Winter's thoughts like a billboard: "I only wish you knew why you will."

Winter laughed and shook his head. "Just do me a favor, chief. I don't think Tat Man is going to start killing people indiscriminately. Blatt doesn't want that, and Tat Man probably needs the job. But just in case, and since you used her for your purposes, I would appreciate it if you'd have the Invisibles keep watch over Gwendolyn Lord for me."

Only after years of knowing the Recruiter could Winter see the faint flicker of something like irritation in the eyes of that expressionless face. “Do you think me so poor a servant of the Lord that I would leave that lovely creature unprotected?”

Winter laughed again, or made a sound that was something like laughter anyway.

“Meanwhile,” the Recruiter went on. “I’m going to give you a series of letters and numbers that you can use in the usual way if you need to contact me. Are you ready?”

“Yes.”

The Recruiter quickly rattled the series off. Just as quickly, Winter memorized them.

“You want more coffee?” he said then.

“Please.”

Winter set his glass aside and rose to collect the Recruiter’s mug. He carried the mug into the kitchen and filled it from the coffeepot.

“You do realize what she is,” the Recruiter said behind him.

“What do you mean . . . ?” Winter began to answer, turning. But his voice faded away when he saw that the Recruiter was gone.

He took a sip of coffee from the mug. “How does he do that?” he murmured.

# 21

Tilda Bach lay wide-awake, staring into the dark. She knew what she had to do, but she did not know if she had the courage to do it. Right this minute, she was so afraid it felt as if all the strength had drained out of her. Her limbs felt hollow. She thought she might not be able to move for fear.

What was she afraid of? She was afraid—she was terrified—of the shape beside her on the bed. The body rising and falling with soft, groaning breaths. Her husband. Martin. The father of the child inside her. She could feel the warmth of his body where she lay. What if she did try to move? What if she woke him? Would a hand shoot out of the shadows and grab her? Would his grinning face be the last thing she ever saw? And what if she didn't move? What if she fell asleep where she lay? Maybe that's what he was waiting for. Maybe then he would rise up above her while she lay helpless and unknowing, and put his big hand on her throat . . .

But there was not much chance of her falling asleep.

In the quiet between his breaths, she could hear the battery clock ticking on the wall. Time was running out. After she had come back from seeing Pastor Mike—after she had found Martin waiting for her, sitting in the living room, sitting in the shadows, smiling that demon smile—she had become convinced that she could not wait much longer. The thing that had gotten into Martin, the demon that was living inside him—it was like the baby growing inside her, except the opposite. While the baby was filling her day by day with more life, somehow making her own life bigger, somehow making her soul bigger, the demon inside her husband was day by day draining the Martin out of him, taking full control of him, devouring his soul, replacing his soul with itself. She had seen things like that happen in the movies. Where a person was possessed by some supernatural entity. And for a while, the living light of human feeling could still rise to the surface and shine in his eyes. And then finally, no, the struggle was over, and there was only red evil and a hunger for death. And sure, that was the movies. She had always figured it was pure make-believe. Spooky nonsense some writer came up with to give you a creepy thrill while you ate your popcorn.

She did not think that anymore. She knew better now.

When Tilda was little, eight and nine years old, she had had a friend named TJ. TJ was a boy with a bad leg. The doctors said they would have to operate on the leg but they couldn't until he was older. So TJ had a painful limp and had to swing his leg in a big arc every time he took a step. He couldn't play sports and the other boys teased and bullied him. Tilda was the only friend he had. She liked TJ because he wasn't like the girls, always talking, gossiping, backbiting. He would listen to her and she could tell him about her father and the things her father did when he was drunk. She and TJ would spend time alone in the woods together. Sometimes they would show each other their bodies. Other times, they would just sit and talk.

Once, TJ had said to her: "You can't imagine a thing unless you've seen it." She asked him what he meant. He said, "I've tried it. I've tried to draw a picture of a monster no one's ever seen before. But you can't. All you can do is put pieces together from things you have seen, like lizards and gorillas and stuff. You can't make up something totally new, something that isn't real already."

One day, she had gone over to see TJ at his house, and she found the house was empty. TJ's family had moved away. She never saw her friend again. She could not find him on the internet. She didn't even know his real name. She thought about him often, though, still. Tonight, lying frightened in the dark, she thought about what he had said to her about making up monsters. She understood it now. The people who made movies about demons taking people over—they may have made those demons up, but TJ was right. They could not have made them up if they weren't somehow already real.

She had tried to explain some of this to Pastor Mike when she talked to him. After all, if a pastor didn't believe in demons, who would? But she could tell he did not believe in them, not really. He had thought she was just another kooky church lady in his congregation. It was obvious in the way he looked at her. Patient. Condescending. Unbelieving. And she knew if he didn't believe her, no one else would believe her either. How could they? Why would they? Everyone loved Martin. She loved Martin. Martin was wonderful. Everyone said so.

But the man sleeping beside her in her bed was not Martin. Not anymore. The demon had eaten him from the inside out.

After she had come home from the church that day, after she had found Martin sitting in the dark waiting for her, smiling that smile that was not Martin's smile but the smile of the thing inside him, she knew she had to do something. To save herself. But more important than that, to save her baby.

She had not told Pastor Mike about what she found in the shed. She had told him about the printouts of that poor woman tied up and gagged, but he had thought she was just talking about pornography, some pictures Martin had printed out so he could erase them from his devices where they might be discovered. For all Tilda knew, that's what those pictures were. Just printouts from some porn site. She had only glimpsed them for a moment. She couldn't be sure. She had scanned through all the local news sites and there were no stories about missing girls, or murdered girls, or anything like that. The pictures may have just been pornography and Martin's bloody T-shirt might have gotten bloody because he cut himself working at his table or on his job or something like that. She couldn't bring herself to tell Pastor Mike about the T-shirt, though.

After she came home, she realized the truth: she had to go back into the shed. She had to get the pictures and the T-shirt and bring them to Pastor Mike. Then, if they were what she thought they were, he would go to the police with her. The police would believe the pastor. They would not believe Tilda, the bar girl they all knew, the bar girl who used to put out for them to get out of DUI arrests, the bar girl now making a big show of being with Jesus and talking crazily about demons.

So Tilda had marshaled all her courage and, earlier today, she had once again waited until Martin went to work. She had once again gone into the shed, her heart nearly bursting with fear.

But the box was gone. Whatever had been in the box: that was gone too.

Which meant Martin must have known she had been in there. He must have seen her come out of the shed as he drove up to the house. He must have guessed she had found the hidden things and gotten rid of them.

He knew she knew about the demon. The demon knew she knew. The demon would want her silenced. Maybe Martin could fight the demon inside him for a while. Maybe not. Maybe he didn't even want to fight it anymore. In any case, her time was running out.

She drew a long, slow, trembling breath. Slowly, quietly, she lifted the sheet that covered her. She had thought her heart was close to bursting earlier, when she returned to the shed. She had not known then what real terror felt like. She knew now. Her heart was not just slamming against her chest like some sort of great beast trying to escape her body. It felt like it had swollen, like it was huge, overflowing up into her throat, choking her. She hesitated. She worried that the chemicals of fear coursing through her body would poison her baby and make her get born sick or crazy or something like that. But she knew if she did not find out the truth about this demon, the demon would strike her down and the baby would not be born at all.

Slowly, quietly, she sat up in bed. She found it so hard to breathe that even that, even just sitting up, made her pant like she'd been working out. She moved barefoot in the dark around the end of the bed. She crept flat-footedly, trying not to make a sound. It didn't work. A floorboard creaked. She stopped, holding her breath, her heart pounding, her legs weak. But Martin didn't stir. He went on snoring softly. She started moving again. Creeping. Around to Martin's side of the bed. To his bedside, his bedside table. His phone was there, plugged into its charging wire. If there was proof anywhere—pictures or videos or communications; anything—it would be there, in the phone. She lifted it. Her hands were so shaky, her muscles so weak, she had to use all her strength to detach the phone from its wire.

Martin moved. Tilda nearly gasped aloud. She stood gaping as he murmured and rolled over onto his back. But almost at once, his breathing became regular again. He was sleeping deeply. She licked her dry lips. They remained dry.

She did not know Martin's password. She had known it once but he had changed it a few months ago and she had not asked him for the new one. He was not the sort of man you needed to snoop on. He had not been before now anyway. Now she was afraid to ask him. That was why she had to do it this way, with him right there in the room.

Martin had a phone that could be opened with fingerprint ID. He preferred it to the face ID models. With a trembling hand, Tilda held the phone against his finger. She gently pressed his finger against the surface. She only touched his fingernail, but her hand was shaking so badly, she thought she was sure she would jostle him and wake him up.

But it worked. The phone opened. She drew it back quickly to keep its light from shining on him. She held it close to her body as she stepped back. She turned so she could carry the phone into the next room for a full examination of its contents.

But then the baby moved.

There had been little flutterings before, but this was different. Before, she had not been sure it was the baby moving. It could have been anything. A muscle spasm. Gas. This time, though, it was unmistakable. A definite, intentional motion. The life within her was stirring. A new person coming to be!

Taken by surprise, she gave a soft cry and dropped the phone.

It landed silently on the edge of the bed. But her cry had awakened Martin.

"What?" he said softly.

Tilda grabbed up the phone.

"What is it?" he said.

She sat down beside him, slipping the phone back onto the bedside table behind her. She touched his hand gently.

"The baby moved," she said.

Martin sat up quickly. "She did?"

"Uh-huh. I felt her."

He made a soft noise: "Huh." Then he laughed. "Wow." He wrapped his arms around her. He put his head in her lap so that the side of his face was pressed against her stomach. She held him there. A tear ran down her cheek.

Martin hugged her and listened for the baby.

# PART THREE

# A CLOUD OF POWER

*For me, this was the beginning of the end, I think. After Thaddeus Blatt and his pentagrammed thug left my apartment, I sat alone for a while and thought about everything that had happened since I'd joined the Division. A friend dead. A lover tortured; dead. Myself—well, dead, too, in a way. The boy I had been was dead. I had become—something else. Something other than I had been when I joined up. Something other than what I thought I was meant to be. I had become a man who arranged the deaths of other men. A man who sometimes pulled the trigger himself. Protecting our country. That was the idea. But now, the Recruiter was telling me our country was corrupt, our leaders were a bunch of grinning skeletons dancing on the strings of a blackmailing puppet master. Thaddeus Blatt, maybe.*

*But Thaddeus Blatt—he was telling me something different. He was telling me it was the Recruiter who was the corrupt one. The Recruiter had acted on his own to transform the Division into a bureau of assassins, assassins he was planning to unleash on one of his fellow Americans—namely, Thaddeus Blatt.*

*I believed in the Recruiter. He was just about the only thing I did believe in. But there was something about Blatt's story that was too plausible for comfort. The Recruiter's reasons for suspecting Warren*

*Gentry had been blackmailed did seem kind of flimsy, as Blatt said. And what about this Isabella Gonzalez story?*

*I went to my computer. I looked up Isabella Gonzalez. There was no news about her on the US sites, but the BBC was carrying a small story about her. They said there was a rumor she'd been kidnapped, as Blatt had said. There was a rumor the kidnapping was part of a gang war between Isabella's father and the El Coba cartel. The BBC didn't have anything solid on the story, that's why there wasn't much there. But it sounded like Blatt had been telling me the truth. And in all honesty, it sounded exactly like the sort of hit the Recruiter would dream up to get Gonzalez and El Coba to kill each other.*

*But I still had my assignment. Maybe that would lead me to the whole truth. I had to find out if Warren Gentry had been blackmailed by Thaddeus Blatt. I had to find out if it was Blatt who was behind Kemal Balkin's sex and extortion operation. And I had to find out just how powerful and widespread that operation was.*

*Gentry was easy enough to follow. He had a regular routine. He took a long run every morning at 6 A.M. He was at his desk working by 8 A.M. He had built up his investigative website into a small business that operated out of a second-floor office on Dupont Circle. He had a team of a dozen people, reporters and technical staff. He made calls, had meetings, ate lunch in a nearby bookstore-slash-café. Then he went home and lifted weights in the gym in his apartment building.*

*Once or twice a week, he went to a private sex club where men gathered to do the sorts of things they do in these places. This particular club specialized in all-male sadomasochism, so there was a bunch of guys tying one another up and hitting one another with various implements and so on. I followed Gentry there a couple of times. To be honest, the whole scene didn't really fit with the Recruiter's theory. I mean, this sort of thing may not be strictly biblical and so on. But if you belong to a club like that . . . like, if you're a registered member—how can you actually be blackmailed for it? Right? Maybe Gentry was doing something else, too, something secret and illegal, with children or something like that. But this—this was right out in the open. He didn't wear a disguise when he went to the club or change cars or look over his shoulder to see if anyone was following him. It didn't seem at all that he was afraid of being seen or recognized. One night, he went with a group of buddies. They took pictures of one another outside the club, laughing and giving thumbs-up. How do you blackmail a guy who's posting his sex life on social media?*

*So since all the man's secrets weren't particularly secret, I decided I might as well confront him face-to-face. The next time he went to this club, I broke into his apartment and waited for him there. It was a little dramatic, I guess, but I wanted to see if I could catch him off guard and scare the truth out of him. His apartment was in a sort of fashionable red-brick castle not far from the Circle. A one-bedroom with wooden floors and a view of the courtyard. There was some artwork on the wall that was a little—what's the word I want?—louche, let's say. But nothing excruciating or pornographic. His sex toys were stowed neatly and discreetly in a box in his bedroom closet. This was the guy's life. As I say, he wasn't exactly hiding it.*

*He came home about two in the morning. I was sitting in the bedroom, in the dark. Sitting in a wooden chair, a white chair hand-painted with pictures of roses and nestled in a corner across from the bedroom door. To pass the time, I was examining one of these toys of his. It was the weirdest device. I couldn't figure out what you would do with such a thing. I was sitting in the shadows, turning it this way and that, looking it over. I heard Gentry come in and close the door.*

*The light went on in the living room. His footsteps approached. Then he came into the bedroom and saw the shape of me in the semidarkness. He gave a short, high-pitched scream and flew back against the wall with his hands up, like he was pinned there. His eyes bugged out so wide with terror I could see them even with the lights off. It was a funny reaction coming from him because he had the face of a hero. Square jawed and smooth featured. White-blond hair. And he was a big muscular beast too. He didn't look like he would be afraid of anyone. But there he was, cowering like a frightened child.*

*"Don't turn the light on," I said.*

*"I won't! I won't, I swear!"*

*"Take it easy. What the hell are you so worked up about?"*

*"Are you here to kill me?"*

*I laughed. "If I was here to kill you, Warren, you'd be dead, believe me." I held up the sex toy, turning it so he could make out the shape in the dark. "What the hell is this thing?"*

*"What?"*

*"What are you supposed to do with it?"*

*"Oh."*

*I could see his body relax a little. He was starting to calm down. There was a small worktable by the wall with a swivel chair in front of it. He pulled the chair out and settled into it.*

*"God," he said. "You scared me."*

*"Really, what is this?" I asked again.*

*He told me what the device was for. You don't want to know. I grimaced and tossed it onto his bed. I was sorry I had touched it.*

*"You don't need me to kill you," I said. "You're taking care of that yourself."*

*"Excuse me. Excuse me, who are you? Why are you in my apartment?"*

*"I want to ask you some questions."*

*"Are you gonna kill me then?"*

*"I'm not going to kill you at all. Who wants to kill you?"*

*"Are you kidding?" He ticked the names off on his fingers. It was an admirable list. He was doing investigations on all kinds of people. Politicians, activists, a couple of business executives. The stuff he had*

*on them—it wasn't just the usual dirt, cheating on their spouses or something like that. He was going after big-time corruption. Bribery, extortion. He was even after one respected social justice activist who might have murdered his mistress. This guy wasn't like the "journalists" you see on TV. He was the real deal, a genuine reporter. He went after everyone on all sides, no fear or favor.*

*"Well, I don't work for any of those people," I told him.*

*"No," he said, "you're government. I can tell."*

*"How can you tell that?"*

*"I just can."*

*"That's kind of insulting."*

*"That's why I thought you might be an assassin. In real life, only governments and gangsters have assassins."*

*"So listen," I said. "Do you know a guy named Thaddeus Blatt?"*

*"Sure. Investment guy. Connected up the waz. Thinks of himself as a behind-the-scenes kingmaker. Always trying to make deals, build coalitions in the government. People pretend to take him seriously because he has money but I don't know how many people take him seriously-seriously. Like every billionaire I ever met, he's about one-tenth as smart as he thinks he is."*

*I smiled at that. It was pretty much what the Recruiter had said about him too.*

*"True or false," I said. "You were going to run an embarrassing story about him and you spiked it."*

*"Who wants to know?"*

*"I do. And while I'm not specifically here to kill you, I am a trained assassin so you don't want to piss me off."*

*For a second or two, we just sat there. I could hear Gentry breathing. Finally, he said: "Okay, it's more or less true. Blatt had some insanely stupid idea that it would be a good thing for America to make friends with the mullahs in Iran. This is what I mean about billionaires. They sit around on their tax-protected islands coming up with brilliant ideas on how to make the world a better place and they have absolutely no clue how anything actually works. 'Oh, let's make friends with Iran, then everything in the Middle East will be swell.' It's like they're six-year-olds but rich, so people act like what they say makes sense. Politicians especially. Politicians need money to stay in office so when a billionaire says something laughably stupid, they believe him. Or they pretend to. I mean, if you want really realistic ideas, you should ask shopkeepers and moms or people like that. People who do stuff. But they don't have the same amount of money."*

*I smiled again. That sex toy had put some images in my head I would have preferred to unsee, but other than that, I kind of liked this guy. "So how come you didn't run the story?"*

*"Well, ultimately, you know, there was really nothing there. According to my sources, Blatt had made some phone calls, given some gifts, nothing illegal or more illegal than usual. And nobody was interested in his stupid idea. When your idea is too stupid even for a congressman who wants your money, you know you're talking crap. Eventually, Blatt let it go."*

*"He never contacted you?"*

*"I got a call from one of his lawyers when he found out I was looking into the story. He did his tough-lawyer routine. I told him to get stuffed. Once we got past all that, he was actually pretty helpful. But his story was the same as my source's. It wasn't worth printing."*

*Gentry gave me some names and over the next couple of days, I asked around the Hill to confirm what he'd told me. Whatever had happened, it didn't seem to have anything to do with Kemal Balkin's operation or blackmail or anything like that. Either the Recruiter had gotten some bad information or had made a bad deduction based on his biblical dislike of oddball sex. Or he was just exercising due caution. That was a possibility too. In any case, I felt my work was pretty much done. If Blatt was working with Kemal Balkin, it had nothing to do with Warren Gentry.*

*I made an appointment to deliver my operation report to the Recruiter. The night before I went in, the Isabella Gonzalez story broke on the news. It turned out she actually had been kidnapped in Mexico. She'd been released after federal agents staged a raid on a hideout in Houston, Texas. The DOJ spokesman told reporters they had tracked the girl down following tips from within the El Coba cartel, which was believed responsible for the kidnapping. There was video of the girl being hustled to a helicopter by the agents. She looked about fourteen and her face was bruised. The spokesman said she'd been worked over while in the custody of the El Cobas and possibly sexually abused. The kidnappers hadn't been caught yet.*

*I remember sitting in my apartment that night with a glass of whiskey—sitting in the dark looking out the window at the moonlight on the river. I was thinking about some of the things I'd done, the people who'd died because of me, the pictures I'd seen at Kemal Balkin's villa, and the things Thaddeus Blatt had said about the Recruiter, about him getting out of control and doing things he was not supposed to do.*

*It's not that I thought I had done wrong. There are people in the world who have to die so that the rest of us can live. That's just so. That's just how it is. And there are people who have to die so that free countries can go on being free and so on. So I wasn't mourning any of the people whose deaths I'd arranged, or struggling with guilt over that. That would have been hypocritical. Someone has to take on that work. For a while, it was me.*

*But the truth was, the truth deep down was, I hadn't really done it because it had to be done. I had done it for the Recruiter. I had done it because I was a lost young man who needed something to believe in and I had come to believe in him. Maybe I didn't believe what he believed but I believed in the man himself. And now, I was wondering, you know: What if Blatt was right about him? What if the Recruiter was a bad guy? Or had become a bad guy somewhere along the way? What if my best friend was dead and a girl I'd loved was dead and I had become the kind of man I'd become—and the person I did it for was not the hero I thought he was. What if instead he had become the villain of the piece?*

*Like I said, I think, for me, this was the beginning of the end.*

# 22

For a long time after Winter stopped talking, Margaret Whitaker sat in silence and he sat in silence too. Once again, she had the sense that there was a new distance between them, a barrier that had not been there before. He was holding something back again. And, again, she wasn't sure she wanted to know what it was.

It had not always been pleasant, listening to these stories of his, these stories he told her about the sorts of things her government was getting up to behind the scenes. A woman like Margaret, a nervous old woman—that was the image she liked to torture herself with—might well be happier being kept out of the loop on such unsavory business. Because of course what Winter said was true: the things she did, the activities she enjoyed, activities like reading a book or having a glass of wine with a friend, watching a history show or a travel show on television or taking walks on the nearby campus, or doing her work of helping middle-class people straighten out their middle-class problems—these activities could only take place as long as men like Cameron Winter were out there somewhere killing people on her behalf. That was the plain truth, wasn't it? Just like Winter said. There were bad men in the world who wanted to do bad things, and their children had to be orphaned and their wives had to be widowed and sometimes the cities in their awful countries had to be bombed to rubble and people in those cities killed more or less at random, so that decent people in decent countries could continue to do the decent things they did.

And the truth was, she could live with all that—as long as she didn't have to think about it too much. But when she was with Winter, she did have to think about it. Which was bad enough. And now she also had to think about this: What if the people in charge of doing all this killing on her behalf—what if they turned sinister or corrupt or just plain crazy? Wouldn't that make her complicit in evil, even more evil than the regular evil required to keep the world spinning?

She finally said: "You had put an awful lot of faith in the Recruiter. I can't help wondering what it must have been like for you to have that faith shaken."

Winter was staring blankly down at the brown rug, but he looked up when she spoke as if she had awakened him from a trance. "What it was like?"

"Yes. What effect did it have on you?"

He shook his head very slowly. "Well. I guess the worst part was . . . it made me doubt myself. You know? It made me doubt my own ability to judge reality. To make moral choices."

"Yes, I can see how that would happen. And that self-doubt—is that still with you?"

One corner of his mouth lifted. His hands were clasped under his chin. His fingers were poking up under his lips. It was as if he was unconsciously mirroring Margaret's customary pose.

"It's funny you should ask that," he said. "I was just recently asking myself the same question."

"Yes. I sensed that. I sensed that's why you were telling me this whole story. So—what do you think? Are you still struggling with this? This lack of confidence in your own judgments?"

He gave a small, helpless shrug. "I don't know really."

"Well, let me ask it another way. If the Recruiter came to you tomorrow and he asked you to do something for him, would you do it?"

Winter's eyes widened as he drew in a deep breath. Again—again—she thought he was keeping something from her. And again, she did not ask what it was. She did not want to know.

"I would," he said slowly.

"For all your doubts."

"Yes."

"And why is that?" Margaret asked. "I mean, as you say, you don't seem to share his certainties. You don't share his religious faith. Even his patriotism seems more—I don't know—more passionate than yours."

Winter spoke hesitantly, as if he was feeling his way to what exactly he wanted to say. "Somehow. I always felt that he . . . that he was not what he said he was. That he was more complex than the way he liked to talk. I always felt the Recruiter was using this hyperserious way of speaking to mask his deadpan irony and at the same time, he was using his deadpan irony to mask the fact that he was altogether serious. Does that make sense?"

"Well, you've hinted at that before. But no. I'm not sure I understand it."

"Well, the patriotic jingoism seemed to be like a joke but the joke seemed to me like a mask for his deep love of the idea of America. The religious fundamentalism—it was a joke. But the joke masked his deep and steadfast faith in God. Maybe I projected that onto him. You know? Maybe he had no sense of humor about himself at all. But I think he did. I think he understood that real faith requires irony and irony is nothing without real faith. And I understood that. I believed in that. I believed in the man who embodied that. The man himself, like I said. Which is funny, you know, because I'm not sure the Recruiter approved of that. Me putting my faith in a man, a person, even himself. But I did. I do. I would die for him, his ironies and his certainties both. I would kill for him."

"Even now."

"I think so. Yes," said Winter.

Margaret swiveled in her chair for another long, silent moment. She had a suspicion—or at least the beginning of a suspicion—that these considerations were not wholly consigned to the past. Really, when she thought about it, she had a suspicion that the Recruiter had come back into Winter's life in some way that he was not telling her. She swiveled very slightly in her chair, considering whether she should question him about that, whether she wanted to hear his answers.

"So," she said then. "Let's talk about Gwendolyn Lord."

Winter let out a startling laugh. Was it a laugh of relief? Margaret wondered. Or was the relief hers because she had changed the subject? No, she thought. It was a laugh of delight. That's what had startled her.

"So it's going well, I take it."

"It is," he said, trying not to grin. "It's going strangely. But well."

"Strangely how?"

He sat straighter in the armchair. He shifted his shoulders as if to break free of some restraint. "Like I said before, there's just a lot about it I don't understand. About her and about me with her. We've only known each other a little while. We've only gone out together twice. But suddenly, it all seems very high stakes somehow."

"You like each other."

"Well, yes, but . . ."

"But?"

"It's just mysterious. The inevitability of it. For instance, why is she . . . ?"

Margaret waited. Watched him. With that odd mix of emotions she felt around him now, that sense of being sad and glad at once. He just seemed so different than he had been. So much more youthful. Fresh. Awake. Alive. It was good to see it, gratifying to see it, a sign that her work had been well done. But it also underscored that other feeling she had. That he was leaving her behind. Abandoning her to her life, so bland and brown and tan. He was falling in love—had already fallen maybe. And it made her painfully aware that she had lived past the age of love without ever having really loved at all.

"Why is she willing to become my lover?" Winter finally said.

"Is she?"

"I think so. I think she is. We almost became lovers the other night. One of us chickened out. I'm not sure which one. But if she's so religious, isn't she supposed to be a perpetual virgin or something?"

"Well, she's a widow, dear, so that's off the table."

"But you know what I mean. Isn't she supposed to want to get married and have priests say words over us and that sort of thing?"

"My experience is that different people live out their faith in different ways."

"Mm. I guess that's true."

"What about you?"

"What about me?"

"Do you want to become her lover?"

"Well, yes. Yes, of course I do."

"Let me rephrase that. Do you want to get married? That's what's really troubling you, isn't it? You're worried that if you begin this, there will be no stopping it. That it will go on forever."

"Yes. Exactly. Forever. Exactly."

"And do you want that? Do you want it to go on forever?"

"Oh . . . I don't know. I don't know what I want. I told you, I've been out with her twice. Two dates. How could I know whether we should be together for the rest of our lives? It's a ridiculous question."

"Well, it might be. But you haven't answered it."

He moved his hands around in the air as if trying to conjure the answer out of nothing. After a few more tries, his hands fell—fell to his thighs with a slapping sound. Whatever he'd been trying to say, he had given up the effort.

"You tell me," he said. "You're the mental health professional. You tell me what's supposed to happen next."

Margaret still had her fingers steepled under her chin. She was still swiveling back and forth a little in her tan leather swivel chair. "You know, I don't think I will tell you. I think I'll let you figure it out for yourself. But I will tell you this. Because you don't know how you feel about the Recruiter. And you don't know how you feel about Gwendolyn. And you don't know how you feel about your life, your past, the things you've done and the things you're about to do. I'll tell you this. Ever since your adventure with Charlotte, you seem to have discovered something. Am I wrong about that?"

"No. I feel that too. I feel that I've found something. But I'm not sure what it is."

"Well, that's what I will tell you. It's you. I think you have discovered yourself, if you can face it. I think you have discovered your real self, as you truly are and always were. Before Charlotte returned, you had this idea that you had become something different than what you were supposed to be. You were making an effort to recover that original self that you had lost. The idea was that you were intended to be a quiet, contemplative academic who studied poetry, but a series of chance events had turned you into a cold-blooded assassin, and so you had come to this university to try to recapture the person you were meant to be. And, in fact, you became a professor—but a professor who, almost inexplicably, keeps finding himself in situations more suited to a government agent."

Winter was listening closely, nodding as she spoke.

She went on: "But now, it seems that whole narrative was too simplistic. Now, you feel you've opened up a locked room inside your mind and you've found a different, more complex version of yourself, a version that might not simply be this English professor you've been trying to become. It might also include the man you were. It might be that your work in the Division was not random at all, not a mistake at all. Perhaps it's just as much a part of who you really are as the professor who reads Keats and Shelley."

"Well . . ." Winter said slowly. "Well, wow. I haven't really thought about it that way. I'm not sure how I feel about that."

Margaret went on swiveling. Watching him. Glad for him. Sad.

"Well, I think you should think about it," she said. "And I think you should understand: The next decisions you make, the next paths you take—you're right, they're going to last forever. Because they're going to bring you face-to-face with something you've never confronted before."

"Okay. What's that?" said Cameron Winter.

"Cameron Winter," Margaret said.

# 23

Winter was still thinking about this the next afternoon as he sat in a rented SUV, parked across from a little playground in Tulsa, Oklahoma. The SUV's engine was off. The driver's side window was down. The heat of the day washed over him, a thick heat like a liquid atmosphere. He was wearing a T-shirt, but his skin felt warm and sweaty underneath. His baseball cap was damp against his forehead. He watched the man in the playground and the two children with him. The children were dancing in the mist thrown off by a large playground sprinkler. Winter could hear them squealing and laughing.

He found this a poignant scene. The man was so large and lumbering, the little boy and girl so small, so spry. He was struck with the sadness of it. The broken marriage. The precious time stolen from the wreckage. The things that had gone wrong and would never be made right. How much of it could have been avoided? How much of it was written in the stars?

Because, of course, these were the questions he was asking now about his own life. How much of what had happened to him was an accident? Losing Charlotte, joining the Division, the end of his career there with its traumas and doubts. Or were these events the emanations of his personality working itself out in time, a kind of destiny generated by his own interior workings? Or was it something else again? Maybe the accidents of his biography were put to the purpose of some unavoidable outcome—the purpose of God, as it were? It was all so impossible to fathom.

The decisions you make now will last forever, Margaret had told him. Because they will bring you face-to-face with yourself.

*Well, there's a paralyzing thought*, thought Winter.

Catty-corner across the park, a car pulled up to the curb, a maroon sedan. Winter sat and watched as the car's door opened and a woman rose out from behind the wheel. He couldn't see her clearly from that distance, couldn't make out her face very well. She was dressed in shorts and a T-shirt. Her hair was unkempt, flying all over as she hurried across the street and strode into the park. Winter saw the man spot her approaching. He spoke to the kids dancing in the sprinkler. The kids stopped dancing and stood still.

This was the children's mother. She spoke to her ex-husband briefly. Gathered the little ones up. Led them away, off to her car, holding their hands, one of each in each of hers.

The man watched them go. Waved when they glanced back at him. Turned away as the mother and children got into the car. He wedged his fingers in the pockets of his jeans and started walking back to the road, back toward Winter.

This was Ralph Lorenzo, the guard from the county jail. He spotted Winter as he reached the sidewalk. He stopped where he was, and stood uncertainly.

"You better get in," Winter told him.

Lorenzo did not move. He was a big man, physically powerful and accustomed to authority. He didn't take orders from smaller men without rank. A half smile creased his big, flat, featureless face.

"Oh yeah?" he said. "And why's that?"

Winter glanced up and down the sidewalk to make sure no one was within earshot.

"Because I know you murdered Owen McKay," he said then. "And if you don't talk to me, you're going to go away for it."

Lorenzo considered. He sniffed to show he wouldn't be intimidated. Nevertheless, he moved toward Winter's SUV. Came around to the passenger side. Pulled the door open. Sank gigantically into the seat.

He shut the door. "You can't prove anything," he said with a nasty grimace.

Winter shrugged. He was looking out through the windshield at another family coming toward the park, a mother and her three children, two by her side, one in a stroller. "That's not going to matter in the end, Lorenzo," he said. "In the end, when all the secrets come out, it's going to come down to who could've done it, and you're the guy." He glanced over at the much bigger man. Lorenzo's eyes were narrowed, his cheeks red. His anger was palpable, like the liquid heat flowing in through the windows.

"Man, there is a pall of fear in this town," Winter went on. "The police won't talk to me. The sheriff won't talk to me. Everyone who will talk to me has the same look in his eye. That watchful look. Frightened. Ashamed. You pulled it off the best, I'll give you that. Inviting me over. 'Sure, ask whatever you want. I'll tell you whatever you want to know.' It was a nice trick. But you know what bothered me about your story?"

There was a long pause while Lorenzo shook his big head at the windshield, angry but cornered and even more angry because he couldn't think what to do.

"No," he said finally. "What bothered you?"

"The timeline. Owen McKay was arrested in the night, but he wasn't brought in into the jail until your shift, the afternoon shift. What happened in the time between? Did they take him to the city jail first? Question him at the cop shop? Taking witness statements. Getting IDs. Or maybe just stalling on orders from someone on high."

"Something like that. So what?"

"So what happened during the night, Ralph?"

"What do you mean? How the hell should I know what happened?"

"Well, I know. I can guess anyway. I think a cloud of power passed over this city. A swarm of powerful men like a cloud. I think they swarmed the county sheriff and the city police force, your mayor, maybe your governor, for all I know. But there were enough of them to enforce a regime of silence. Fear and silence. So the cops clammed up, and the sheriff clammed up, and pathology reports were rewritten. And, in general, people got the message: Know nothing, say nothing. Just go on about your lives and everything will be fine. Fear is a primary emotion, Ralph. It's not that hard to spread it if that's what you want to do."

Lorenzo gave a derisive laugh, but he did not speak again. There was nothing he could say.

"A swarm of powerful men descended on this city in the night," Winter said again. "And one of those men was covered with tattoos, wasn't he? He was the tip of the spear. He was the enforcer. I've met him. He's a savage. Insane. A killer. He was the one they would have sent to see you."

Winter glanced at Lorenzo again, but only glanced at him. He could see the big man was grief-stricken at his own humiliation and he didn't want to humiliate him more.

"What did he do, threaten your children? I saw the place where the wedding band used to be on your finger, so I figured it had to be that. Listen, there's no shame in this. It was a clear choice. The whole town was covered. You had no one to turn to, nowhere to go. A guy like you, ex-military, you've seen death, dealt death. You must have known what the Tat Man was the minute you saw him. What he was capable of. What'd it come down to? You had to kill a killer to protect your family. No big deal. You'd done it before in the war. I've done it too. So that's what you did."

"You can't prove that," Lorenzo said again, but there was no force in it this time, no strength left in his defiance.

"Well," said Winter. "Even by your own telling, you're the only one who could have pulled it off. You brought McKay into the cell. You dismissed the others. You were there alone. It didn't have to be more than a few seconds. You shot McKay with that almost silent device the Tat Man gave you. And out you walked. Then you manned the cameras, watched the hallway. You said, 'No one else went in the cell or went by the cell.' Which was true enough. The shrink came down and opened the door, and there was the corpse of McKay, just where it had been since you shut the door. That's the only way it could have happened, so that's the way it did happen. There's no such thing as an impossible murder."

"What do you want, Winter?" Lorenzo said with sudden savagery. "If it's money, you're screwed, man. The wife took everything in the divorce. You saw where I live. I haven't got a dime."

"Too bad. As soon as I saw your trailer home, I was looking forward to pillaging your untold riches. But how about this instead? How about you give me some information? The cops had McKay in custody all night. The guy was out of his mind. Raving. He must have said things to them. And when the powers that be swept through here, when they told everyone to keep their mouths shut or else, there must have been things people knew, things they had to hide. But I'm sure there's been gossip. Whispering man-to-man, right? What did McKay say that night?"

Lorenzo's tongue swept over the inside of his lip. He shook his head. "You're not gonna believe this, but I don't know. Nobody's told me anything, and I didn't ask."

"You're right. I'm not going to believe that. You work with cops. You know cops. McKay must have said something to them. Cops must have heard something. Some of it must've gotten back to you."

The big man raised his big shoulders and let them drop. "Like you said, McKay was raving. That's all I know. Screaming about what was inside him. It was still inside him. He just kept saying that."

"Talking about the gizmo in his brain."

"What?"

"When he said it was still inside him, he meant the gizmo in his brain," said Winter.

"No," said Lorenzo. "That's not what he meant. That's not what he said."

Winter drew a slow breath. "What did he say then? What was he talking about? What was still inside him?"

Lorenzo shifted in his seat, turned to face Winter. Stared at him with hard eyes full of pain. "The evil," Lorenzo said. "He was talking about the evil. He kept saying the evil was still inside him."

Winter gave a laugh. Then the laugh died. The look on Lorenzo's face killed it. The two men sat silently, staring at each other.

"And there's something else," Lorenzo said after a while.

Winter waited.

"At the end. Just before. When I pulled the nail gun out and pointed it at him and just before I pulled the trigger. There was a second, just a second at the end when he knew what was going to happen. You know what he did?"

Winter could only shake his head.

"He smiled," said Lorenzo. "He smiled at me. He said, 'I never should've let them turn out the light bulb.'" Lorenzo snorted. He turned away. He looked out the window. "Those were his last words. I don't even know what they mean."

# 24

Winter was relieved to find a nonstop flight from Tulsa to St. Louis. That very night—the night of the day he spoke to Ralph Lorenzo—he was sitting in a strip club on a lonesome Missouri two-lane about an hour from the airport. He was watching a naked woman dance on a table.

It wasn't his table. And it wasn't much of a dance. A customer seated halfway across the dark room had tipped the bare-breasted waitress a couple of bills. In return, she had set her drink tray aside, removed her shorts, and climbed up on his table. Once there, she began to move around in an aimless, haphazard way with a bored look on her face. The customer gripped his overpriced cocktail and gazed up between her legs. Seated at a table against the wall, Winter gently swirled his own overpriced cocktail and looked on. He found the scene more depressing than sensual.

The customer's name was Patrick Griffin. He was a man in his early seventies with flaccid features that looked as if they'd melted into the melted flesh beneath his receding gray hair. He was big-bellied, soft, and, as of right that moment, dull-eyed, less like a man gazing up at the Promised Land, and more like a mouse mesmerized by the snake that would eventually devour him.

Until about eighteen months ago, Griffin had been the warden of Osage State Correctional Facility. He had retired then and announced he was planning to move south. But he hadn't moved south. Not yet anyway. For the present, he was still living on his own in a small green clapboard house not far from the prison. Winter had gone to his house to speak to him, but had arrived just as Griffin was pulling out of the driveway in his long, sleek Cadillac. Winter had followed the Cadillac, hoping to find a place to speak with Griffin. This—this strip joint—turned out to be the place. Winter figured it was as good as anywhere else. Dim, except for the colored Christmas lights casting a muddy glow over the shadows. It was not so noisy he'd have to shout but, with the heavy bass beat of the music from the speakers, it was not so quiet he'd be overheard either. And, along with the naked waitress dancing on the table, and another girl giving a lap dance in a corner, there was also a stripper on stage, twining herself around a metal pole, so the attention of the other seven or eight men in the room was fully occupied.

Winter waited for the girl on the table to finish her dance. As she was climbing down from the table, he picked up his drink and carried it across the room. Griffin was studying the girl's breasts as she put her pants back on and recovered her tray. He turned, surprised, as Winter slipped into the chair across from him.

"Can I help you, son?" Griffin said in a manner not altogether friendly. He had a flat local accent with a nasal twang.

"I think you can," Winter said. "My name is Cameron Winter. I want to tell you a story."

"Well, Mr. Winter, I do like to hear a story from time to time, but frankly I come to this place to look at women's tits and drink and you're interfering with both those activities."

Winter placed his phone on the table so that Griffin could see the photograph of Owen McKay. It was a very long, unpleasant minute before Griffin dragged his baleful gaze off Winter's face and looked down at the picture.

"Owen McKay," said Winter. "Do you recognize him?"

Griffin sniffed. "I do not. And unless and until you explain to me why you are distracting me from my study of the female anatomy, I don't think I am going to say anything else. I'm too old to punch your lights out, but I'm still young enough to invite my friend the bouncer over there to punch your lights out and to enjoy watching him do it. So say what you have to say and make it quick."

"They changed McKay's face," said Winter. "That may be why you don't recognize him. But I'm guessing he used to be a man named Gregory Finch. I checked the records, looking for convicts who died at Osage—who died young while serving life sentences or on death row. Finch—McKay—was transferred to Osage prison while you were warden there. He had been convicted of committing three murders—brutal killings of young women. He beat the needle by arguing diminished responsibility but he was given life without parole. A 'light bulb.' Isn't that what convicts call it? Shortly after his transfer to Osage, he was reported to have had a heart attack and died."

"Well, that is a very sad story," said Griffin. "I think I'll be calling the bouncer now."

"It's not really all that sad," said Winter. "Because I don't think McKay did die. He and Frank Burton, who was on Osage's death row, and Trey White, who was doing a light bulb like Finch here—I don't think any of them died as they were reported to have done."

Griffin made no answer to this. He lifted his overpriced drink to his melted face. The Christmas lights shone on the glass as he drank from it, green and red and yellow. The lights were reflected in his eyes too as he gazed past Winter at the naked woman pole dancing atop the bar-slash-stage.

Griffin set his glass down. He crunched some ice between his teeth.

"That is one very flexible female," he murmured. "What did you say your name was again?"

"Cameron Winter."

"And who are you exactly, Mr. Winter?"

"I'm an English professor."

Griffin snorted. "I was 101st Airborne, Professor. What are you, military intelligence or something?"

Winter sighed. He hated when people identified him as a government agent. He wished he could wash the stink of that right off himself, but it just wouldn't go. He adjusted his phone until it displayed a photograph of Harris Turner.

"I'm guessing that's Frank Burton as was," he said. "He got a new face too, I guess. He raped and murdered a young woman in Connecticut recently. Owen McKay murdered his wife and child in Oklahoma."

"Uh-huh," said Griffin.

"Before Burton—or Harris Turner as he called himself—before he killed this sixteen-year-old girl, he got upset watching a movie with his wife. The scene that upset him was a scene at Osage prison."

"*The Midnight Hour*," Griffin said. "Not a bad little picture. I hosted Clarence Snyder at my home for dinner. Surprisingly regular fellow for a movie actor."

"Glad to hear it," Winter said. "Some of those people can be real narcissists."

"Ain't it the truth. Let me ask you something, Professor Winter. Look over your shoulder for a minute."

Winter looked over his shoulder. The pole dancer was kneeling on the bar, bent forward, holding her breasts up to the face of a man seated on a stool there.

"I'm sure a lad as pretty as you are has seen some very fetching bosoms in his day. How would you rate those comparatively speaking?" Griffin asked.

Winter faced him, trying not to let his rising irritation show on his face. Griffin kept his eyes trained on the dancer.

"You must know I can't answer any of these questions of yours," he said.

It was Winter's turn to remain silent. His gut was twisting with anger and frustration and he didn't want his voice to give it away.

"So what is it you're looking for?" Griffin asked.

Winter spoke between his teeth. "Three people are dead, Mr. Griffin. A woman, a girl, a child. Two men who were reported to have died in your prison murdered them. I want to know what happened, how it happened. And I want to know before the third man, Trey White . . . before he kills someone too. I want to find him before that happens."

The thumping, tuneless music from the speakers filled the space between them as Griffin raised his glass again and drank again and crushed ice between his teeth again. Winter watched the expression on the man's melted features. Despite his elaborate show of nonchalance, he was not without conscience. That was Winter's sense of him anyway. He thought Griffin wanted to forget these things and was bothered that Winter had brought them up.

"I'm not looking to fix the world here, Mr. Griffin," Winter said. "If you could just tell me how to find the third man. Trey White. If you could just give me a lead on him so I could reach him before he kills someone, that would be enough. I could live with that."

Griffin rolled his eyes. "Hell, I don't know which king of creation you take me for, but I don't know anything about all that. This whole rigmarole didn't start with me. How could it? The decisions were made way above my pay grade. I mean, you must know that."

"How high above?" Winter asked. "The Department of Corrections?"

Griffin made a whiffling noise and lifted the edge of one hand to the level of his hairline: *Higher.*

"The governor?" said Winter.

Griffin didn't answer in words, but a gesture of his head said yes.

Winter wiped the sweat off his upper lip. He cursed.

"It's a cruel world, son," Griffin said.

"That means it had to have come down from the federal level."

"It would mean that, I think, but I don't know it for sure."

Winter considered. The thumping tune from the speakers, the Christmas-lit murk, the smell of male appetite—they all fell into the background of his mind.

"Were there only three?" he asked. "Three prisoners."

"As far as I know. Only three from my facility anyway."

"And how'd that go down? What were you told?"

Griffin hoisted his shoulders. "Not much. Not anything, when you come right down to it. They signed consent forms and were taken away by the governor's orders, not all right away, you understand, but one, then another, then another. And I was given to know that they had passed away in the infirmary and the DOC would be informing the nearest and dearest. Then I was told in no uncertain terms to keep my face shut and my butt puckered. And that's all she wrote."

"And you don't know what happened after the prisoners left?"

"Not a hairlike thing. I mean, if I had been running the show, all three of those murderous sons of bitches would have been put down like the mad dogs they were. But where they went after they left my custody and what happened to them there, I do not know."

Winter cursed again. This was too big for him. Crazy big—not to mention just straight-up crazy. How was he supposed to handle something like this? Something that came all the way down from DC?

When Griffin drank this time, he drained his glass. When he set the glass down, the last two remaining ice cubes rattled in it. Winter could barely hear the rattle under the pound of the music. But the bare-breasted waitress heard it. She came out of the shadows instantly.

"I wouldn't mind a refill, darling," Griffin told her. "And when you come back, maybe you could climb up on my table again and let me bask in the experience of that fragrant flower of yours."

His hands folded on the tabletop in front of him, he watched with a small, contented smile on his lips as the waitress's backside went ticktocking away.

"You've kept all this secret until now?" Winter said to his profile.

"I have. I have. For good or ill," he murmured dreamily. "Not sure why I'm telling you, to be honest. Except I'm sorry about the killings. The women. The child. I'm not surprised, mind you. But I am sorry about it, I truly am. Plus I don't have much to lose anymore. Job's over. Wife's gone. Children don't ever come by for a visit. No use dwelling on it. When the word comes down from on high, a man in my position has to do what he's told. That's the law of the world. Still. I wouldn't want to just sit here, gawking at titty while Trey White goes off and does what he does to some poor woman or other. He was a real monster, that one."

"But there's nothing else you can tell me," said Winter. "A lead. A name. Someone. Something."

"Not a molecule. That's all there is, there isn't any more."

Winter sat there a few more moments, trying to think of some angle he hadn't tried, some other question he hadn't asked. He was tired of this feeling inside him, of being defeated, of being a failure, of being too slow to outrun the tragedy, and too weak to take on the powers that be.

The waitress returned. Griffin tossed a few bills on the table. She swept them up and took her shorts off.

The girl climbed up on the table and started swaying around. Griffin looked up between her legs and went dead-eyed again.

Winter's chair scraped as he got up without another word. He left the strip joint with the heavy bass of the music beating his retreat.

# 25

Winter lay awake that night, watching the light beneath the door of his hotel room. He knew the tattooed man would come for him—come for him soon. Maybe here. Maybe now. This would be a good time and place for it to happen. He had no gun with him. He had no more security than the lock on his door. The sinister powers that be didn't want any more bodies lying around, or so it seemed to him. But they had killed Warren Gentry to keep him from printing his story, so they weren't making a hard-and-fast rule about it. Given a chance to threaten him, the Tat Man would find it hard to restrain himself from going beyond mere threats to murder. This time, he might collect the tattered remnants of his sanity and use a gun, do it quick, even if it meant missing out on all the fun of slow torture. Winter watched the light beneath his door and thought: if the door should burst open, if Tat Man should step in and pull the trigger, there wouldn't be a hell of a lot he could do to stop him.

And so it might come to pass. Because Winter knew too much but he didn't know enough. Too much to be ignored, but too little to go public and expose this whole fatal mess they'd made. He could now piece together the events that had led to the killing of

Owen McKay. He thought he could anyway, more or less. But he had no proof. He had no witnesses. His story would just be another conspiracy theory on the flood tide of conspiracy theories that washed through the internet every single minute of every day. It might get some attention. It might not. Even if it did, it would simply be carried off by the next absurd story and the next. And if, in the meantime, he should get stabbed to death in a mugging, or hit by a car, or if he should shoot himself seven times in the back of the head or simply disappear without a trace, who would there be to speak for him, to take up the search for the truth where he'd left off?

Well, he lived through the night, so that was a positive development. And his rented car didn't explode when he turned on the ignition. And his plane didn't crash on the ride home. All the same, he arrived at his apartment in the late morning feeling half dead with exhaustion. He tried to catch some sleep in the greater security of his own apartment, but he was disturbed almost at once by a text message from Dean Copely. The dean was inviting him to attend an "informal discussion" with him and Lori Lesser on the subject of the 101 English course he was assigned to teach next term. The text annoyed him so much, he couldn't settle down to sleep right away. Just as he thought he might drift off, his phone rang. He saw on the readout that it was Gwendolyn Lord, so he answered.

"You sound like I woke you up," she said.

"No, I'm awake. I'm only pretending to be asleep to get your sympathy."

"Poor thing."

He laughed wearily.

"I was just wondering if you wanted to hang up and call me back and invite me out to a movie tonight. Sort of like a midweek surprise to let me know you're thinking about me. I would find that incredibly flattering and charming."

Winter paused only a second to wonder if he could make the long drive to her place without falling asleep at the wheel, high throttling into a guardrail, and dying in a fiery crash. He doubted it.

"What a great idea," he said. "Can I just surprise you by inviting you in the middle of this conversation and save some time?"

"Oh, all right."

"What movie am I surprisingly inviting you to?"

"It's called *These Little Ones*. It's about a Christian community that adopts seventy children. It's based on a true story and it's supposed to be very touching."

Somehow, Winter managed not to groan aloud. He thought he would almost rather stick a screwdriver in his nose and scour out his brains before sitting through a movie of that description.

"Sounds great," he said enthusiastically.

"Oh, it won't be so bad. It'll be good for you to have an emotion. You might even like it."

"I'll pick you up at seven."

He cut the connection and let his phone hand sink down onto the mattress beside him. At least now he didn't have to worry about Tat Man bursting into his apartment and killing him since the assassin couldn't possibly torture him as much as this film she was dragging him to. Relieved of that anxiety, he fell quickly into a sound sleep.

He awoke near noon, muzzy-minded but refreshed. As his vision cleared, he saw a message on his phone. It was an anonymous text on an app he had never downloaded. Puzzled, he opened the phone and read the message. A time and a location, that was all it said. Then he watched with mixed feelings of admiration and annoyance as the message disappeared, taking the app with it.

"How does he do that?" he muttered.

Twenty minutes later, he was out in the heat of midday, on his way down to the lake. He looked very lakeshore appropriate in shades and a khaki cadet cap. He wore a white short-sleeve shirt untucked over white slacks that flared at the bottom just enough to hide his ankle holster and his smaller Glock—the six-shot 43—secured within.

He blended well with the crowd of swimmers, sand diggers, sunbathers, and kayakers gathered on the strand. Hands in his pockets, body relaxed, but eyes alert and watchful, he strolled on the beach until he caught the scent of jasmine. He followed the tendrils of the scent as they gathered into an atmosphere. In this way, he reached the place where the sand ended, a patch of sparse grass bordering a grove of box elder. Here, secluded in a little stain of shade, were two beach loungers, one empty, the other bearing that offense against nature that was Fulu Fulu, the latest undercover iteration of Stan-Stan Stankowski.

The federal agent was only barely undercover in fact. He was wearing an absurd formfitting Chinese concoction that looked like a cross between a bathing suit and an evening gown. It was bright red with gold flower designs. Of course it was, Winter thought bitterly. And, he also thought bitterly, the suit actually looked pretty good on Stan-Stan who, again, had somehow become miraculously petite and slender and shapely. Not to mention Asian, for the love of God, with pink hair and enormous sunglasses, and an herbal cigarette which now seemed to poison all the air around with its jasmine stench.

"I can't wait for this assignment to be over," Winter muttered, settling into the lounge chair beside him.

"Honored friend," said Stan-Stan, in his soft, mellifluous, vaguely sensual voice. "My soul is gratified by the sight of you with your internal organs still internal despite the efforts and desires of our tattooed associate."

"I've been expecting him every hour," Winter said.

"The iris of caution blossoms in the garden of longevity," said Stan-Stan, or Fulu Fulu or whoever the hell he was.

Winter suppressed a sigh as he gazed out past the shade to the sun-dappled lake water. A graceful Lido with a bright-white sail skimmed serenely into and out of his field of vision.

"So peaceful," Stan-Stan/Fulu murmured with a musical tone. "One could almost forget the storm clouds gathering over the palaces of power."

Winter answered softly, speaking out of the side of his mouth. "What did these palace idiots do, Fulu Fulu?"

"Now, now, my friend. The processes of our imperial government are complex and inscrutable. As hurricane winds may grow from the fluttering wings of a butterfly, so the greatest catastrophe may have its source in a single sentence inscribed by an obscure supernumerary in an unread four-thousand-page bill entitled something like the Diversity, Equality, and Trustworthy Homeland Act."

Winter allowed himself a dark laugh. "So Thaddeus Blatt was desperate to save his zillion-dollar investment in Thaumatix after Isaiah Kahn drove his motorcycle into the Donner Pass and he paid off some ambitious government underling to give him permission and funding for this insane experiment of his."

"Mr. Kahn was the sort of person who mused aloud about his impossible dreams. Mr. Blatt apparently is the sort of person who took these musings too much to heart."

"What was the idea?" Winter asked. "He thought he could implant some bug into a psycho-killer's head and turn him into an angel of good citizenship? Was that it?"

"For a man with the mind of a Westerner, you have much of the wisdom of Chan within you. But yes. The heads of three psycho killers, to be exact."

"And let me guess. They gave these psychos new identities and then released them into the wild and then lost track of them."

"Lost track of two of them, unfortunately, it is so. They were monitoring Owen McKay quite closely, but did not realize in time that their experiment had failed. It was only after he killed his wife and child that they rushed to cover their tracks by having him eliminated in his padded cell. As for Harris Turner, he had slipped out of sight over time, too far for them to trace his location until he acted in an unfortunate manner that gave his location away."

"Raping and killing a sixteen-year-old girl," said Winter.

"Just as you describe it in your blunt Western way."

Winter's personal ethos was stranded in the eighteenth and nineteenth centuries so normally, he would never curse in front of a woman. But since Stan-Stan was not, in fact, a woman, and had he been a woman would not have been a lady, Winter let fly with a particularly ugly series of expletives.

"May I remind you that the female sensibility is as delicate as a cherry blossom?" Stan-Stan remarked softly.

Winter repeated the words a second time. "So a woman, a child, and a teenager have been slaughtered. And now—what? They're waiting for the third murderer to sacrifice some innocent lamb so they can find him and kill him by way of covering up what they did?"

Stan-Stan—or Fulu Fulu, whichever—raised his herbal cigarette to his lips and took a long and languorous draw. The pungent smoke spilled in slow spirals out of his mouth as he replied, "This is more to the point of why I called you here, my honored friend. Mr. Blatt and his illustrious illustrated companion are also willing to kill anyone who might expose them in a manner plausible enough to force even a government-friendly news media to report it and thus to require action on the part of the authorities."

Winter spat out his reply, "But the authorities are in on it!"

"Only in the most supplementary manner. After all, no one knows who wrote the relevant sentence into the Diversity and Equality bill. But it does have the president's signature on it. So while no one in particular can be held responsible, everyone must work together to ensure they are not all held responsible."

"So a cloud of federal power descends on any municipality that might catch on to what's happening. And Thaddeus Blatt sends crazy Tat Man to supply the bloodshed and terror that no one approves of but no one particularly forbids because it makes all the rest of it work."

"To be fair, the tattooed man has an employment history that would cause a good deal of suffering within the civil service if he should choose to reveal it. No one has the talent to kill him, and everyone benefits from his being alive."

"Amazing," Winter said. "To think I once worked for this collection of jackasses."

"Which brings me to the reason I have requested this meeting," Fulu-Stan went on. "Though, of course, it is always a moment to treasure when I have a chance to converse with so honorable an acquaintance for any reason whatsoever."

The federal agent drew jasmine-scented smoke again. Winter, meanwhile, shook his head in the direction of the kayakers paddling past on the glittering surface of the lake. The laughter of children on the beach was carried to him on the subtle movements of the summer air.

Then Fulu-Stan continued. "Your inquiries have fallen on Washington's elite like a rain that waters the weeds of their suffering. If these inquires of yours should suddenly cease because, for instance, some tattooed maniac cuts your heart out and swallows it even as it beats its last, there would be many in the gathering places of the powerful who greeted the event with a discreet sigh of relief."

"You wouldn't be threatening me would you, you son of a bitch?" Winter said.

"Threatening you? Heavens no, my friend. I am merely warning you of a threat, as is appropriate to my deep respect for an angel-faced yet overly persistent friend of many years. And . . ." Here he paused to further pollute the air beneath the trees with a sickly sweet cloud of jasmine. "And I am conveying an offer to you as well. A way perhaps that we might all reconcile your continued existence with the peaceful sleep of those who serve our nation in unelected and yet significant positions which are, may I add, largely invulnerable to the normal consequences that accompany dishonesty and failure."

"They want me to stand down and keep my mouth shut."

"I hope you understand that I correct you only with the greatest of respect. They want you to stand down, keep your mouth shut, and help them find the Recruiter, who is, after all, the original source of their anguish."

Winter made no other response than to turn his head and glare at the agent's delicate profile, which was half concealed behind the enormous sunglasses, which were themselves half concealed by a spill of pink hair. Fulu Fulu Stan-Stan did not return the look but continued to gaze out at the lake and the far shore and the pale-blue sky above it.

"The Recruiter and his so-called Invisibles seem to have lived up to their names by all but vanishing off the face of the earth. They have left only an occasional trace of themselves in the inexplicable scandals and other misfortunes that sometimes occur for no discernible reason in the lives of some of the very government functionaries whose sleep your inquiries have disturbed. Which, if I may say so, means the Recruiter and his Invisibles have gone underground while leaving you all alone out in the open where sleep-deprived bureaucrats may turn their vengeance upon you in the form of allowing our tattooed colleague to do whatever he has in his unfortunately disordered mind to do. So it is all part of one sinister yet somehow admirably intricate pattern."

The midday sun was high and hot, but a cool breeze came in off the lake and dispersed the stench of jasmine for a moment. Winter drew in the fresh air gratefully. The leaves of the box elders chattered as the soft wind stirred them. Winter, conversely, seethed in silence.

"I pose to you a slightly delicate question, my honored friend," Fulu-Stan went on. "Have you had any recent contact with your honored master?"

Winter snorted. "With the Recruiter? No, of course not."

"I see you choose to deal in untruth."

"I see you choose to dress up as a pink-haired Chinese girl, but I don't bother you about it."

"A fair point, but an irrelevant one, under the circumstances. Which include, should you refuse this offer, your almost certain death in an extraordinarily painful manner at the hands of our inky friend."

Winter shook his head at the view. "So the deal is: you would blame the Recruiter for the murder of Warren Gentry, and whatever other parts of this mess you need to cover up, and that would solve both the Thaumatix screwup and erase the embarrassing history of the Division at a single blow."

"It's so efficient it's difficult to believe it was dreamed up by a government functionary," Fulu-Stan said. The herbal cigarette had burned down almost to its dull-gold filter now. Fulu-Stan let his hand waft down to the side of his lounge chair. The cigarette tumbled from his listless fingers. It landed in the sparse, sandy grass, where it continued to send a thin tendril of stink up into the air. "The Recruiter trusts you more than he trusts any man alive," Fulu-Stan murmured with gentle tact. "You may be the only man alive he does trust. I'm sure if he did come to see you, he left you with a method of reaching him discreetly. I'm sure if you summon him to a meeting, he would attend. And we would attend. And all would be well."

Winter stretched his back, which was stiff from travel. Then he swung his legs off the lounge chair and stood over the graceful figure of Fulu Fulu in her red-and-gold bathing costume.

"Sorry, honored friend," he said, speaking into the distance. "There's a reason they call the Invisibles the Invisibles. I haven't seen them."

"From the seeds of lies grow the thorns of misfortune," said Fulu Fulu.

Once again, Winter's response, delivered as he turned to walk away, would have been uncharacteristically impolite had Fulu been a lady—or been almost anything rather than whatever it was he was.

# 26

In the early evening, Winter drove north to take Gwendolyn to the movies. The scenery along the way was beautiful: summer pines bending over the edges of endless lake water like angels bending over a cradle. But anxieties harried him through the long ride. How could he prove what had happened at Osage prison? The sorts of nameless government shadows who could descend on a city and intimidate the local police into silence—they could only be stopped by being dragged out into the open, exposed in the media, put on display before the public. But the current government was in favor with the media. Most of the important journalists were more intent on covering for them than exposing them. And Thaddeus Blatt and the Tat Man were willing to do murder to keep the curious silent, while the politicians and the press looked the other way.

It was frustrating stuff. Enraging even. There was a third killer still on the loose. When the gizmo in his brain failed, there would be another slaughter of innocents. And the truth was, Winter could not think of a single thing he could do to stop it.

He parked outside Gwendolyn's building as the summer darkness began to fall. He took a deep breath and released it, clearing his mind for her company. At this point, he reflected, it would almost be a relief to be bored to death by this crappy happy-slappy Christian movie she wanted to drag him to. He stepped out of the Jeep.

A wind was rising in the leaves of the sidewalk trees. The heat of the day was beginning to taper off into a cooler evening. He stood for a moment and shifted in his clothes: an untucked shirt over slacks, his khaki cadet cap, his hidden ankle holster and Glock. He scanned the scene, wondering if the Invisibles were ranged about him, blended into the background, where they were keeping watch on Gwendolyn for him as the Recruiter had promised they would do. He took another long breath, full of the deepening dusk. Then he went into the glass foyer and pressed Gwendolyn's buzzer.

"Come on up!" she sang out over the intercom.

The door lock snapped open. He pushed into a drab, nondescript hall. Rode the elevator up to the fourth floor. Walked down another drab, nondescript hall and reached her door just as she opened it for him.

She was wearing a white summer dress with a print of red roses. All complexity melted away when he saw her. She may have been stepping out to greet him, but he would never know for sure, because, without thinking, he crossed the threshold and took hold of her. He kissed her and the door clicked shut behind him. He kissed her neck and cheek and whispered her name and she flowed up against him.

It was only later that it struck him how natural it had been to make love to her. Dramatic in its way, but also as inevitable as a change of seasons, with the same commonplace abundance of beauty that overflowed the senses so that they couldn't fully take it in. Even when it was over, as he lay naked on his side and looked and looked at her where she lay naked on her side and looked at him—even then, his mind and heart couldn't quite comprehend everything that had happened to him and that was happening to him still. He went on looking until Gwendolyn grew flustered and pulled the sheet up to cover herself.

"Don't," he murmured. He gently tried to tug the sheet back down with his finger.

But she held onto it, smiling. "Stop. You're staring at me."

"I'm not staring at you. I'm gazing at you. It's an entirely different thing."

"Well, it feels the same. It's embarrassing me."

He sighed and gave up on the sheet. He stroked her cheek with his fingers instead. He brushed a strand of her hair back behind her ear and let his eyes move intently over her elfin features. She murmured and rested a fingertip against his lips. He kissed it.

"You just did this to get out of going to the movie, didn't you?" she said softly.

"Not this, no. I would have done anything else but not this. This I did for itself. Missing the movie was a bonus."

"Well, you were nice to agree to take me to see it, even if you didn't."

"I was nice. More than nice really. It was a kind of willing martyrdom. Like agreeing to have my skin cut off and my flayed body set on fire. And to pay for the tickets."

"You're horrible. I'll never ask you to ask me to take me to the movies ever again. My mother said I shouldn't."

"Did she?"

"She said I should play hard to get."

"No, don't do that. Defy your mother and be easy, for my sake."

He gathered her to him and kissed her, body to body. He whispered her name and pressed her face against his chest. After a moment, he felt dampness on his skin.

"Are you crying?" he said.

"It's all right. I'm happy."

He laid his cheek against her hair. He drew in the perfume of her. "It's all so damned strange, isn't it?" he said.

"Mm, no. It isn't strange at all."

"It's not?"

"No. You just don't understand it, so it seems strange."

"Well, explain it to me."

"My mother said I shouldn't. She said it would scare you away."

"That woman always underestimates me." He drew back so she would look up at him and he could study her face. Her cheeks were stained with mascara now. He brushed one of her tears away with his thumb.

"Tell me," he said. "It's making me crazy. When I came in, I wasn't even thinking about this. I didn't know I would do it. I didn't know if you would. If it would be all right with you."

"Of course it was all right. I wanted you to."

"I thought maybe—I don't know—maybe it would be against your religion."

"Mm," she said, and kissed him gently. "I'm a good girl, but not that good. And anyway, I don't think God can be against this."

He kissed her back. "Really, you're making me slightly insane. Tell me what we're talking about."

"No, you'll laugh at me."

"I won't. Or if I do, it won't be a mean laugh. It will be a nice laugh, I promise."

A fresh tear spilled down her cheek. She hid her face against him again. After a moment, she kissed his cheek. She whispered into his ear.

"We were made for each other, Cam. In heaven, where things are made, we were made for each other."

He almost did laugh but managed to stop himself.

"Don't laugh," she said. "You said you wouldn't. I knew it from the minute I saw you, the minute you looked at my ring. It's serious. It's special. It doesn't happen to everyone. But it's happened to us. It's a gift. We have to be grateful."

He smiled to himself and held her so she wouldn't see. Because she was right: He did find it laughable. But it was sweet too. It made him feel protective of her, as if she must be very innocent and vulnerable to believe such a thing.

She nuzzled him, wiping her tears off on his shoulder. "I know you don't believe me. You can't, because you don't believe in God. But of course there is a God. Otherwise, who made everything? And he made this, and it's a gift to us, and you have to be grateful to him. That's why I know he's not against this."

"Well, I'm grateful for that anyway."

She pinched his arm.

"Yowch," he said.

"Just take the gift, Cameron. All right? Don't be too smart for the truth. Take the gift."

"I will," he said. "I did! I have."

"There's just one condition, okay?"

"Uh-oh," he said. "What's the condition?"

"You're not allowed to die. Not until we're old and wrinkly and ready to go to heaven together. I belong to you now and you have to take care of me. And if you died, I'd fall to pieces—for good this time."

It gave him another restless night, all this—this sort of talk from her. He couldn't tell if she was teasing him or flirting or being serious, but he thought she might be serious and it made him edgy.

Later, when she was sleeping beside him, he lay awake. He thought again about the tatted killer he felt sure was coming for him. The wait had made him tense before. It was suspenseful before. But now it was frightening. He was afraid—afraid for Gwendolyn, for what it would do to her if the bastard got him. How had he gotten himself into this situation with her? So fast? Faster than fast. Like arriving at a destination to find himself already waiting there to welcome him. All this stuff about gifts made in heaven and so on—it seemed like girlish nonsense to him. But he had to admit it fit in with what he felt about her, what he had been feeling about her from the start.

It came into his mind then, as he lay there in the shadows, that he hadn't told her that he loved her. Not the first time he'd made love to her nor the second as their evening together drew to a close. Because it was all just that natural—natural as the seasons changing. His love was just there, so he hadn't thought to talk about it. He had the urge to wake her up and tell her about it now, but she was sleeping so peacefully, her face so close he could feel her breath on his shoulder. He ought to tell her as soon as she woke up, he thought. Because he did love her. And it occurred to him once again that he had always loved her somehow. But by then he was falling asleep too, and his thoughts were almost like dreaming.

He woke up and it was morning and he had a sense that something wonderful was happening, then he realized it was Gwendolyn and also the smell of bacon. He sat up and pushed the Glock and its holster under the bed and pulled his slacks on. Then he wandered sleepily into the living room and through into the narrow kitchen. She was there at the stove, wearing a teal-blue nightshirt that ended mid-thigh. She was making bacon and omelets.

He came up behind her and put his arms around her and kissed her hair. "I woke up and thought something wonderful had happened. Like when you wake up as a kid before you remember it's Christmas morning. Then I realized it wasn't Christmas morning, it was you."

"Are you sure it wasn't just the smell of bacon?"

"No, that's what I thought at first." He kissed her again and she tilted back into it with a low murmur, smiling. "I love you," he said.

"I know! You forgot to tell me yesterday."

"I didn't think of it because it all just felt so natural."

"Mm. Go pour yourself some coffee and sit down while I finish. I love you too, by the way."

She made a good omelet—a hell of an omelet actually, he thought. The best omelet of all omelets anywhere. And he liked how bright her apartment was, and the white curtains and white rugs that softened the light from the windows, and he even liked the flowery posters that decorated the wall. He must really be gone for her, he thought, because he hated flowery posters but he liked these posters because they were hers and feminine like she was.

"So tell me about the gun," she said.

"My gun? It's a Glock. Very light. Six shots."

"That isn't what I meant."

"Don't play around with it. It's got a tricky safety, makes it easy to accidentally blow your head off."

"That isn't what I meant. Tell me about the man in the cell in Tulsa and what's happening with all that."

Winter hesitated. It was not that he did not want to tell her, but he did not want to worry her about the Tat Man, or worry her any more than she was worried already. She was a girl who thought God gave people gifts. How could he explain to her that God had given him the gift of a lunatic assassin who wanted to eviscerate him just for fun?

"A rich businessman got the government to fund an incredibly reckless experiment. It resulted in people being murdered, and now the businessman is trying to cover it up, and the government is trying to cover up the cover-up."

"And you're trying to expose all of it, so you're in danger."

He made a gesture. He couldn't bring himself to speak the whole truth of it out loud.

"And now I've made it even worse for you," said Gwendolyn. "Because you have to take care of me. Plus you're not allowed to die, remember?"

"I remember. But as much as your happiness means to me, my darling, I wasn't planning on dying in any case."

She put a bit of omelet in her mouth and lollipopped the fork a moment as she thought all this through. Then she drew the fork out and wagged it at him and said, "What was the experiment? The stupid experiment they're trying to cover up?"

"They put some sort of gizmos in the brains of three killers. They were supposed to turn these psychopaths into nice guys. And they did for a while. Then they didn't. Twice. And people got killed. So now I need to find out who the third killer is before he murders someone too."

She sat back in her chair, raising a glass of orange juice in one hand as she brushed her hair off her face with the other. Winter understood with sudden certainty that he would never get tired of looking at her. He did not know how he knew this, but he did. The sight of her soothed him somehow.

"I was right then, wasn't I?" she said. "It really was demons. That's what Owen McKay meant when he said it was still inside him. He was talking about the demon. Right?"

Winter made a gesture. This seemed absurd to him, but he had to admit it wasn't entirely inaccurate.

"I'm right, right?" Gwendolyn went on. "They tried to make the evil in him go away with a machine, and it worked for a while, but then the demon found a way around it."

Winter suppressed a patronizing smile. *What a loopy dame*, he thought lovingly.

Gwendolyn pushed her chair back and stood. There was a small sideboard behind her. She went to it and opened one of the drawers. The pattern of Winter's breathing changed as she leaned down to the drawer and her nightshirt rode up on the back of her thighs. Then she turned around with a slender chain in her hands.

"You have to wear this."

He sipped his coffee. "What is it?" But he could see now it was a cross, a cheap metal cross on a cheap metal chain. "I can't wear that, sweetheart," he said.

"Sure, you can. Why can't you? It will protect you. From demons anyway."

"I don't believe in it. It would be fake. Hypocritical."

"No, it wouldn't. You'd be doing it for me, and I believe in it. That's all that matters. Please. You don't have to wear it. Just carry it with you. It will make me feel better to know you have it."

"What, do you keep a collection of these?"

"Sure. So I can give them to people. What's wrong with that?"

He hesitated another second, then figured what the hell. He took the cross and stuffed it and the chain into his pants pocket.

As he did, he was still thinking about the sight of her bending over the drawer. He stood up and drew her to him.

"You don't have to thank me," she said.

"I wasn't going to thank you."

He lifted her off her feet and began to carry her back toward the bedroom.

"I have to get ready to go to work," she told him.

But now she was laughing.

# 27

The next morning, Lori Lesser unveiled her latest attempt to end Winter's academic career. Winter knew he ought to pay attention, but all he could think of was sex and murder.

He had tried to postpone this meeting with Lori and Dean Copely, but every avenue of escape had been cut off and he was stuck with attending. Still, even as the meeting was taking place, even as Lori was maneuvering to get him fired, she and her plans were the last things on his mind. In fact, his mind was so full of images of passion and savagery, it was as if he was watching some crazy thriller movie playing in his head.

The meeting took place in Dean Copely's office. It was a large, stately library of a room on the top floor of the building called the Gothic. There were walls of tall bookshelves. There were large windows giving sunlit glimpses of the campus outside: white stone temples and towers glimpsed through the green crowns of trees. There was a wooden ceiling carved with vines hanging over a majestic walnut desk with brass inlay. The chairs were club-worthy studded red leather. The sofa was a royal scarlet that matched the central color in the elaborate design of the carpet. And here and there were numerous framed photographs of the dean with his wife and three children. His wife and three children were all wearing radiant smiles—smiles that Winter had preserved for them by silencing the dean's underage Thai prostitute.

Winter was enthroned in one of the leather chairs, the dean in another across the rug from him. The dean always reminded Winter of a character in some comic strip or other, a pencil sketch of a businessman or a nerd: the egg-shaped head, the glasses, and a few lines suggesting a face and form floating within a gray suit.

As for the assemblage of secondhand clothes, cuddly bosom, wild eyes, and frizzy hair that was all Winter saw of Lori Lesser, it was tucked into one corner of the sofa. Her hand and her mouth were both moving as she talked and talked in that buzzy tone of hers, at once amicable and terrifying.

What was she saying? Winter sometimes wondered as the meeting dragged on. But too late: He had lost track of it and was too distracted to catch up. It had something to do with racialism and historic injustices and the systemic metaphorical violence of favoring the poetry of John Keats over whatever blithering doggerel had been scrawled by lesser and justly forgotten versifiers of some oppressed minority or other. So he assumed, anyway, because Lori was always talking about such things, and because some of her catchphrases seemed to leap out at him as if made momentarily visible in the office air.

The inner Winter, however, was somewhere else altogether. In bed with Gwendolyn for one thing. Because he couldn't quite get over the semimystical feeling that having sex with her had been something more than just sex. It was a feeling he had never experienced before. He couldn't quite put it into words. He could conjure images of their coupling, and that was stirring. But the images were nothing like the way it had actually been. Thinking of her body was little better than watching a scene in a movie. It was a pretty picture, but did not convey the inner experience of being with her. That had been more than bodies, either hers or his. It had been something they became together that was larger than them both. Which struck him as the sort of hackneyed sentiment one might find in some horrible pop song. But it hadn't felt like a horrible pop song at the time.

". . . in order to make a beginning in understanding our own privileged positions and how they manifest . . ." Lori Lesser was saying.

Winter didn't want to get sentimental about this. It was just sex, after all. But there was something more to it, something he wanted to capture and preserve in his imagination. But he simply couldn't find the language to preserve it with. He tried, as was his habit when at a loss for words, to think of a poem that would express what he was trying to express. He was startled to discover he could not think of a single line. Maybe it was Lori's jabber that was distracting him, because now and then it did pull him back into the present moment. He gazed at her, at her mouth moving, her hand moving, and he wondered how he could ever have found her attractive at all. Had it just been his solitude and her comforting woman's shape? Was he as frail and impressionable as that?

But never mind. He returned to his own thoughts, and this startling realization that of all the poets who had written of love, not one had written of what had happened to him with Gwendolyn. He asked himself: How could that be? What were poets good for if not for capturing the experience of love? And the answer came to him: Words, as hard as the poets tried, could never really capture that simultaneity of flesh and spirit that was involved in genuine passion. If they wrote "I crave your mouth, your voice, your hair," it did not speak the soul of the desire. Whereas if they wrote, "Thou Angel bringst with thee / A heaven like Mahomet's Paradise," then where were the lips and breasts and warmth of flesh that made it real in this, the living world? Elizabeth Browning came close, he thought: "I love thee with the passion put to use / In my old griefs, and with my childhood's faith." Yes, that said some of it. But for all the high claims of poetic diction—the claims it could transubstantiate the particularities of life into their greater meanings—now that he had been through such a moment with an actual woman, he could not find a single verse to remember it by.

"I think what Lori is trying to get at here," said Dean Copely. And Winter turned to him with the same expression of grave attentiveness he had turned on Lori and with the same level of attention, namely none at all.

Because, as the dean spoke, Winter's mind had moved on to recalling the drive home from Maidenvale and his phone conversation with the despicable Arthur Dimmerman, the attorney who had threatened him in the Thaumatix offices.

It was he who had called Dimmerman as he drove. Because now that he and Gwendolyn had parted, all his frustration and anger had come back to him. Something about his night with Gwendolyn had overcome his paralyzing sense of failure and strengthened him with fresh resolve. He found he could not simply sit idly while the third killer's gizmo failed and another innocent victim died.

So he called Dimmerman and gave his name to the assistant who answered. He was not surprised when, almost instantly, Dimmerman's voice came over the dashboard speaker and filled his Jeep with the human equivalent of growling.

"Winter," he said—and he did not mean it in a nice way.

"Seems we have a problem, Dimmerman," Winter said.

"I have no problems," the lawyer answered in that pinched, nasal voice. It was an instrument designed to communicate scorn. "You have a problem. You couldn't just leave it alone, could you? You couldn't just go home like I told you to and forget what you should never have known in the first place."

"Yeah, yeah, yeah. And now, you're going to destroy me, I know."

Dimmerman laughed. A single laugh. A laugh without any trace of laughter in it. "We're way past that, fool. Way past that. You'll be lucky if I destroy you. That's your best outcome. You should pray that I ruin your life, Winter. Because the alternative is much, much worse."

Winter had to swallow his irritation before he answered. He could already tell it was useless to appeal to Dimmerman's conscience. It'd be like appealing to the conscience of an alligator. But to what else could he appeal?

"A woman is dead, you preening thug," he said, stiff-jawed. "A child is dead. A sixteen-year-old girl was raped and murdered. There's one more of your killers out there, Dimmerman. Whatever he's going to do, he's going to do it soon. Help me find him."

There was a pause. A second's pause. Winter could only hope it meant the alligator was wrestling with his sense of fair play. But he doubted it. And sure enough, Dimmerman then said, "I don't think you understand the higher stakes here, Winter."

"Higher stakes?" Winter nearly shouted the words at the dashboard.

But the dashboard spoke back to him without any feeling at all, certainly no feeling resembling shame. "Look," Dimmerman said—and as he went on, Winter could hear the lawyer choosing his words with legalistic care. "For reasons I can't discuss over the phone, it would be best for everyone concerned if we could resolve our differences in an amicable manner. But you're making it very difficult for me to be that charitable. Do you understand?"

A thought came to Winter then, an awful thought, so awful it gave him a feeling in his stomach like there was tangled fishing line in there, hooks and all. Steering with one hand, he dragged the other hand across his mouth as if to wipe away the venom on his lips. He said, "You know where he is, don't you? Trey White. The third killer. You already know where he is."

"I have no idea what you're talking about."

"You know but you're not bringing him in because you're hoping the gizmo won't fail this time. You're hoping you can still salvage your investment, Blatt's investment. And you're willing to risk some innocent's life on the possibility."

"This is not your problem. Your problem is shutting up before it becomes more useful to cripple you than leave you alone."

For the next several moments, there were no more voices in the Jeep. Only the sound of the engine. The sound of the wind rushing by the windows.

"I want to meet with Thaddeus Blatt," Winter said then.

Dimmerman gave another one of those laughless laughs. "You're as close to meeting with him right now as you ever will be."

"Tell him I said this," Winter replied. "Tell him I said it's no good him coming after me. Tell him it won't settle anything, not a thing. Tell him I said: His world is full of the invisible. He'll understand what I mean. His world is full of the invisible, and whatever he does to me will come back to haunt him a hundredfold. He knows this is true. Our acquaintance goes way back. He knows who he's dealing with."

Again, there was a pause. Winter figured Dimmerman was just constructing his strategy.

The lawyer's scorn-filled voice came into the Jeep again: "You were offered a chance to solve that problem. There was some possibility that Mr. Blatt would be grateful to you if you did solve it. That possibility remains. It will remain until it doesn't remain. Do you understand? All you have to do is lead us to the Recruiter and, as far as you're concerned, this whole experience will be a memory. Don't be an idiot, Winter. Take the gift."

Winter was startled to hear the lawyer snarl the very words that Gwendolyn had whispered to him. *Take the gift.* It was a moment before he could formulate a response. In that moment, Dimmerman cut the connection.

"So," said Dean Copely. "I think the issues are pretty clear."

Winter blinked and the present came back to him. Here he was, sitting in Dean Copely's office. There was the dean's comic strip figure on the studded red-leather chair. There was the disheveled pile of stuff that signified Lori on the sofa. There were her bright and furious eyes. Sunlight poured through the large windows and pooled on the rug.

"There's no reason to make a whole melodrama out of this," the dean went on. "This university prides itself on maintaining the highest standards when it comes to both education and professional ethics. I'm sure we can find some middle ground that will satisfy both your dedication to your subject and Lori's concerns about inequality."

"I don't think so," Winter answered at once. Sitting there thinking about his talk with Dimmerman had made him irritable all over again. He had to work to keep the harshness out of his voice. "I don't think there is a middle ground. I have a job here. I teach poetry to young people. Poetry is a thing. It's a thing that does a thing, or tries to do it. It tries to use words to unite the material world with its greater meanings. That's very difficult to do. Only a very few people have done it well in all of human history. I teach the ones who did it better than anyone else. Because they were trapped in a moment when the greater meanings seemed to be slipping away. To teach anything less, anything less than the best, would be selling my students short, wasting their time."

"But that's just a matter of taste," said Lori Lesser, smiling horribly. "That's just your socially conditioned response."

"No," said Winter. "It's actually not." He stood up. He smiled horribly back at her. "Judging the quality of poetry is my expertise. If it were just a matter of taste, Lori, there would be no poetry at all. Look," he went on. "I really am sorry. I'd like to help you here. But I can't. You two will just have to figure this out on your own."

"Winter," Dean Copely pleaded desperately.

"This isn't going away, Cam," said Lori Lesser, in her most pleasant singsong. "We'll take it up again when classes start in the fall."

But as he walked to the door, Winter was already thinking of other things.

# 28

Martin Bach sat in the shadows. He was thinking about Tilda. He held a claw hammer in one hand. He tapped the hammer's head against the palm of his other hand as he considered what to do about her.

In many ways, he was reluctant to kill his wife. She was not the type of woman he liked to work on, for one thing. There was a certain kind of girl whose suffering excited him. She was not that kind. He wondered if maybe the fact that she was carrying a baby might add to the experience. The possibilities there intrigued him. But even with all that considered, he did not want to take the risk of striking so close to home.

He knew he was being followed. He'd been aware of the man on his trail for weeks. The man in the blue Buick. Martin assumed he was an agent of the same mysterious cabal that had gotten him out of prison in the first place. The people who had forced him to choose between living in a cage like an animal and enduring their bizarre, experimental surgery on his brain. In the end, the lure of freedom was too great. He let them castrate his mind and deprive him of the joy of his desire. Now they had sent the man in the blue Buick to watch him, to make sure he did not recover that joy.

But he, Martin, had developed a way to lose the Buick man. He was good at that sort of thing. He was good with devices of all kinds. He guessed that the man was tracking a signal from the machine they had installed in his head. After a series of simple experiments, he had figured out a way to intercept the signal. It was easy then to first imitate the signal, and then block it, so that the man was actually following a cheap store-bought transmitter instead of the thing lodged in his skull.

Martin had tested this ruse a couple of times. He had come and gone from one of his worksites without the agent even knowing he had left. The agent had sat there in his blue Buick for over three hours, believing Martin was still inside the site. Finally, when Martin was sure the trick worked, he felt free to celebrate the unexpected return of his passion. It had been a somewhat hurried experience. He'd had to choose a grubby little homeless tart for a subject, someone no one would miss. He'd had to finish her more quickly than he would have liked, too. It did not satisfy him the way the old killings had. But at least he knew he could avoid his follower whenever the need arose.

But what good would that do him if he satisfied himself on Tilda? There would be no way of hiding her disappearance. And they—whoever they were—would know right away what he had done. That was the whole reason they were following him in the first place—because they were worried he would do something like that. They were afraid he would recover the manhood of his soul, the meaning of his life. They wanted to keep him a womanish slave to love and mercy.

He sat in the shadows and considered all this. *Tap, tap, tap* went the head of his hammer on his palm.

He was inside the Harkney house. The Harkneys had hired him to update the wiring here. That was one of the contingencies of the house's sale. The place was empty, all the furniture and most of the decorations gone. The family had already moved away. Martin was sitting in a crawl space beneath the kitchen. He had been replacing some of the old circuits down there, lying on his back in the cramped space with a sheet of protective plastic under him. He'd laid out the sheet to catch paint chips and bits of insulation and copper splinters as they fell. But it had occurred to him while he worked that the plastic and the space might provide a tidy way to get rid of Tilda's body when he was through with her. He was thinking that over with the hammer in his hand, as he sat with his back propped against the wall in the crawl-space shadows. *Tap, tap, tap.*

He didn't particularly want to kill Tilda, but the problem was this. Tilda might know about him. Or she might not. He wasn't sure. He had been trying to convince himself she didn't. That would solve his dilemma right there. But he had spotted her snooping around the shed. He had caught her trying to open his phone up too. At least, he'd thought that's what she had been doing. He had removed his souvenirs from the shed and erased the recording of the suffering tart from his phone, and it was bad enough he had had to do that. But if Tilda knew, if she knew already, that would not be enough. He would have to get rid of her.

He sat and brooded, frowning to himself. Upstairs, the doorbell rang.

Martin caught his breath. His hand went still. The hammer hovered in the air above his palm.

It was probably just a deliveryman at the door, he thought. Someone from some company that had not been notified about the Harkneys' change of address. At first, he thought of simply waiting there in the crawl space until the deliveryman went away.

But then he thought, no. He would go upstairs and find out who it was, make sure the problem was resolved. That would set his mind at rest if he decided to use this place for his own purposes later.

The doorbell rang again as he was climbing the ladder out of the crawl space.

"I'm coming," he called out.

He rose into the kitchen. The house was bright and spacious, especially with all the furniture and curtains gone. The afternoon light spilled unfettered through the wall of western windows that looked out on the wooded acres of backyard. Martin moved through the splashes of sunlight in the large living room and came into the foyer at the foot of the main staircase. Even before he reached the door, he could see his visitor through the door's sidelights. He was surprised to recognize Pastor Mike.

"Pastor!" he said as he pulled the door open. "What are you doing here?"

The young man was wearing a short-sleeve denim shirt. It gave him that youthful look he liked to parade before the female parishioners. Martin remembered he had admired this man once. But that was before his true soul had returned to him. The memory of his admiration was embarrassing to him now.

He let the pastor in. There was no furniture to sit on, so the two stood awkwardly in the empty foyer at the base of the stairs.

"I was chatting with Sara Harkney," the pastor said. "She told me you were working here." The pastor was much smaller, much more slender than Martin, a wavering reed beside a stone colossus. Martin was still gripping his hammer and he thought it would be easy to clutch the pastor by the throat, hold him suspended in the air and whack him over the head like driving in a nail. "I just wanted to stop by and chat, take advantage of the chance to catch you alone," the pastor said.

Martin narrowed his eyes as if he was curious to know what the pastor's private business with him could be. But he wasn't really as curious as all that. What *could* it be? A leak in the church cellar, some damage to the roof, something he was supposed to fix for free as an act of Christian charity-slash-self-justification? It amused Martin to think he had once cared about such things. But it also made him feel ashamed. He had been so desperate to get out of prison that he had allowed these anonymous men to turn him into the sort of whimpering eunuch who went poodling after priests and churchwomen, doing their chores for them like a slave.

"Tilda came to see me the other day," the pastor said. "She was concerned about you."

Martin straightened where he stood. Well, now he actually was curious. "About me?" he said. "What's she got to be concerned about me for? I'm all right. I'm fine."

The younger man nodded quickly, averting his eyes, embarrassed. "Well, yes, you looked perfectly fine in church Sunday. That's exactly why I thought I should talk to you. It sort of worried me. About Tilda, not you. Tilda had this crazy idea . . ." He gave a nervous half laugh. "I'm almost embarrassed to say it."

"No," said Martin. "Go on. I want to know. What's she worried about?" He smiled to encourage him. Martin knew he had a sweet smile. Women turned limp and stupid when they saw it. Pastors too, who were just like women really. Male or female, they were all the fluttery same.

"Well, look, this has got to be just between you and me," said Pastor Mike. "Technically I'm violating a confidence here. It would be as much as my job is worth if it got out that I had spoken with you about this. It's just that I'm really concerned about Tilda."

"I don't want to get you in trouble, Pastor, but if you're concerned, I'm her husband, I would like to know if something's wrong with her."

The pastor continued to dither. Martin really was tempted to cave his head in. "Well, it sounds ridiculous I know," he continued finally. "Tilda—she had some crazy idea that you might be possessed—by a demon."

Martin stared—gaped—at him. "A demon?"

"I know," said the pastor, shaking his head. "I know, I know. The thing is: I've been pastoring awhile now and . . . Well, I've found that women have a tendency to take these sorts of ideas a bit too, you know, literally. But I thought, all the same, it might mean that something was going on between you two that I should know about. Some kind of marital problem where maybe I could be of some help."

"A demon?" Martin said again. He started to grin. "You've got to be kidding me."

"I know!" said the pastor. He laughed. "I mean, I'm not going to do an exorcism, but I thought maybe if you needed some counseling . . . I don't know. Something."

Martin also laughed. "A demon," he said, yet again, shaking his head.

Then both men stood and laughed some more.

And Martin thought: *So that's that. She knows.*

# PART FOUR

# THE ALIEN CORN

*You have to understand. I had never once challenged him. The Recruiter, I mean. Never once. He had given me my assignments and I had carried them out and I had never been anything but a good soldier, as good as I knew how to be. There would have been no point in raising objections really. He always knew what I thought before I thought it anyway, so why would I bother saying it out loud? Half the time, he answered me before I spoke to him. And you know, the Division had given meaning to my life, a purpose to it, even a kind of passion to it after Charlotte went off her own way. But it had also covered me in blood. In death. Not that I minded that so much. The people I killed needed killing. But if I lost my faith in the Recruiter, then I would lose my faith in the reason for the killing, and what would I be left with?*

*So now here I was in the brick building again, the Division offices in DC, sitting across from him again where he sat stone-faced as always with his hands clasped on the desktop. I had filed my mission report on Warren Gentry and he had summoned me here for a follow-up.*

*"Many people have said many things about me, Poetry Boy. Called me many names," he said. "But no one has ever called me effervescent. No one has ever accused me of having a sparkling, sprightly sense of fun, or a blithe and abandoned air."*

*"They just don't know you like I do, chief," I said.*

*"And yet, you're trying to tell me that Warren Gentry, a man who makes his living exposing the idiocy and corruption of our government, would kill a story simply because Thaddeus Blatt asked him to?"*

*I shrugged. "There was no story. The plan didn't go anywhere."*

*"So says Gentry."*

*"And Blatt. They both say it. And what do we have that proves otherwise? I mean, you said it yourself: No money changed hands between them. And if Kemal Balkin has something on Gentry, I never saw it. His picture wasn't in the trophy room."*

*"As I understand it, the trophy room was where Balkin displayed his high-level acquisitions. Gentry's just an independent journalist."*

*"Still, there's no evidence Balkin had anything on him. Why would he?"*

*"Well, he is a pervert," the Recruiter said.*

*"This is Washington, chief. If you're going to start persecuting perverts, you're going to need a bigger division. Anyway, he's just a gay guy."*

*"Last time I checked the holy Bible, homosexuality was still an abomination before God."*

*"He's seen worse."*

*"Be that as it may."*

*"We can't just assume anyone who runs afoul of Leviticus is in Kemal Balkin's pocket," I said. "Gentry goes to those clubs where they wear leather and smack each other around. He's not ashamed of it. He and his buddies take selfies outside the place and post them on social media. How could Blatt blackmail a guy like that?"*

*I couldn't tell whether the Recruiter was just staring at me blankfaced and motionless like he usually did or if he had actually turned to an obsidian statue of personified moral indignation. The silence went on so long between us, I began to sweat. I sweat a lot around the Recruiter.*

*Finally, he spoke, but very slowly, "I'm trying to think of the words with which to explain the nature of sin to a man so soulless he's little more than a dumb animal."*

*"I'll wait."*

*"I suppose I could try to detail the strategies of Satan, how he convinces us we can erase the pain of our shame by calling good evil and evil good, and how in this way, he entices us further and further down the road to our spirit's destruction. But I know the very idea of Satan's existence would shatter like glass against the stone wall of your mistakenly cherished sophistication—where so much of reality has shattered before."*

*As almost always with the Recruiter, I did not know how much of this was irony and how much, if any of it, was supposed to be taken seriously. There were plenty of gay agents in the Division. And sure, the Recruiter tormented them with his idea of their sinfulness, but he tormented all his agents about anything he thought might be a weak point in their psychology. That was his whole modus operandi. It was how he tested our breaking points. But he sure as hell never hesitated to use an agent's homosexuality if he thought they could seduce some jihadist into a fatal patch of trouble or something like that. So while I had to imagine he was telling me something here, I thought it had to be something other than what he was pretending to tell me.*

*He went on: "Maybe it would save time if I simply said that just because your vacuous modern sensibility leaves you feeling comfortable with the idea of men torturing one another for sexual pleasure, that doesn't mean Gentry isn't doing other things as well—things that might even dent your faithless complacency and, more to the point, the faithless complacency of the public at large and so leave him vulnerable to extortion."*

*By now, to be honest, I was totally confused. Was it possible this whole assignment had sprung up out of the Recruiter's disapproval of*

*Warren Gentry's private life? That wouldn't have been like him. Which made me nervous. Thaddeus Blatt claimed the Recruiter was going off the rails. That he'd drifted way beyond the outlines of our brief. Maybe news of Kemal Balkin's trophy room had made him paranoid, or maybe it had just made him furious, too eager to expose whoever was trying to manipulate members of our government with their various, not to mention widespread, abominations against God.*

*"Can I ask you something?" I said.*

*"You can ask."*

*"This Isabella Gonzalez kidnapping."*

*"I thought I already lied to you about that. What more do you want?"*

*"Was that one of our hits?"*

*"You think I would manipulate a pair of drug lords so that one of them might kill the other and incidentally help us strangle the flow of poisonous filth into our country, potentially saving the lives of thousands?"*

*"Well, when you put it that way, yeah. That sounds exactly like what you would do."*

*"So?"*

*"Well, the girl's not a drug lord. She looks like she's only thirteen or fourteen. And I saw her on the news after she was rescued. She was banged up. Like someone had knocked her around. Plus the cops said she might have been molested."*

*At last the Recruiter's obsidian seemed to melt back into too, too solid flesh. He sat back in his chair, his hands sliding toward him across the desk until they settled down to rest on his stomach. His expression didn't change, but he did draw in a long, audible breath through his nose, which made me wonder if he was sighing.*

*"It's possible you should begin to think about a new line of employment," he said.*

*"Why? Because I don't think we should smack little girls around to get our work done?"*

*"Because you wonder if we would. You wonder if I would allow that. And because if you had the slightest understanding of the true structure of the moral universe, it would have begun to occur to you by now that there are operators ascendant within our government who may soon seek to wreak a terrible vengeance on me and my division for having done exactly what they themselves assigned me to do. Which, by the way, is behavior also in character for those steeped in the sin whose nature I can't explain to you because you are drowning in unbelief like a pig wallowing in quicksand."*

*It's hard to describe what I was feeling then, the nausea of uncertainty inside me. Did he want me to leave the Division? To quit? To abandon him when his superiors were planning to destroy him in order to cover their own tracks? Where would I go? What would I do? Who would I be then?—that was the real question.*

*"Are you asking for my resignation?" I said. I didn't recognize the sound of my own voice when I said it.*

*And of all the unreadable gestures the Recruiter had ever made to me, the gesture he made then was the most completely mysterious one of all.*

*"Warren Gentry is working for Thaddeus Blatt now, Poetry Boy. For no money, as far as I can tell. That was what brought him to my attention. That—not his various abominations before the Lord. Gentry's a good investigator. And that means there's a storm coming. And if you've lost your faith in what we do and how we do it, you will not survive it. You should get out while you can."*

*I remember—I don't know, maybe half an hour later—standing on the Mall with the spire of the Washington Monument rising into the blue sky on one side of me and the image of the Lincoln Memorial's shimmering in the reflecting pool on the other. My hands were in my pockets and I felt I should be heading somewhere, walking somewhere, but there was nowhere to go. So many dead. My best friend. A woman I loved. The man I thought I was supposed to be. And why?*

*I just stood still there. Could I believe in my leader? Could I believe in my country? Could I believe in myself?*

*There was nowhere for me to go.*

# 29

"So," said Margaret Whitaker. "Let's talk about Gwendolyn Lord."

Winter laughed. "How did I know you were going to say that?"

The therapist sat stately in her therapist chair. She steepled her fingers under her lower lip and swiveled very slightly this way and that. She already had a sense of how the rest of this session was going to go. How the rest of their therapy was going to go. She was certain now that she'd been right when she began to suspect that their work together was nearing termination. The thought of that was painful to her. She was going to miss these talks with Winter. Though she knew her attraction to him was simple countertransference, a normal part of the therapeutic process, it did not feel like countertransference. It felt like love, or at least what she thought love would have felt like had she ever really been in love. And while he, in leaving her, would be leaving to begin the life that was awaiting him, she, in losing him, would be beginning that journey to what was awaiting her—her and all flesh—the end of things, an end she could already sense approaching.

"How is it going with you two?" she asked.

He hesitated only a second before he answered: "We spent the night together."

Margaret nodded slowly. She was slightly surprised to find this had no effect on her. But then, her feelings for him were not—not primarily—physical. They were rather a desire for a life she might have had, a life more like life than the life she had led. "So I take it her religious beliefs didn't get in the way."

"She said they didn't matter because we were made for each other—in heaven, where things are made apparently."

"She said that?"

"Pretty much word for word."

"Well. Okay. How do you feel about that? Knowing you as I do, I have to assume you don't believe it."

He massaged his eyes with his fingertips. He was hiding his face from her, Margaret thought. That didn't matter though. She could still sense his excitement and pleasure at what was happening to him.

"I'm in love with her," he said.

Margaret had felt nothing much at the news he and Gwendolyn had spent the night together. But she felt this. She felt it like a red-hot pang. She reminded herself that preparing Winter to find a relationship like this one with Gwendolyn was everything she had been working toward. It didn't help.

"And the feeling is mutual, I take it," she said. "Gwendolyn's in love with you too? You being made for her in heaven and all."

He smiled. Smirked, Margaret thought. He was wearing a pair of black jeans. He reached into the right-hand watch pocket, that obscure little pouch just below the beltline where people used to keep their pocket watches in the days when they had pocket watches, and their coins in the days when they had coins. He drew out a metal cross on a metal chain.

"She gave me this," he said. "She wanted me to wear it for protection against demons."

Margaret lifted one eyebrow. "Demons?"

"I know. Don't get the wrong idea. She's a highly intelligent woman. She just really believes in all this stuff."

"I can't help but notice you're not wearing it."

"How can I? I'd feel like a hypocrite. Not to mention a superstitious idiot."

"But you haven't left it at home either."

"I've been transferring it from one pair of pants to the next."

"Why's that, do you think?"

He snorted. "Damned if I know. I'm touched by it as a token of her concern, I guess. But also . . . Can I tell you something without your laughing at me?"

"Absolutely not. Nothing cracks me up like the confidences of my clients. Why? Are you going to tell me you believe in demons now? You're going to become a supernaturalist just to please your girlfriend?"

He laughed and rolled his eyes. "Doubtful. No. But . . ." Winter tucked the gleaming trinket back into his watch pocket. He leaned forward in the client's armchair, his elbows on his knees. He did not look at Margaret. He looked into the air between them, as if he were searching for something there. "You know how we were talking last time about finding myself, finding who I really was. I was thinking . . . It's not that I believe Gwendolyn and I were made for each other in heaven or anything. But I do have this sense that I loved her even before I met her. That there was an image of her already in my mind and so I knew her when I saw her in real life. Is that crazy?"

"Go on. I'll let you know when you're crazy."

"I was thinking, well, if there was an image of her in my mind, then maybe . . ."

The pang of sorrow in Margaret's chest had resolved itself into an almost-pleasant melancholy. She could see that Winter was beginning to crack the puzzle on his own. Her work was just about done.

"Maybe?" she said.

"Well, maybe there was an image of me in my mind too. So I would know myself when I found me in real life just like I knew Gwendolyn."

"And what is that image?" Margaret Whitaker asked.

He plonked back in the chair. He sighed. "After that meeting with the Recruiter . . . After he suggested I should resign because I didn't have enough faith in him to face the coming congressional investigations . . . I stood in the Mall and I felt . . . just lost, you know. Adrift. Because who would I be without him? As long as he was sending me on missions, I didn't have to believe in anything. He did the believing for me. So who would I be now? And I guess ultimately that's why I decided to turn myself into . . ."

In her melancholy, Margaret smiled gently. "Poetry Boy," she said. "An English professor."

He nodded. "Right. Right. So I teach at the university and try to write books I don't want to write. And then I keep going off on the trail of these insane crimes, these insane murders, because really I'm not what I'm pretending to be. Or at least, that's not all I am. I'm also something else. Something the Recruiter saw in me from the beginning. And without him, ever since I left the Division, what I've really been is . . ." His mouth opened and closed but no more words came.

"What?" said Margaret. "You've been what?"

"A killer without a cause," said Cameron Winter. And then his eyes grew bright and he looked up and smiled at her.

And he said it again: "A killer without a cause."

# 30

When he came out of Margaret's office building, he stood on the sidewalk in the bright morning light, the first heat of the day enclosing him. He stood, going nowhere, his fingers in the pockets of his jeans. He was aware that he was standing just as he had stood when he had left the Recruiter's office that day years ago, and that he felt now exactly the way he had felt then. Just as stymied. Just as lost. Just as uncertain of who he was, and what he was supposed to do next. It was as if the time between that day and this had never passed, as if he were back in DC by the reflecting pool with no real sense of himself, nowhere to go.

A killer without a cause, he thought.

Maybe the whole point of his therapeutic journey had been—to paraphrase the poet—to arrive where he had started, and to know the place for the first time. To discover that his life had not been an accident, or that its accidents had somehow been put to the service of a mysterious intention, a journey to a destination as inevitable as it was unexpected. The idea filled him with a dread almost indistinguishable from excitement. He did not know if he was terrified or thrilled. Or both.

He straightened. *What now?* he wondered. He drew a deep breath. He removed his hands from his pockets. He took a single step.

A black car pulled up sharply to the curb beside him.

Winter pivoted, tense, alert. He had the Glock in his ankle holster. He had his hands by his side. He was ready to move, to dodge and draw, as the car's passenger window slowly came down.

He saw Arthur Dimmerman sitting behind the wheel. At first, he was surprised. Then he was not surprised.

Dimmerman said nothing.

Winter heard the car's doors unlock. He forced his breath to slow. His eyes went over the car: a BMW coupe, two doors, tight in back. He stepped to it, peered in to examine the rear seat and the floor. No ambush. No one there. He opened the passenger door and lowered himself into the seat next to Dimmerman.

Even before he shut the door, the bimmer was moving. The tires let out a single high syllable as the car cut into the passing traffic. Dimmerman drove swiftly through the city streets. The Capitol dome was in front of them, then gone. The campus was beside them, then gone. They were on the highway. The lake in the distance sank sparkling away. Neither man said a word.

Winter stole a glance at the attorney. Expensive blue suit. Pink shirt open at the collar. Coiffed sandy hair. His profile—could a profile be coiffed? Winter wondered. If it could be, Dimmerman's was.

"I see you've been promoted to chauffeur," Winter said.

Dimmerman couldn't hide the flash of anger in his eyes, the twist of anger on his lips. But he said nothing.

"No, really, congratulations," said Winter.

Dimmerman said nothing.

They drove on in silence.

The city faded. There were summer trees all around them. Suburban exit signs came quickly, one after another, then more slowly with longer intervals between. Beyond the highway's pavement, there was nothing but forest and fields. The bimmer went fast, but Winter felt Dimmerman was holding it back, keeping it within spitting distance of the speed limit. He didn't want to deal with the police.

They left the highway. They went past gas stations and a diner. They turned and went past low buildings, shops and garages. Another turn. No buildings now. A thin line of trees with an open field beyond, that's all. The lonelier the road became, the more Winter was aware of the Glock on his ankle and the tension in his ready gun hand.

Dimmerman slowed the bimmer down and turned onto a dirt road, no more than a path really. All at once, they were surrounded by sunflowers, as if they had been rushed by a summery mob. The tall green stalks clustered at the windows and blocked the view. The yellow blossoms seemed to lean toward them, alien eyes peering in through the glass. Winter could not help but look back at them. Weird they were, beautiful and alive. Only when the car began to ease to a stop did he face forward again. He looked out through the windshield. He saw the dirt lane open into a clearing up ahead.

The bimmer came to a slow stop with its front fender at the place where the tall blooms ended. Dimmerman shut off the engine. The sunflowers gathered close on either side, peering in at them. Winter's right hand edged down along the side of his knee, closer to the Glock.

Dimmerman gestured at the top of the windshield. Winter ducked his head and looked out and saw the helicopter descending.

Winter did not know one brand of private chopper from another, but he could see this was a luxury machine. It descended majestically out of a pale-blue sky dotted with high small clouds. Even inside the car, the windows closed, he could hear the uncanny quiet of its propellers.

Dimmerman gave him a sour look. Winter smiled, just to annoy him. He popped the door open and stepped out.

Winter walked past the last sunflowers toward the clearing. He could hear birdsong and the buzz of bees joyful among the great petals. Lines from Keats's "Ode to Autumn" flickered in his memory, meaningless. The birdsong stopped and the bee-buzz was overcome as the muted throb of the chopper grew louder. Soon, Winter felt the wind in his hair. The petals of the flowers, shoulders high, trembled in the wash from the propellers. The leaves shuddered and the stems swayed.

Winter stepped out into the clearing, the flowers at his back. He stood and watched as the chopper's skids settled slowly into the grass. The pilot cut the engine. Winter heard the bees again as the propellers slowed. The chopper door came open.

Winter had not seen Thaddeus Blatt in person for years, not since that day in his apartment when Blatt showed up accompanied by the man who would become Tat Man. Winter was impressed by how little Blatt had changed in the intervening time. He must have been close to sixty now, but he looked no different, or not much. Short though he was, he was still solid and muscular in his pale slacks and tight aqua shirt. He hadn't lost any hair to speak of, and whatever marks age had scored into his features had been surgically removed as cleanly as the marks of corruption. His posture straightened as he emerged from under the propellers. Winter remembered he had read somewhere that Blatt had recently traded in his second wife for a younger model. Maybe that was what kept his step so springy as he walked toward him over the low-cut grass.

"Winter," Blatt said with a friendly smile. He stopped about five yards away, not close enough to offer his hand. That saved Winter the trouble of refusing to shake it, which would have made him feel petty. "You asked to see me." He spread his hands as much as to say: *Here am I.*

Winter nodded. "I want to find Trey White. The third murderer. I want to get to him before your gizmo experiment fails on him, too, and someone else gets murdered."

Thaddeus smiled sadly. He shook his head, as if with regret. "It's a problem for me, Winter. Legal. Reputational. I offered you a solution: You draw out the Recruiter. He takes responsibility—for this and all his crimes. And the whole thing is over. But you turned me down. So as things are . . ." He finished with a shrug and another sad smile.

Winter sighed. "Oh, hell, Blatt. I don't care what happens to you. Getting justice done is beyond my power here. I just want to prevent more innocent people from getting killed. Tell me where Trey White is and I'll take care of the rest."

Blatt's regretful smile was sympathetic now. "I understand. I do. But listen, there's nothing to worry about. The situation is well in hand. We've got this. You're not required to play the hero here."

Winter gave a humorless laugh. "Yeah, I'm not reassured. A child has been murdered already. A teenaged girl was raped and murdered. A mother was murdered. That's not to mention the doers, the guys you experimented on, the guys you had Tattoo Man put down. No loss, sure, but just by way of an accurate body count. Which would have included me, too, if Tat Man had had his way. It's time to end the experiment, Thaddeus. Send that ink-stained lunatic to take Trey White out. I don't care. But do it now, before some other innocent gets killed."

The two men stood facing each other, surrounded by the vast flower field in the warmth of the sun. The chopper sat by like a great dark insect. The bees hummed and frolicked amid the blooms.

"Well, you know, that's another thing," Thaddeus Blatt said. "Even if I had the Recruiter. I don't want to end this. Not yet. It's too early. I mean, I don't want to sound grandiose or anything, but long term, the implications of what we're doing are world changing. If this works? We're talking about putting an end to crime. Putting an end to human evil. Right? How great a potential benefit to mankind does there have to be before it occurs to you that—you know, tragic as it is—a death here and there is not that high a price to pay?"

"I don't know, Thaddeus," Winter said, shaking his head. "How much misery do you have to add to the world before it occurs to you that, rich as you are, you might still be an idiot? Your theory might be wrong?"

Thaddeus Blatt's sculpted features were brightened by a sparkling white grin. That bright row of chompers couldn't have been natural either, Winter thought. Why didn't the guy just buy himself a whole new body?

"People always say that though," Blatt said in a friendly tone. "When one of these transitional moments comes along. They always say things like: Don't sail the ocean sea, it's dangerous. Don't try to build a flying machine. Don't go to Mars. You would not believe the effort and expense that went into securing the permissions and authority and equipment that were required to get this project underway. Three tries is all we could manage. That's all we're going to get. And yeah, okay, we had setbacks on two of the three. But there's no evidence as of now that the third attempt is failing. The opposite, in fact. We've got a close eye on it and it all looks fine. If there's any sign of trouble, it will be taken care of. You have my word on that. All right? But imagine. If it succeeds. Imagine what that would mean, Winter."

Winter rubbed his eyes. He knew he was wasting his breath. What was a child's life when compared to a billionaire's big idea? What was a young girl's rape and murder in balance with his dreams of glory? If Winter had never felt the full weight of his anachronistic existence, he felt it now. He had been haunted by his helplessness and failure since this whole thing had begun, but here in this sunflower field he felt the burden of them was overwhelming. Should he threaten Blatt? Talk tough? What the hell was he going to threaten him with? A professor with a headful of poetry and a six-shot Glock on his ankle, versus this man who descended out of the sky like a titan, who manipulated governments like a puppet master god?

"Anyway," said Blatt. "I didn't come all this way to discuss my private business with you. I want to talk to you about something relevant to your own life. You mentioned one of my employees."

Winter nodded. "Your private assassin. Tat Man."

Blatt laughed. "Tat Man. I like it. I'm gonna call him that from now on. You recognize him though, right? You remember the way he used to be."

"I remember," Winter said.

"I'm afraid he's had some kind of psychic break since then. He's become increasingly unmanageable. As you experienced in your apartment, I'm sorry to say. That was not at all what I intended. I want you to know that."

"Oh good. That makes me feel much better," said Winter.

"The truth is, I could use a man with skills like his but with a little more—self-discipline, I guess we'll call it. I mean, let's face it: Your talents are being wasted while you bore twenty-year-olds talking about poetry no one gives a shit about anymore. And say what you will about me, I am a very, very generous employer."

"We haven't got time for me to say what I will about you," Winter told him.

More laughter, more bright teeth. "I know, I know. But whatever my flaws may be, I'm not the bad guy here, Winter. That would be your homicidal, jingoistic, Bible-thumping, homophobic friend, the Recruiter. I mean, you think *I'm* lawless? What about him? Him and his 'Invisibles.' Moving around in the shadows, interfering with my legitimate business interests. Damaging my reputation with my investors. Talk about a psychic break. The man's completely out of his mind."

"Right. This must be the same pitch you made to Warren Gentry when you brought him over to your side," Winter asked. "'Stop investigating my plans to arm the lunatics in Lunatic-stan and help me bring down the real evil of the Division.' Right? That's why he recognized me right away for what I was—because you'd told him all about me." Winter shook his head. "The Recruiter thought you were blackmailing Gentry because there was no money trail. But you didn't have to pay Gentry. And you didn't have to blackmail him either. You just offered him the Division, the best story of his life. He was a reporter. The real kind. They don't make many of them anymore, but he was one. You traded him a great story about us in exchange for killing a minor story about you."

"Gentry would have paid me to help him expose what your murdering boss was doing."

"He would have. Until he realized what you were. Then he found Jesus and turned on you and started working to expose you. And you sent Tat Man to pump some bullets into him."

"That's the way the Recruiter tells it . . ." But Blatt stopped there. He raised his two hands as if in surrender. The bees buzzed in the sunflowers, and Winter thought of Keats again . . . "more, / And still more, later flowers for the bees . . ." "Look. Look," said Thaddeus Blatt. "I don't want to stand here relitigating the past. This is about—let's call it two competing visions of the future. All right? Yes, I admit, people—a few people—have been murdered in the course of what I'm trying to accomplish. But what I'm trying to accomplish is to get rid of murder altogether, get rid of the bad guys, heal their sick minds, make the world a better place. The Recruiter—how many people are dead because of him? Right? And for what? He just wants to go on, taking the bad guys out one by one, here and there, whac-a-mole, same as people have done forever. And what happens? You kill one, two more rise up. It's—it's nihilistic, really. Help me get through this, and we have a chance to eradicate evil itself. Like, all of it. I mean, just being blunt here, that should be an easy choice to make."

Winter closed his eyes and breathed and opened them. He was beginning to grow weary of this conversation, or maybe of the world.

"Thanks anyway, Blatt," he said.

Blatt threw up his hands and let them fall to his sides with a slap. "You can't say I didn't try," he said.

"No," said Winter. "You tried." He could not keep the weariness out of his voice. "But you were right: it's an easy choice to make."

Blatt gave an oh-well tilt of his head, and started to turn back to his luxury helicopter. He paused though. He glanced back at Winter. "You do know how foolish . . . well, *foolish* . . . that's not the word I want. I mean . . ."

"Anachronistic," said Winter.

"Right. Right. Anachronistic. You do know how anachronistic you're being, don't you?"

"I do," said Winter. "I do."

Once again, Blatt threw his hands up. "I tried."

"You tried."

Blatt walked back to his chopper and climbed in. The bird's engine coughed. A banditry of chickadees took flight out of the sunflowers. "And gathering swallows twitter in the skies," Winter thought. The chopper's rotors began to spin with their strangely quiet flutter. How odd it was, thought Winter, that he kept thinking about "To Autumn," in the heat of July. The chopper's skids rocked and lifted. The helicopter rose into the air. Probably it was the final stanza's intimations of death that had brought the poem to mind, Winter thought. He tilted his head back to watch the big black whirlybird rise and rise, then dart away over the trees.

When the chopper had risen above earshot and grown small in the distance, and the buzzing of the bees could be heard again, and the chickadee song could be heard as well, Winter turned to head back to Dimmerman's BMW.

And there stood the Tat Man.

He stood amid the sunflowers. He must have been hiding among them all this time. Winter realized he should have thought of that, but he hadn't, he just hadn't. Now it was too late. Tat Man already had his pistol drawn. It was leveled at Winter's chest, dead center. He was only ten yards away or so, too close to miss.

Winter was fast. He didn't waste time thinking. He dove to the side. The Tat Man pulled the trigger and the gun made a soft spitting sound. Winter felt a stinging shock in his shoulder. He hit the ground and rolled and reached for the Glock in his ankle holster. It seemed to him he was quick on the draw, quick enough to get a shot off before the Tat Man fired again. But time—or his sense of time—had taken a strange turn and become haphazard. Yes, the gun was in his hand, but when he tried to lift it, the Tat Man was already standing beside him. Impossible he could have reached him so fast, yet there he was. He brought a heavy boot down on Winter's wrist and pinned it to the soil. Winter tried to lift his hand but he was too weak, way too weak. His fingers trembled and went limp. The Tat Man, smiling, bent down and plucked the gun out of his grip. Winter realized then that he had been shot not with a bullet but with something else. A dart? A capsule? He didn't know. He couldn't think. Whatever had been injected into his bloodstream, it was sending his mind haywire.

He knew only that he ought to be afraid. This was the last of him for certain. He was helpless. He was done for. He ought to be terrified. But the drug had robbed him of fear.

All he felt was sorrow. All he thought of was Gwendolyn. He was not supposed to die. It would shatter her, he thought. He felt as if his heart were breaking.

The world wavered once then went away.

# 31

Once, years ago, during his time in the Division, Winter had been punched so hard, he developed an abdominal hernia. He was in prison in some Communist hellhole or other at the time, but somehow, the Division managed to get him sprung. As soon as he returned home, he had to have surgery. He had never been under anesthesia before. He found it a wild experience. "Count backwards from one hundred," the doctor said. Winter got to ninety-eight and he was in the recovery room. Like that, like a crash cut in a movie, or a magician clapping his hand. There was no puff of smoke, no wave of a wand, but time disappeared and the surgery was over. He had opened his eyes and turned his head on the pillow. And there was the Recruiter. He was sitting in a chair by his bedside, his arms on the chair arms, his back straight, his face stony and expressionless.

Winter said—these were the first words out of his mouth when he came to—he said: "How can you believe in an afterlife when they can just turn you off like that? Like a light bulb."

"That's so you don't have to endure the long centuries till the end of days," the Recruiter answered gravely. "You'll open your eyes and you'll be in the kingdom of heaven. Not you, of course. You'll be damned. But the people of God, I mean."

As it had been then, so it was with him now. It seemed to him no time had passed, and he was suddenly aware he was in motion. Through the heavy fug that still hung in his mind, his situation came back to him. He had the sense to lie still and keep his eyes closed. To tense with subtle stealth in order to test his range of motion. His hands were bound behind him. That was metal he felt on his wrists, so he was in cuffs, heavy cuffs, not a zip tie. His back was bent forward and his legs were bent at the knees, so he was enclosed in a small space. He had to fight down a shudder of panic at that. Was he in a coffin? Had they buried him alive? But that made no sense. If they had wanted him dead, he'd be dead. He stole a blurry look through half-lowered eyelids. He was in a vehicle. A loud one. Bouncing. Not on a road. In air. Judging by the thwapping rhythm of the noise, he was in the back of a small chopper. The seats were behind his back. He couldn't turn to look at them without alerting whoever was there that he was awake. He forced himself to remain still.

The sound of the rotors changed. He felt the machine lurch into a descent. His stomach was already sour from the drug and the motion made vomit come up his throat. He swallowed it back down and suppressed a groan.

The chopper dropped swiftly, then swiftly slowed. Winter's stomach churned, but he did not move or make a sound. He felt the delicate landing, the skids finding their place on the surface. He heard the engine noise cut and die away. He heard the door open.

"All right," someone said. Winter thought it was Tat Man speaking but he wasn't sure.

Then, his ankles were gripped roughly. He was dragged out of the back of the chopper. He dropped and his back hit the ground hard. He grunted and coughed. He couldn't help it.

He was grabbed by the front of his shirt. He tried to stay limp as he was hauled to a sitting position. He let his head loll to one side as if he was still unconscious. But it was no good. He was smacked in the side of the face—with a gun barrel, he thought. Not hard but hard enough.

"Open your eyes," Tat Man said.

There was no use carrying on the charade. He opened his eyes and looked into the killer's round face. It was a mad face, bright yet somehow dead, like the face of a crazy snake. Tat Man grinned. He held up a pistol. It was a Glock, not Winter's, bigger, a 19, with maybe a fifteen-bullet mag, maybe more.

"Walk or I'll blow your kneecap off," Tat Man said. "I want to."

With a growl, he dragged Winter up off the ground. Winter struggled to get his feet under him. He had a single second to take in his surroundings. His glasses were gone. His eyesight was all right, but not great. The world looked fuzzy. He caught a glimpse of cornstalks, taller than a man. Then the Tat Man grabbed him by the back of his shirt collar and jammed the barrel of the Glock into the back of his neck. It hurt. Winter grunted. He told himself again that if Blatt wanted him dead, he'd be dead, but the thought didn't comfort him much. Tat Man was so crazy he might kill him just for sport. And he was sure to kill him eventually.

What happened next happened fast. Tat Man held his shirt, and kept the gun pressed into his spine, and marched him forward. The world was jostled around him. Cornstalks. A small white building. He stumbled as he tripped over his own feet. Then he was inside. In a hall for a moment, then pushed through a door into a small room.

The first thing he saw there was Arthur Dimmerman, waiting for him. Then he saw the shiny black walls made of some material he couldn't name. There was a metal chair in the middle of the floor. Nothing else, not a single thing.

The Tat Man shoved him again. Groggy and with his arms cuffed behind him, Winter lost his balance and fell to the floor. The floor was hard and white, made of some kind of acrylic like in a lab. As Winter lay there, Tat Man tried to kick him in the stomach. The kick landed off target and hit him higher, in his ribs. Winter let out a strangled gasp. Drops of vomit flew out between his teeth.

"Knock it off," Dimmerman said to the Tat Man. "That'll only make this harder. We'll be done in an hour at most, then you can do whatever you want to him. Meanwhile, have some patience. Try not to act like a lunatic."

Muddy as his mind was, Winter had to force himself to take that in, remember it. This was the plan. They were going to question him. For what? The Recruiter's location probably. His contact number. Then when they got the information, Dimmerman would hand him over to Tat Man and Tat Man would torture him to death for his personal pleasure. He thought of Gwendolyn again. He knew the thought of her would be worse than the Tat Man's torture. The agony of knowing what his death would do to her—that would be worse.

Winter tried to say something—something nasty—but he couldn't get his face organized. Noises came out of his mouth, but no words.

"Get his shoes and his belt and empty his pockets," Dimmerman said.

Tat Man went to work. He pulled off Winter's shoes. He pulled off his belt, fast like drawing a sword. He reached into one pocket of his jeans, then another, then another, then the last. He pulled out Winter's wallet and his keys.

"The ankle holster too," said Dimmerman.

"I got that already," said Tat Man. "And his glasses. And his phone."

"All right then, put him in the chair."

Winter's mind was beginning to clear. Not all at once, but intermittently. It was like the moon coming out from behind clouds. There were moments of bright-white clarity. Then the clouds passed over again. He told himself to stay cool. He told himself to have patience. The drug had left him weak and sick. If he tried a move on Tat Man now, the assassin would slap him down easy as a schoolyard bully with a kid half his age. All Winter could do was force the bright moon of his clear mind out into the open as much as he could. Pay attention. Watch for his chance.

And there would be a chance, he told himself. He knew there would be. They had made a mistake, and he was going to make them pay for it. God was his witness. If there was a God. Maybe there wasn't. But there was a Gwendolyn. So he could not die.

"Get up," said Tat Man. But he didn't wait for him to stand. He grabbed him by the shirtfront again, getting plenty of chest hair in his grip this time. Winter gritted his teeth and growled with pain as Tat Man dragged him to his feet. He grunted when Tat Man shoved him down into the chair, hard.

"Try not to kill him yet," Dimmerman said dryly.

Tat Man walked around in back of Winter, out of his sight. He jammed the barrel of the Glock into his neck again, a stunning blow and stunningly painful. Then he drew the gun away, out of Winter's reach. He had just wanted to let him know it was there.

Dimmerman, meanwhile, stepped up in front of him. "He wants to kill you now," he said to Winter. "You know that, right? If you try to hurt me, it'll be the last thing you ever do."

Winter tried to grin. It wasn't easy. He wanted to say something—something like, *It might be worth it.* But he still couldn't get the words in order. Anyway, what good would it do him? Dimmerman was right. If he made a play now, he'd wind up with his brains all over his face. The best he could do was stare death at Dimmerman as the lawyer unlocked his cuffs, then brought one arm around and cuffed it to the chair arm, then brought the other arm around and pulled another pair of cuffs from his jacket pocket and cuffed that arm to the other chair arm. He did it efficiently and fast. It only took a couple of seconds.

Dimmerman moved away. His leg hit the chair as he did and Winter heard the chair leg scrape against the floor. Winter couldn't see either man now, the lawyer or Tat Man. Or wait—yes, he could. He couldn't see them clearly, but they were dimly reflected on the shiny black surface of the walls. They were faint bright shapes in the gleaming darkness.

Dimmerman pressed something against the back of Winter's head. Something metal. Not a gun this time. Something else. Winter peered at his own reflection to see what it was: a short helmet of some kind, colored gold. It rose up the back of his head and curved over the top to cover half his pate and press close against his temples. Winter heard a buzzing noise and felt the two pieces of the solid metal retention strip come together beneath his chin. They tightened around his throat until he began to gag. His tongue stuck out.

"Too tight?" said Dimmerman.

The buzzing noise again, and the retention strip loosened. Not much. Just enough so he could breathe.

Winter's mind was growing clearer and clearer. Even though his reflection was indistinct on the wall, he understood now what the helmet was. It was the same sort of helmet he had seen during his tour of Thaumatix. The guy in the wheelchair had used one. The helmet had read the guy's mind so he could speak and guide a computer.

Dimmerman came back around in front of him. Dapper and coiffed, Winter thought bitterly. And also soulless. When he handed Winter over to Tat Man at the end of this, he would not even think about it. He would not lose even a wink of sleep.

"We need to find your Chief," Dimmerman said. "We need your method of contact, passwords and so on. Plus we need to know what you know and who you've told about our project. I know you're trained to resist torture, so we won't bother with that, not now anyway, not for this. This—well, you can fight the machine for a while if you want, but there's no way the information won't show up somewhere in your brain soon after your mind clears from the drug. And then we'll get it. And then . . ." The tone of Dimmerman's voice changed. Handcuffed to the chair, Winter lifted his head to look at him. Up till this moment, the lawyer had been delivering a bland recitation, giving him the facts of the case in phrases with no emotional charge. But now—Winter could tell—his words had become delicious to him. He was rolling them around on his tongue, tasting them, sucking the juices out of them. They made his eyes brighten. His thin lips curled into a dreamy smile. "Then I will give you to—what did you call him? The Tat Man. I will give you to the Tat Man, and he will tear you apart. Tear you apart. Slowly, Winter. And while you are suffering, and while you are dying, I want you to think of me. I want you to think of what I told you would happen if you toyed with me and I want you to think: *Now—now it is happening to me, just as he said it would.* And then die thinking that. Thinking of me, Winter."

He fell silent, but hesitated there a moment, as if drunk with pleasure, as if Winter was already being torn to pieces. The very thought of it sent Dimmerman into an ecstatic daze.

But Winter was not thinking of Dimmerman. Not even a little. He was forcing the bright moon of clarity to shine in his still-cloudy mind. He was thinking that the handcuffs that held him to the chair arms were strong, good quality, with a double locking mechanism. But he could move his hands a little, slide the cuffs along the arms a little, maybe just enough. He was thinking about the fact that the leg of the chair had scraped when Dimmerman had bumped against it. The chair legs were anchored in thick rubber rings so he could not move it without wrenching the chair free, but the legs themselves were not bolted down. That was good, too.

Winter saw Dimmerman blink and come to himself.

"Well, we don't want to distract you, so we'll be next door, watching, and reading your mind, until we know what we need to know. And then Tat Man can have you."

He made a gesture over Winter's shoulder to where Tat Man was standing. He cocked his head: *Let's go.*

Winter was thinking about the fact that they were going next door, that they would watch him from a nearby room so as not to distract him. They would not be able to see him until they reached that room, so maybe for the next few seconds, while they walked down the hall, he would be invisible to them. Maybe fifteen seconds, or twenty, maybe even a little more if he was lucky.

He was thinking: Maybe just enough slack, maybe just enough time. And the chair wasn't bolted down. And there was Gwendolyn, so he was not allowed to die.

Dimmerman held the door of the room open and Tat Man walked out into the hall. Dimmerman took a last look at Winter, a look dreamy with pleasurable expectations.

Winter was thinking. He could hear Tat Man's footsteps. That was also good. If he listened closely, he would hear when they went through the door into the nearby room so he would know when they would be able to see him again. He was forcing the bright-white light of clarity to stay longer and longer in his mind. He was trying to pay attention to everything.

Dimmerman walked out and closed the door and Winter heard him bolt it from the outside.

On the instant, Winter started moving. The slack on the cuffs was better than he'd hoped. He found he could work his hand around and down to the front of his jeans, to the top of the right-hand pocket. He listened to the men's footsteps in the hall outside. At the same time, he managed to work his thumb into the small, obscure pouch at the top of his pocket, his watch pocket. Tat Man hadn't searched that pocket. Why would he? No one carries pocket watches or spare change anymore. No one carries anything in a watch pocket. Winter heard the footsteps in the hall stop and he knew that Dimmerman and Tat Man had arrived at the door of the nearby room.

Winter dug his thumb deep into the watch pocket and wrapped it in the chain of Gwendolyn's cross.

He heard the door open down the hall. He drew the cross out quickly. He worked his hand to gather up the chain. He closed his fist around the cross so neither the cross nor the chain was visible. He heard the door to the nearby room shut. Dimmerman and the Tat Man were now in there. They could watch him, or they would be able to watch him soon.

Winter was panting with effort. Tired out. He sat still and steadied his breath. He heard a short buzz and, after a second or two, he felt the metal of the helmet grow warm against the back of his head. The shiny black walls of the room began to lighten.

Something was happening. Winter squinted at the wall in front of him. He gripped Gwendolyn's cross in his fist.

He gasped. He cursed.

Fleetingly, he saw his mother's face.

Winter stared, his mouth open. There she was, his mother, right there in the dark of the walls, wavery like something seen underwater, but unmistakably herself. She was not as she was now, in her sixties, but as she used to be when Winter was small. Lovely, but glassy-eyed and distant, unreachable. He forced the childish longing for her from his mind, yet he felt the sorrow of his childhood loneliness as her image faded away.

There followed an image of a town house, dim as if seen through fog. It was the house he had grown up in. His heart greeted the sight of it like the heart of a lost man who stumbles on a familiar place. And there was Charlotte—Charlotte when she was a girl at the height of her perfect, porcelain beauty. For a moment Winter was mesmerized by the sight of that face, mesmerized as he had been in the days when he had loved her so much.

He had to shake himself, growling with the effort to bring himself back into the present. This thing on his head, it was downloading his imagination, it was dumping his mind—his soul—onto the walls around him. Dimmerman was right. He could not fight it. Even if he tried to bury his thoughts of the Recruiter, it would read them before he could hide them away.

He gripped Gwendolyn's cross more tightly in his fist. He felt the edge of it digging into the flesh of his palm. *Good*, he thought. Maybe the pain would distract him. He gripped it harder. But more images appeared on the shiny black walls nonetheless. Sweat beaded on his forehead and began to run from under his arms down his sides, dampening his shirt.

There was his father on the black wall now. There was his old friend Roy. Seemingly random words floated like clouds and burst and were gone. *Breath. Leaf. Thorns.* He needed something to distract him, something to fill his mind with information that would be useless to the men watching in the nearby room.

He tried to recite a poem.

"She walks in beauty like the night," he whispered aloud.

But then, there was Gwendolyn. And, in a panic, he thought: *no, no, no.* The poem had reminded him of her, of that night in the restaurant when she had reached out for his hand. He changed tack. He whispered: "Much have I travell'd in the realms of gold, / And many goodly states and kingdoms seen . . ."

The words appeared on the wall screen as if carved there in stone. A faint image of the sea arose, the Mediterranean. The words and the water melted and ran down the walls and poured into a nothingness above the white floor. But there was Keats's face. Winter focused on a thought of the poet dying in his room above the Spanish Steps in Rome, lying on the little bed with his damp hair plastered to his brow. The tuberculosis had eaten away his lungs. He was only twenty-five. Winter tried to fill his mind with the sorrow of it. The poet's face became water and fell like tears.

"Thou wast not born for death, immortal Bird!" he whispered aloud to the fading image of Keats. He could only call up fragments of the poem. "Perhaps the self-same song that found a path / Through the sad heart of Ruth, when, sick for home, / She stood in tears amid the alien corn . . ."

He focused on the recited words as if he could see them—and he *could* see them in the brightness of the bright black walls.

At the same time, he began to work his hand, to move the metal in his hand and maneuver Gwendolyn's cross up his palm to the tips of his fingers. He thrashed his head in the chair, as if struggling against his own thoughts. But that was just to distract Dimmerman and Tat Man in the next room so they would not notice what he was doing with his hand.

"Thou wast not born for death," he said through gritted teeth. He loved Gwendolyn. He could not—must not—die.

He lost track of the poem. He quickly, desperately returned to the other. "Round many western islands have I been, / Which bards in fealty to Apollo hold . . ."

There was an island on the wall. And the witch Circe who made men into swine. And a Greek ship, a trireme, with its sails thrust out like a warrior's chest . . .

"Then felt I like some watcher of the skies / When a new planet swims into his ken . . ."

The black shiny walls around him had filled with stars and planets. To distract the watching men, he cried out as if in anguish and pitched his body forward. Meanwhile, his hand, as if convulsing, covered the handcuff that was linked to the chair and maneuvered the tip of Gwendolyn's cross into the cuff's keyhole. Shaking his head wildly to create more distraction, he gave his cuffed wrist a sharp twist and turned the cross counterclockwise, freeing the double lock bar. Then, as if convulsing, he twisted the cross clockwise and opened the main lock bar.

"Or like stout Cortez when with eagle eyes, / He star'd at the Pacific . . ." he recited hoarsely.

He giggled, high, like a madman when a picture of the conquistador Balboa appeared—because Keats got it wrong, it was Balboa who discovered the Pacific, not Cortez, and Winter's mind always made the correction whenever he reread the poem.

He gripped the arm of the chair to hide the fact that the cuff on the chair arm was now open.

Then, with a final and triumphant cry—"Silent upon a peak in Darien!"—he collapsed backward, slumping in the chair as if exhausted, and he let his mind go free.

The performance had sapped what little strength the drug had left him. It was now as Dimmerman had said it would be. He didn't have to think of the Recruiter, or of his contact number or their password or the people he had spoken to about the case—Gwendolyn and Livy Swain and Ralph Lorenzo and all the others. The thoughts just burbled up to the surface of his brain somehow and he could feel their images populating the depths of the shiny black walls all around him.

He shuddered in the chair and hung his head and sobbed as if he were weeping in grief—grief and defeat and despair.

But he was not weeping. He was thinking: *Come and get me, you bastards.*

And sure enough, though the time seemed long, though minute after minute passed without a sound from outside the little room, though the information in his brain drained out of him and the images appeared and disappeared on the walls around him until, when he raised his face, he saw his mother again and felt the grief of his oldest loneliness—even so, ultimately, sure enough, Tat Man and Dimmerman had what they wanted. They were done with him.

Winter heard the door of the nearby room open down the hall.

The effects of the drug still weighed on him. Winter felt limp and wasted and he was not sure how fast he could move.

But fast, as it turned out—he could move fast. He wrenched his body to the left and brought his free right hand over, carrying Gwendolyn's cross. He could hear the men's footsteps as they came down the hall toward him, so he knew they could not see him for the next fifteen seconds or so. That was how long it took him to unlock the cuff around his left wrist, working the cross in, turning it counterclockwise then clockwise until he could yank the ring off his wrist and free his hand.

He heard the bolt in the door turning. He was on his feet. He saw the door begin to swing in. He grabbed hold of the heavy metal chair and tried to lift it. It stuck in the rubber rings that held it to the floor. The cross was still in his hand and pressed painfully into his flesh, but there wasn't time to care. He was frightened by how weak he was, how fixed the chair was, but he commanded himself to be not weak but strong. He let out a low, deep growl, wrenched the chair free, and hauled it up into the air.

The door came open. The Tat Man walked in first, the Glock tucked into his belt. Dimmerman was right behind him.

Winter gave a roar and rushed at them.

He saw the Tat Man's startled face and swung the chair with the whole force of his body. Still, it was a feeble blow. The chair legs hit the Tat Man in his chin and chest, but weakly. Tat Man staggered back against Dimmerman. But he would have steadied himself and drawn his gun if Winter had not struck again.

Winter struck again. Bringing the chair legs to bear this time and charging forward so they ploughed into Tat Man straight on. It still wasn't forceful enough to hurt the killer, but it threw him back and he stumbled into Dimmerman and they both fell to the floor.

Winter raised the chair above his head and hurled it down on top of Tat Man as hard as he could.

And he ran.

He had no other choice but that. If he had tried to fight the Tat Man in his condition, he'd have been beaten and killed in a moment, every chance lost. Instead, he took the only gamble left to him. The entryway, the door at the end of the hall. He sprinted for it on his stocking feet, praying that the door would be unlocked, praying that he could get it open, get out, before Tat Man could draw the Glock and fire.

It was a short stretch. He was at the door in a second. He heard a wordless shout behind him. He heard the clatter of the chair being shoved aside. He could feel the final seconds passing before the gunshot. He grabbed the doorknob, turned and pulled. The door opened—just a crack—Winter whisked through it like a wisp of smoke. Tat Man had his gun out, quickly pointed it, pulled the trigger. The gunshot went off, loud as a bomb in the tight space.

But Winter was outside with the door swinging shut behind him. He heard the bullet ricochet.

He spun round, ran blindly, and plunged into the corn.

# 32

He went on running. His shoes were gone. Leaves and stalks that had fallen and dried crunched underneath his socks and sometimes stabbed him painfully. He did not slow. His glasses were gone. The stalks and leaves and husks scratched his face and hurt his eyes. He clawed through them. The handcuffs, still attached to his right wrist, slapped at his flesh and scraped him. The helmet felt heavy on his head. The retention strip felt tight around his throat and made it hard to breathe. He imagined that Dimmerman would tighten the strip with his remote and strangle him. He imagined the Tat Man would run up behind him in the corn row and shoot him down. Fearing that, he dashed out of the row and crashed through the stalks into the next row and then the next one. He hoped he was out of range of the helmet's remote. The stalks rose up above his head but did not close over him. He could see the sky, pale and misty blue. But there was nothing else, no hint of what direction he should take. He was gasping for breath and there was no strength left in his legs. "Except the Will which says to them: 'Hold on!'" he thought. He went on running.

Were they chasing after him? He couldn't know. He didn't dare turn to look behind him. It would slow him down. Surely, whether they were following him or not, they could track the helmet. He could not figure out a way to lose them or how to make a stand and fight them. He knew he could not run much longer. He went on running.

He cut across another row. Something stabbed him in the sole of his foot and he cried out in pain and tumbled sideways through the cornstalks. He turned his body and got his balance back but had no idea which way he was facing. He ran. He did not know if he was running back the way he came. He saw—he thought he saw—something white showing through the green and yellow of the corn. Was it a building? Was it the building he had just come from? He was gasping for breath so hard he sobbed. His legs felt as if they were turning to mush. He smashed through stalks, his cheeks lashed by them. And suddenly, he broke through the edge of the cornfield, stumbling wildly forward as if the field had spat him out.

There was a narrow dirt path ahead of him. There was an old shed on the far side of it. That was the white building he had seen through the corn. Not the building he had come from. It was a small structure of tired clapboard, its their paint peeling. It looked abandoned, but he couldn't be sure. The door was closed and latched as if the place might still be in use.

Gasping hoarsely for breath, he limped across the path toward the building. His lungs were sore. His feet were cut. His socks were wet with blood. The strength was gone from his legs. His face stung and was also bleeding. There was a pain in his right hand, a bad one. It had been there all along but now it forced itself upon his attention. He looked down at it. His hand, with the cuffs still dangling from the wrist, was clenched tightly into a fist, so tightly it took him an effort of will to open his fingers.

Gwendolyn's cross. It lay in his palm in a slather of blood. It was bent out of shape from how hard he'd gripped it. It had opened a gash in his flesh and sunk into it, the bloody chain dangling.

He gasped as he dug the cross out of his palm. He stuffed the cross and its chain back into his pocket. He wiped his pain-burnt palm on his shirt as he stumbled, panting, toward the shed.

It would not be long before they caught up with him. They would track the helmet till they found him. By foot or by car they would run him down. He had minutes at most.

He reached the shed. He lifted his bloody hand to the door latch, a hook latch. He had to rotate the hook to free it. His hands were so shaky, his fingers so weak, he tried three times and could not do it. He cursed and tried a fourth time, using all his focus. The latch snapped free. The door swung outward.

He stumbled inside. Except for the wedge of sunlight pouring through the slightly open door, the shed was windowless, dark. He looked around. He could make out tools on the walls, hanging on hooks, sitting on shelves. A saw. A wrench. An oilcan. Old tools, rusted. There was a wooden stool. There was a workbench. For a moment, he was too tired to think. But he had to think so he forced himself. His eyes scanned the wall in the shadows. He felt the time passing. He knew the Tat Man was coming near.

He saw a bolt cutter, a small one. That was his best bet. He took a faltering step to the wall and wiggled the cutter off its hook. He worked one finger of his left hand under the retention strap around his neck. The pressure of his finger made him gag as he tried to pull the strip away from his throat. If he positioned his head just right, he could put a little distance between the metal and his flesh, just a little. Still, his hand was shaking so badly, he stuck himself with the blade of the bolt cutter as he worked it under the metal. He coughed, feeling the blood trickle down his chest. His eyes filled with tears but he did not stop. He maneuvered the blade under the strip and slid it to the place in the center where the strip's two halves came together.

He heard the car then. Not far away, only a little distance. But it did not sound as if it was moving all that fast. Because they were tracking him, Winter thought. Because Dimmerman was reading the map on his phone and giving Tat Man directions. Winter guessed he might have as much as a minute left before they reached him. Winter wrapped his hands around the bolt cutter and squeezed. The handle dug hard into the gash in his palm. The pain was exquisite, like a dentist's drill on a raw nerve. The tears spilled out of Winter's eyes and streamed down his cheeks. A strangled squeal of suffering came out of him. He squeezed the handles harder, then harder. With a thrill of hope, he felt the blade sink into the gap and begin to spread the strip apart.

The car outside came closer. He could hear the gravel on the dirt track crunching.

And then, he felt a shock of black agony. He heard a loud crack. The bolt cutter blades had broken through the metal strip. Winter gagged again as he twisted the blades to force the two sides apart. Quickly, he set the cutter down on the wooden stool. He grabbed the strips in his two hands and bent them back and peeled the helmet off his head. His hair was plastered to his head with sweat—like Keats's hair on his deathbed. Sweat poured down his brow.

He could hear the car approaching. He heard it slowing on the dirt path. It was just outside the shed. He heard it stop. He couldn't see through his tears and had to wipe his face on his sleeve. That took time, too much time. The car engine died and the car doors opened. He could feel the seconds ticking away as if his very flesh were keeping count of them.

He picked up the cutter. He picked up the stool. Unsteady on his feet, he carried the stool to the right of the door. He set it down in the darkness there beyond the wedge of sunlight. He heard the footsteps approaching the shed from outside. He heard

Dimmerman say something but the lawyer's voice was low and he couldn't make out the words. He placed the helmet on the stool and then moved away from it, moved to the other side of the wedge of light, into the shadows to the left of the door.

He stood there in the dark and waited, the cutter in his bleeding hand. In the next few seconds, he knew, he was going to die—die or live, one way or the other. He would not let the outcome fall between. In the deepest place of himself, where his instincts knew the way of things, he understood that his chances were not good, if he had any chance at all. It wasn't just his weakness or his trembling exhaustion or the fact that Tat Man was a killer and was trained for this and had a gift for it as well. It was also his—Winter's own—sense of irony, or his sense of the irony of the gods. He felt it was like the gods to let him find Gwendolyn and fall in love with her and grasp at last what the poets were trying to do with their words, to let him glimpse all this, then just kill him for the joke of it. This was the sort of cruel and hilarious gods he believed in, if he believed in any gods at all.

He knew that Tat Man would be wise and cautious. He knew the killer would come in slow. He knew he would keep his gun hand close to his side where it was hard to strike at. He knew he would be ready for Winter's one last desperate attack.

But he also knew they were tracking the helmet. That they could probably see where it was to the very inch. It would be to their left as they came through the door. Dimmerman would be pointing that way now as Tat Man approached the shed. Tat Man would turn in that direction first. Anyone would. Winter would have, if it had been him coming to kill the Tat Man instead of the other way around.

The killer was at the door. The door swung slowly outward. The wedge of light spread across the shed's floor. It reached the edge of the stool on one side, and stopped about a yard from Winter's feet on the other. The Tat Man's shadow filled the light.

The Tat Man said softly, "Come on, Winter."

His hand—his gun—appeared at the edge of the doorway, pointing at the stool, at the helmet. Then it started to swivel Winter's way.

Winter screamed in fury and terror and brought the head of the bolt cutters down on Tat Man's wrist, then instantly drew the instrument back and jabbed the blade at him.

He hoped to stab Tat Man in the throat or eye. But he only hit his chest and barely pierced him. It was enough though, just enough. Tat Man dropped the gun on the shed floor when the cutter hit his wrist. He cried out and staggered back a step when the blade stuck him.

And in that single second, Winter dropped the cutter, swept his arm down, and grabbed the gun.

Even Winter was surprised the trick had worked so well.

His chest heaving from the effort, he pointed the Glock at Tat Man's chest.

"Back up, back up," he panted. He could not muster more voice than that.

The Tat Man grinned and raised his hands and backed slowly away. Winter could see Arthur Dimmerman behind him. The lawyer's face was pale. His mouth was open with surprise and fear. Tat Man backed up and Dimmerman backed up. Stalking them, Winter stepped out of the shed and into the sunlight. He squinted in the sudden brightness.

His face was bloody and wet with tears. The gun felt slippery because his hand was soaked in blood. His hand was trembling. His shirt was bloody and his bloody socks left marks where he stepped. His lungs hurt and his legs were weak. He was so tired he was afraid he might lose consciousness. But he would not lose consciousness. He refused. He had beaten them. Somehow he had beaten them. He was going to get in their car and drive the hell away. He loved Gwendolyn, so he would not die.

"My friend, my friend," the Tat Man said. "Where do you think you could go?" As if he were reading his mind, Winter thought. "Our security team is already working. Some are on their way here. Some are using your information to track down your friends. It is all finished."

Winter pressed his elbow against his side to keep his arm steady. He raised the barrel of the Glock and pointed it at Tat Man's face. "Give me the car keys," he said.

"Maybe we can make a deal," Tat Man said.

"Give me the keys to the car."

"Don't be an idiot. This is all fantasy. You and I are little men. Pawns in all this. If they can use us, we make a living. When they are through with us, we die. Where will you go? Really, where will you go?"

"Look in my eyes, Tat Man. Give me the keys."

"He's right," said Dimmerman. His voice was high, breathy. It trembled. "Give him the keys."

Tat Man smiled, gestured with his head at the lawyer behind him. "He knows. The minute you leave, the machinery will go into motion. It's in motion already. You can't stop it. But you can deal with me, man-to-man. Maybe some of your people can be saved. You do not want anything to happen to innocent people, do you, my friend? You do not want anything to happen to your Gwendolyn Lord."

Winter laughed once and shot him between the eyes.

Judging by the expression on Tat Man's face, he was startled to find himself dead. His body stiffened and jerked back, then went slack. He sat down hard, then tumbled backward. His head hit Dimmerman's legs, then slid to the ground. He was staring and his mouth was agape as if he could not get over his surprise.

Winter got this reaction a lot when he killed people. He was a well-spoken man, a man of taste and culture, a gentle man in many ways and given to fine feelings. Cold-blooded killing was not the sort of thing people expected from him. Unless they were very insightful, they did not understand the complete absence of sentimentality in his makeup. He knew there were some men so low that only death could improve their personalities. He did not hesitate to improve them when the need arose.

These ideas flickered through his mind momentarily, and it flickered through his mind that maybe he had even fooled himself in this regard. In the present moment, though, he could not parse these insights. He could not think very clearly at all. A grating, high-pitched noise kept repeating and repeating in his head and it distracted him. What was that noise? he wondered in his haze of slaughter and exhaustion. His eyes shifted and he saw. It was Dimmerman screaming—shrieking really, again and again, like a girl in a horror movie. The lawyer's hands were thrown up in the air as if he'd seen a mouse and gone hysterical about it. His too-handsome face was splattered with Tat Man's blood and brains. Because while Tat Man's expression remained strangely intact except for the black hole just above the bridge of his nose, the back of his head had been blown off almost completely and Dimmerman had been standing right behind him when it happened.

Dimmerman kept shrieking in that horror-movie way. It made it hard for Winter to concentrate. Finally, he was sick of listening to it. Winter stepped up alongside Tat Man's corpse and smacked Dimmerman in the face with the barrel of the Glock. The blow shocked Dimmerman. He instantly fell silent. He stared at Winter, aghast, holding his bloody cheek with one hand.

Winter pressed the gun to Dimmerman's forehead.

"Tell me where to find the third man," he said.

# 33

Martin Bach came out of the Harkney House and stood on the front step in the dappled summer sunshine. It was late afternoon, the beginning of evening, almost quitting time.

The man in the blue Buick spotted Bach at once. The man in the blue Buick was not always the same man. There were three men and they took turns following Martin, sometimes in the Buick and sometimes in other cars. This man, the present man, was named John Stokes. He was in his fifties, a big man with broad shoulders and a paunch. He was bald but for a fringe of silver hair. He had a thick silver chevron mustache. His eyes were gray, tough and merry. He had been a Kansas City police detective for many years before going into his current line of business—which, for the past few months, largely consisted of following Martin Bach.

Following Martin Bach was not an interesting job. There was not much to it. The Buick men had tracking devices on their phones. The devices read the signal from the doodad in Bach's brain and told them exactly where he was. All they had to do was go where he was and keep an eye out to make sure he didn't get up to anything unpleasant. But all Martin Bach ever did was go to work and go home. Now he was at work, rewiring the Harkney House.

Stokes had been watching the baseball app on his phone. It offered video of all the best plays of the week along with commentary, stats, and feature articles. Stokes had the engine running because it was too hot to sit in the car without air-conditioning.

When Martin Bach stepped out of the front door, Stokes caught sight of him right away. He shut off the baseball app and watched him. Bach stood on the house's front steps, scanning the neighborhood: green trees, rolling hills, big houses set on the distant heights, their facades just visible through the leaves. Like Stokes, Bach was a big man. He was wearing jeans and a denim work shirt and a bright-yellow tool belt with tools dangling from it. His truck was parked in the Harkney driveway. But he did not walk to his truck. Instead, he descended the front steps and walked down the front path of the house to the street. With his thumbs hooked in his tool belt, he started to stroll across the street on the diagonal.

With an inner twinge of aggravation, John Stokes realized that Bach was coming toward the blue Buick.

Stokes was annoyed that he was the one Bach had spotted, but all the blue Buick men knew he was going to spot one or the other of them sooner or later. They'd been following him for too long, too close. Eventually, Bach was sure to catch on. The bosses at Thaumatix had told the blue Buick men not to worry too much if it should happen. Bach knew he was part of an experiment. He knew he was obligated to check in from time to time and that, from time to time, the company might keep an eye on him. In the event he should catch them out, the blue Buick men had been told to explain to him that they had been assigned to watch him and that he could call his contact at the company if he needed more information.

As Martin Bach approached the Buick, John Stokes sighed and pushed the Buick's door open. He unfolded his big frame and rose up out of the driver's seat into the muggy heat. He shut the door behind him and stood waiting for Bach to draw near.

Bach gave a friendly, comical little nod as he walked toward Stokes as if to acknowledge the awkwardness of the moment. He smiled. Bach had a nice smile, Stokes thought. Kind of sweet and childlike. The ladies must go for that in a big way.

As Bach came closer, Stokes said, "Hey, Martin."

"Hey," said Bach with a sheepish laugh.

Then, in a single, blindingly swift motion, Bach drew the claw hammer from his tool belt and brought it sweeping around in a backhand arc. Stokes had no time to react. The hammerhead smashed full speed, full force into his temple. Stokes's thoughts became a chaos of electric nothingness. He began to pitch forward, feeling helpless to stop himself. Bach's hand finished its arc up high and then he brought the hammer down again and Stokes was dead.

With the body lying still at his feet, Bach felt very calm and sort of dreamy. His heart beat steadily, not even racing. He calmly holstered the hammer and squatted over the ex-policeman's corpse. He went through the pockets of Stokes's gray slacks and found his car fob. He pressed the button that opened the blue Buick's trunk.

He seized Stokes by his belt and his collar. Stokes was heavy, but Bach was strong. It was not hard for him to lug the body to the back of the car, hoist it up, and dump it in. Some blood dripped from Stokes's head onto the street, but surprisingly little. Not so much that anyone would notice if they were casually passing by. They'd find the dead man eventually of course, but Bach knew the schedule of their shift changes and he did not think anyone would miss Stokes for at least another hour or so.

Which was plenty of time. He would be long gone by then.

He closed the trunk. He used the fob to shut down the car's engine. Then he headed back to the Harkney house to torture and kill his wife.

She—Tilda Bach—was lying on the floor of the crawl space. She was wrapped in Martin's protective plastic sheet. It was bound round her with duct tape so tight she could not budge. Only her face was exposed. Her mouth was stuffed with a rubber ball and taped over. In her terror, with her heart hammering, she could barely draw in enough breath through her nose. She felt as if she was suffocating. She felt as if a gigantic, clawed hand of pure fear was squeezing her to death.

"I'll be right back, Tilda." Those were the last words Martin had spoken to her as he looked down at her over the edge of the crawl space. Then she had heard his footsteps receding on the floor upstairs. She had heard the door open and close. Then nothing. Silence. But not silent silence. The silence was loud with her screaming thoughts.

Her thoughts were a babble of wild prayer. She was pleading with Jesus to save her baby. In a roiling flood of disjointed words, she was telling Jesus that she knew she had been bad, very bad, and done many bad things, but that the baby had not done anything to anyone and had not even had the chance to live her life yet and be a person. She was explaining to Jesus that she had to go on living in order for the baby to live, but after the baby was born, Jesus could kill her and she wouldn't care, if Jesus would only take care of her baby and find another mother for her who was not bad like she was but was good and could teach her baby to be good so Jesus would love her and take her to heaven. She told Jesus that she had tried to believe in him and had tried to change her life and she had changed her life and had been much better than she was before but she knew she hadn't really believed in him the way she was supposed to. She had just wanted her life to be better and because it was better when she went to church and said all the prayers and talked about Jesus, she did those things but she never knew if she was being real or if she was just pretending because it worked for her, and she was so, so sorry for that, she wanted it to be real, she really did, and it was not her baby's fault if it wasn't, her baby would believe in him and do everything he wanted her to do, if he would just let her be born and have a life and live.

This prayer went through her mind in such a rush of hysterical terror, the words soon became a single white blur of entreaty and negotiation. With her whole heart, she offered up the only thing she had left to bargain with, her life, her life for her baby's life and the word *please* over and over until it was not a word at all but part of the general blur of soundless sound, that blur of entreaty that itself became an emptiness of self-surrender.

At this point, she heard the door to the house open again and shut, and she knew that Martin had returned. She heard his footsteps on the floor again, slowly coming toward her, slowly growing louder, closer. She could not breathe for her horror, and her prayer was a mad wordless strain of pleading and the shattering knowledge that everything was over for her except suffering and death and the death of the thing she loved beyond her own life, her baby, who would never have the chance to live.

Then there his face was, in the opening of the crawl space above her, looking down at her. And she was staring up at him with eyes so wide it felt as if they would burst out of her. There was nothing left in the world but her husband's demon face and the death of her baby and she thought she had gone mad because there had to be more in the world than this horror and despair. She wondered if she had already died and was in some hellish fantasy place. She could not find a handle on reality because this reality made no sense to her.

Because the face above her was not her husband's face at all.

It was an awful face, a hideous thing to look at, scarred and swollen and discolored like the face of a monster. Tilda was screaming behind her gag at the sight of it, and trying to thrash out the terror that filled her body even though she could not move. Her head was so full of her screams and prayers and horror that she could not hear what the face was saying to her. The mouth in the swollen, bruised face was moving, but she could not hear the words, could not even hear the sound of the words.

Her breath ran out. Her screams became a whimper. Her thoughts were scrambled with entreaty and surrender and fear. The mouth in the horrible face kept moving, kept speaking, the same words over and over and over—and then over again, until Tilda began to make out the sense of them.

"Don't be afraid," the face kept saying. "Don't be afraid."

The man above the crawl space was gesturing at her with one hand, a gentling gesture. He was trying to calm her.

"I'm going to climb down and free you," the man said. Then he said again: "Don't be afraid."

Tilda had been in a place beyond thought and understanding, but she was beginning to return to the world now and the world was starting to seem real to her again. This was not Martin. This was another man. He was disfigured and terrible, but his voice was kind and he was saying he would help her. But he did not know about Martin, she thought. He did not know that Martin was creeping up behind him right that minute, that Martin was going to kill him, and then kill her baby. She started to try to warn him, but she could not speak.

The man was climbing down into the crawl space.

"It's all right," he kept saying. "Don't be afraid."

Tilda tried to shake her head. Tried to warn him that Martin was coming to kill him and the baby.

The man squatted over her. "It's all right. Don't be afraid. I'm going to take the tape off your mouth. It might hurt a little."

He pulled the tape off quickly, and it shocked her but it did not hurt, or if it did, she couldn't feel it. He fished the ball out of her mouth.

She gasped for breath. She gasped, "Martin is coming."

"No, no, no," said the horrible man. "Martin is tied up. He's in my car. He can't get out."

Tilda tried to tell him this was wrong, that Martin could get out, that Martin was strong and there was a demon inside him and he could do anything.

"Listen to me," the man said. "I'm going to use a knife. No, no, it's all right, don't be afraid. I'm going to use a knife to cut you free. It will look scary, but I will not hurt you. Nothing will hurt you now, but I have to cut you free. Don't be afraid."

"Martin is coming," she said.

He began to work with the knife, cutting the tape and the plastic. "Martin is in my car," the man said. "He's tied up and both his legs are broken. He tried to kill me with a hammer, but I took the hammer away from him and broke his leg. Then I lost my temper and broke his other leg. I've had a rough day. Anyway, he's not going anywhere. And the police are coming. The police are on their way."

For the next few moments, Tilda lay staring up at nothing, trying to understand what was happening, trying to think whether this was real or something else, some other thing she only wished was happening.

"Did Jesus send you?" she asked.

"No," said the man. "I came on my own. Or, I don't know, maybe he did. I'm probably not the right person to ask. Can you stand up? Let me help you."

He put his arms around her. She could feel they were strong and she leaned into them. He lifted her to her feet.

"I'm going to lift you up out of here," he said to her.

"No, no, no," she said on rising notes of panic. "He might be up there."

"All right. All right," said the man. "Don't be afraid. I'll climb up first, then lift you out."

She stood swaying on her feet, weak and sick. She told herself to pay attention and keep standing. The man had climbed out of the space. He was above her again, reaching down for her with both hands.

"He's not here. Let me get hold of you. Don't you hold on to me," he said. "I'm stronger. Let me hold on to you."

He took her under the arms and lifted her out of the crawl space as if she weighed nothing. They were in a kitchen. The man had his arms around her. He was holding her up and moving her toward the kitchen door.

Tilda was still in a daze but she was beginning to cry as she began to make sense of things. She nestled under the man's arm. "Is my baby all right?" she asked him.

The man with the horrible face stopped, startled. He stared at her. "Wait. There's a baby?" he said. Then he looked down at her. "Oh. Inside you. Is that the baby you mean? Yes. Yes, I think it should be all right. I don't know. You should probably try to be calm. Take deep breaths. We'll get you to a doctor. The baby will be all right."

Holding her close, he helped her walk to the kitchen door and out into the empty room beyond.

Tilda was crying hard now. "I prayed to Jesus and you came," she explained.

"Oh. Well, good," said the man. "It's nice when things happen that way."

Tilda sobbed with wonder. "I hear sirens."

"Yeah, that's the police. They'll be here soon. They'll take care of us. We'll be all right."

It occurred to Tilda now to look at the man, really look at him. She turned and lifted her face to his. He glanced down and smiled at her. He winced as if it hurt him to smile. He was injured. She could see that now. His face wasn't monstrous. It was just that he'd been injured and he was bruised and swollen. His eyes were clear, though, behind his glasses. They were clear and kind. When she looked into them, she felt safe. She was not afraid.

He helped her toward the front door. The sirens grew louder outside.

"Are you an angel?" she asked him. "Did Jesus send an angel?"

He laughed once. "Sorry, no."

Holding her up with one arm, the man reached out with the other and opened the door. The sirens were very loud. She saw the police cars pulling up in front of the house, their blue lights flashing.

Tilda's legs buckled under her as the full understanding of what had happened overwhelmed her. She had been rescued. Her baby had been rescued. Her baby would live.

"But what are you then?" she cried out to the man. "How did you get here? How did you find me? What are you?"

The man helped her walk, guiding her out the door and toward the police cars. He held her close. He would not let her fall.

"I'm an English professor," he said.

# EPILOGUE

"What happened next?" said Gwendolyn Lord. "After you shot the man with the tattoos? Then what happened?"

"Well, luckily, Tat Man still had my phone with him," Winter told her, "so I recovered that and alerted my old boss that our code was blown. We have a complex response protocol that probably would have alerted him anyway, but I couldn't be sure. That helmet thing was terrifying. It really did seem to drain my brain of everything that was in it. Anyway, then I called the police to tell them about this Bach character. But I couldn't get them to take me seriously. They seemed to think the whole thing was some kind of joke. Apparently, they had some history with Bach's wife. I don't know. They didn't actually respond until I got there myself. It wasn't far. When I called them from the scene and told them I had broken Bach's legs, that finally got them started. To be honest, I think they showed up to rescue him from me."

"I'm not surprised. Hold still."

"Oh, I'm not going anywhere. I like it here."

Winter was lying on Gwendolyn's sofa, his head resting comfortably on her lap. He was gazing up the soothing contours of her body to her face, which seemed to him to have morphed magically and dramatically from cute to beautiful since he had fallen in love with her.

Gwendolyn was carefully working the tape and gauze off his wounded right hand. He could see that the gauze was stained a sickly yellow. Gwendolyn looked sober and concerned as she worked, which Winter found immensely comforting. When she removed the gauze and saw the wound beneath, he heard her draw in a sharp breath through her nose. She gave him a glance of reprimand but when he obligingly cowered at her displeasure, she softened.

"Poor thing," she said.

"That's the spirit. You're really getting the hang of this."

"Well, you belong to me now, so I'll always take care of you. But let's not push our luck, okay? What is this? What did they do to you?"

"It's all your fault. That stupid cross you gave me. It nearly cut me to pieces."

"After saving your life."

"Well, first it saved me, then it lacerated me."

"Well, that's the way the cross works, so ha ha." She set the bandage aside and took up a tube of disinfectant. She seemed to be paying close attention to his hand, but he thought what she was really doing was avoiding his gaze. He could see that her thoughts were elsewhere. "Will you tell me something?" she said.

"I might. What?"

She spread the disinfectant on his palm, never looking at him. "Well, it's just . . . Brett—my husband—he was never allowed to tell me where he was or what he was doing. I sometimes wonder . . ." She stopped there and worked on his palm. He didn't ask her to go on. But after a moment, she did go on. She said, "I sometimes wonder, if Brett had lived, if that might have hurt us, you know. If the secrecy might have hurt us as a couple."

"What do you want to know, Gwendolyn?"

"You won't mind my asking?"

"Try me."

She took a breath. "The Tattooed Man," she said. "Did you have to shoot him?"

Winter sighed. "I don't know, sweetheart. Depends what you mean. I guess I did. I mean, you did tell me I wasn't allowed to die."

"It was self-defense then."

He laughed once. "No. Not really."

"Well, why did you do it then?"

Nestled in her lap, looking up her curves at her features, loving her intensely, he opened his mouth intending to lie to her, some tranquilizing lie, but he was surprised to hear himself tell her the truth instead.

"He threatened you."

She nodded, still working on his hand, wrapping it carefully in a fresh bandage. "I thought that might be it. It sounded as if you'd left something out of the story and I thought it was probably that."

"Even if he had just spoken your name, I would have done it," he told her. "If he had come back to life and spoken your name again, I would have killed him twice."

She went on nodding. "And will there be trouble about it? Will you be in trouble?"

"I doubt it. I doubt he even existed officially. Even the government didn't know his real name. I haven't heard of his body being found or anything. I don't think it will be."

She wrapped his hand with tender care, never looking at him, her expression thoughtful and sad. "What is it like, killing a person, Cam?"

Once again, he surprised himself. It was a forbidden question in the business he'd been in. You either knew or you didn't know and if you knew you didn't talk about it, and if you didn't know, there was no point in asking. So when he heard the answer come out of him so naturally, as if it were nothing more than another breath, he felt certain for the first time that she was right, that they had been made for each other somehow, that they were two parts of a single thing. He would come to love her more in time, he thought, as he got to know her better, but he would never love anyone else, not like this.

"It's like a suicide that didn't quite come off," he said. "It's like trying to imagine yourself dead, but all you can imagine is a body that looks like you, and you're still there and life goes on and that's the hell of it."

Gwendolyn had finished bandaging his hand, but she still didn't look at him. She stroked the bandage and laced her fingers in his. Her chin trembled and a tear fell down her cheek. "But this is better, right? Being here with me? This is better than that."

"Much better. Better than anything," Winter said. "But . . ." He didn't finish. He decided there was no point in telling her the rest.

"Oh, I know," she said. She flicked the tear off her cheek. She made an effort and smiled down at him. "Brett explained it to me. This is part of you too. There's no point in thinking about it. It's just the way you're made." Still, her lips twitched with what, for her, passed for anger. "How could they do it though? All these billionaires and experts, governors, and the president even. How could they even think to do it? And be so careless? And let it all get out of hand the way it did? What on earth is the matter with them?"

Winter smiled ruefully but continued silent. What was the point in answering? Here in this sunlit apartment with its flowery posters and white curtains and white rugs and the white sofa he was lying on. There was no answer that made sense here, and really, anywhere. People would not hear the answer, even if you gave it to them. And if they heard it, they would not really believe it. They would not allow themselves to comprehend the simple fact: You can drop a pebble down the well of human wickedness and stupidity and wait and wait and never hear the splash. Gwendolyn was right. There was no point in even thinking about it.

"Will anything even happen to them?" she asked. "Thaddeus Blatt. Will anything even happen to him?"

He made a face, considering. "Maybe. Hard to say. My friend, my old chief, is irked with him. You should never irk a man like that. I think he'll make a project out of Blatt now. My guess is, the truth will come out, or some truth, or maybe some other truth, some scandal or other, I don't know. I suspect Blatt's probably going to have a hard time of it over the long run."

"I hope so. I'll never forgive him for making your handsome face all swollen, for one thing. I was so looking forward to showing you off to my mother."

"Maybe she'll like my personality."

"Maybe. She can be very shallow sometimes."

She stroked his hair, which he enjoyed enormously.

"So I guess until your old boss destroys all the evil in the world . . ." she said.

"And stupidity," said Winter. "Don't forget the stupidity."

"Yes, until he destroys all the evil and stupidity, I suppose we'll just have to go on living with them."

"Or until your pal Jesus comes back, yes, it does look that way."

She leaned down to him so that her hair spilled over his face along with the perfume of her hair. She kissed him gently.

"Poor things," she whispered.

"Yes," Winter said. "Poor things."

It might—or might not—have made Gwendolyn feel better to know that Thaddeus Blatt was growing troubled in mind. More than that. He was fearful in both mind and heart. Winter's words kept coming back to him: "Your world is full of the invisible." He knew what those words meant. He sensed they were true. He sensed his old archenemy the Recruiter was out there somewhere with his small army of loyalists, working against him. Stories had begun to appear on social media. Stories about his businesses and his investments. Hints and rumors about his involvement with Thaumatix. Nothing too damaging yet, just conspiracy theory nonsense from unofficial sources. But what was annoying about it was that most of the conspiracy theories were true. Informed by insider knowledge, littered with incriminating details. The sort of thing that could gather steam if anyone in the major news outlets took up the tale. Which was unlikely, since they all admired Thaddeus Blatt. But it was not impossible. It was a threat hanging over him. It worried him. As the death of his tattooed assistant worried him. And the arrest of Martin Bach. And the continued existence of Cameron Winter.

For the present, Blatt had retreated to strategize and regroup. He had suddenly decided to spend what was left of the summer on his private island in the Caribbean. It would be a pleasant family vacation, swimming, hiking, barbecuing, and sunbathing with his new wife and his two children from his second marriage, six-year-old Laura and eight-year-old Ken. They had had a wonderful week this week and the week before and the wife and kids were all asleep now and snug in their beds. And Thaddeus Blatt was alone on the veranda, overlooking the sea. He was sitting in his rocking chair, holding a snifter of brandy. He was gazing out beyond the railing at the wild summer water, the frothing whitecaps stirred by the winds of distant hurricanes, and the vast sky above with its infinite depth of stars. The Milky Way was slashed across the scene as if by a great, magic paintbrush. The night was beautiful and the world was beautiful and he had to trust that all would ultimately be well.

This—this house, this veranda especially, especially at night—this was where he always came to gentle his soul, to quiet his thoughts, to gather himself for the efforts ahead. No one near him but the people he loved. And the housekeeping staff. And the small army of security men watching over them to keep them safe. He could see their black silhouettes patrolling the grassy verge of the cliffs out in front of him. He knew they were behind the house, too, and to the left and right of it. And there were some inside as well, guarding the halls and stairways. Hard veterans of secret wars who could defend him and his family against any and all attackers. So tough they could keep even his anxieties at bay.

And he did have anxieties. No matter what he told himself to keep himself calm, the anxieties kept creeping back into his mind. He kept thinking about those stories in social media. And the death of Tat Man. A real loss. The loss of his most effective operator. There was no one like him when it came to handling the really hard problems. He could get past anything, get in anywhere, do to anyone what he wanted done. Terrible things sometimes, things that spread a paralyzing cloud of compliance over everyone nearby. Even Blatt was afraid of him after he got to know him truly. How would he ever find another workman of that quality?

So there was all that. And there were some unanswered phone calls in DC too. That was worrying. These politicians had taken his donations gratefully enough, but now they didn't want to be associated with him and wouldn't return his calls. He supposed they had to protect themselves. And so far anyway, they'd managed to keep Martin Bach quiet with legal aid and promises. So maybe it would all work out.

But there were other players out there, not so friendly, people who knew more than was good for them, who might need to be taught to keep their mouths shut, a little pressure applied. Winter, for the most obvious one. Winter knew way too much. And he'd told some of it to others, surely to the Recruiter himself. For the present, at least, Blatt felt he had to move with caution. With his support wavering inside the Beltway, it would be wise to keep a low profile for a time. Especially now that Tat Man wasn't around to do the wet work.

He sipped his brandy. He gazed at the stars. He counseled patience to himself. Wait. Wait and see what needed to be done. He knew men like Winter. Winter was a tough customer, but no one was incorruptible, no one was immune to fear. It would all come right in the end. It always did when you had enough money. Money was kind of like magic in that regard.

He sighed. He stood, the rocker creaking behind him. He left his empty snifter on the small table by the chair. He gave a one finger salute to the shadow of the nearest soldier by the cliff. He went inside and climbed the stairs.

It did him good to count his blessings. To peek in on the children sleeping peacefully in their beds. To go into his own room and undress in the darkness with the shape of his wife's body rising and falling beneath the covers. What a gift she was. The youth of her and the firmness and softness of her skin—what gifts. The touch of her was like some life-giving elixir. It had brought the vigor back to him, not just sexually but in all sorts of ways. The nights with her had given him new energy, new confidence, new dreams to dream. It was a good time in his life. The best time. If it had not been so good, he would not have been so worried about losing everything.

He slid into bed. Felt the warmth of his wife's body beside him, the smoothness of her skin against his thigh. He was tired and glad to close his eyes and glad to feel the soldiers around him and the Caribbean around him and all his troubles so far away.

"Blatt."

He opened his eyes quickly. He thought he had heard something. He thought he had heard someone whisper his name. It was a moment before he realized he had been asleep, fast asleep for a long time, hours maybe. He must have been dreaming.

"Blatt."

He caught his breath. He turned his head. A shadow was standing over him in the darkness. The shadow of a man.

He was about to sit up. He was about to cry out. But the shadow lifted his hand and Blatt saw the gun barrel trained on his face. He went rigid and still. His cry turned to dust in his throat.

"Listen to me," the shadow whispered—a whisper so low it was the shadow of a sound.

"How did you get in here?" Blatt started to say—but the shadow's gun hand stiffened and again the words died in his throat and crumbled to silent dust. His mind was racing. His heart was pounding. His fear made him hollow and weak. He did not want to die. And his children. His wife. Even if he lived, their murders would poison his existence with grief.

"Listen to me," came the shadow's shadowy whisper. Blatt stared wide-eyed into the blackness of the gun barrel. "You think you know me," the shadow said. "But you don't know me. I know you. I can see you. I can see you move. I can hear you think. But that's all right. Move where you want, think what you like. Just remember this. If Gwendolyn should dash her foot against a stone—if an arrow should come nigh her—then you *will* know me—then you will truly know who I am."

Before Blatt could stop them, rasping words burst from his mouth. "Winter, I can give you . . ."

But the shadow's free hand lifted suddenly, threatening as a blade. Blatt choked on the dust of his words. Trembling and breathless, he stared up at the shadow's hovering hand.

Slowly, a single finger of the hand lifted.

Slowly, the shadow brought the finger to his own lips: *Shh.*

Slowly, the shadow lowered his hand. The shadow lowered his gun. The shadow turned around.

Slowly, deliberately, the shadow walked away, until he had become one with the darkness.

# ACKNOWLEDGMENTS

My thanks to Captain Felicia Jamison of the San Francisco Sheriff's Office for graciously schooling me on the protocols of a county jail. Thank you also to Michael Bates for sharing his incredibly deep and wide knowledge of Tulsa, Oklahoma. If you ever want to know more about that city—and a lot of other things—check out his blog, batesline.com. And thanks as always to Otto Penzler and everyone at Mysterious Press, including Charles Perry and Luisa Cruz Smith, and to Mark Gottlieb and Robert Gottlieb and everyone at Trident Media.